# *Miami* INTERLUDE

### Linda Bennett Pennell

Black Rose Writing | Texas

This is a work of fiction. Names, characters, businesses, places, events, and incidents are either the products of the author's imagination or used in a fictitious manner. Any resemblance to actual persons, living or dead, or actual events is purely coincidental.

ISBN: 978-1-68513-530-0
PUBLISHED BY BLACK ROSE WRITING
www.blackrosewriting.com

Printed in the United States of America
Suggested Retail Price (SRP) $20.95

*Miami Interlude* is printed in Calluna

*As a planet-friendly publisher, Black Rose Writing does its best to eliminate unnecessary waste to reduce paper usage and energy costs, while never compromising the reading experience. As a result, the final word count vs. page count may not meet common expectations.

# Miami INTERLUDE

# PROLOGUE

In Coconut Grove, there once existed a magnificent estate overlooking Biscayne Bay, where the mouth yawns wide and Bimini is a straight shot across the Atlantic. Built by a fabulously wealthy Yankee, the villa played host to the glamorous, the wealthy, the famous, the prominent, and the notorious—anyone considered entertaining or useful. The source of the man's wealth, like his provenance, was somewhat murky, but the outrageous entertainments he provided ensured all of Miami, and beyond, jockeyed for invitations and flocked to his soirees.

It was the 1920s, and South Florida glimmered with promise as her denizens, newcomers and old pioneers alike, mined the gold of an unprecedented land boom. Because he had resided in Coconut Grove for nearly two decades, it was simply assumed that the Yankee made his money by investing in and developing real estate. Whatever its source, the well of the man's wealth seemed bottomless and his lavish parties never-ending.

But as with all things in life, nothing lasts forever.

# CHAPTER 1

*Summer 1926*
*Dade County, Florida*

Della studied her reflection, tucked a wayward chemise strap back into place, and nodded. She had given it her all and the result was pleasing, if she did say so herself. It was important she looked her best tonight. Art wanted—no, needed—to make a good impression, and as his wife, she was part of the package. She put an arm out at shoulder height, then shook it in quick rhythm. The beaded fringe around her knees bounced as her body shimmied. The twenty-five-year-old matron in the dresser mirror smiled back at her. She still had the right moves. Thank goodness.

She ran her hands over her slender hips and giggled softly to herself. Her lithe figure was in style and all the rage. She needed no breast binding to achieve the desired look. At college, her friends had been very proud of their hourglass figures. They had teased her mercilessly about her boyish figure, but she had the last laugh now.

Lifting the hem of her silk chiffon sheath, she examined her knees. Too much rouge or not enough? Pull her stockings back up over her thighs or leave them rolled down? From what she had heard of Anders Aldridge's parties, stockings rolled down and more rouge would ensure she fit in with the socialites, flappers, alleged gangsters, politicians, and millionaires who attended. According to the *Miami Herald*'s society column, everyone who was anyone in South Florida turned up at some point at Villa Lucca. Tonight, it would be Art's and Della's turn.

At the sound of keys rattling, she met her husband's gaze in the dresser mirror, then twirled around. Art lounged against the bedroom doorjamb and grinned at her with a lascivious gleam. "Any more moves like those, and we'll never get to the party." He waggled his brows. "Do you really want to go?"

She Charlestoned her way over to him and wrapped one arm around his neck. The index finger of her free hand drifted along his jaw as she gazed up into his eyes. "I've spent all month preparing to be a hit for you, my darling. I used last week's grocery money on this dress and had the cobbler fix these shoes so no one will suspect they are years old. I had my hair bobbed so I would be in current fashion. I actually cried as ten inches of it fell to the floor. The hairdresser must have thought me demented. Now that I've gotten used to it, I love it. You wanted a modern, stylish wife on your arm, and you've got her." She patted his cheek sharply. "We are going to that party."

He laughed and held her at arm's length. "Okay, okay. You don't have to resort to violence." His gaze traveled down and back up. He whistled softly. "You will be the most beautiful girl there."

Della winked. "You're not so bad yourself." She raised up on tiptoe and kissed him lightly. "We're already late. Is the car out front?"

"It is, and"—Art raised his wrist and made a production of examining his watch—"we're not late. We are fashionable."

Della tilted her head and pursed her lips in an exaggerated imitation of deep thought. "Hmm. I suppose no one wants to be the first to arrive. You can't make an entrance if there's no one to see it."

"Correct, and I want to be seen by the right people. A lot is riding on making good impressions tonight."

Art took her elbow and guided her to the front door.

She glanced at herself in the foyer mirror, a hand flying to her mouth. "Wait. I almost forgot. My clutch. It's in the bedroom. I'll be right back." Maintaining the desired image demanded having her rouge, lipstick, and powder at the ready.

Once they were settled in the car, Art placed a hand on her knee. "Ready to shine, my love?"

Della nodded. "Ready as I'll ever be."

•   •   •   •   •

Della laid her arm atop the open roadster's door and tried to relax, but her wayward fingers refused to cooperate. They beat a restless tattoo against the door's metal ledge. She wriggled deeper into her seat and laid her head against its tufted leather top. Tonight was going to be special, something she had never expected to experience.

A satisfied smile danced across her lips as she gazed at a huge full moon that made the car's headlamps almost unnecessary. It painted the banyan trees, mangroves, and palmettos lining the road with a silvery glow, casting them in eerie relief. Some might see this stretch of road, overhung by vegetation and Spanish moss-draped tree limbs, as a sinister alley leading away from a hellish swamp, but Della had grown to love this drive away from their old Cracker farmhouse at the edge of the Everglades. Her greatest fear was that Hialeah, with its new horse racing track and other attractions, was growing so rapidly, it would one day swallow them and their farm whole.

The house had originally been a two-room dogtrot built by Art's pioneering ancestors. His grandparents had added more rooms and a wraparound porch to complete the cozy, rambling home she and Art enjoyed. It was not a grand house by any standards, but its high ceilings and broad porch gave relief from summer's heat, while its heart pine walls and flooring held in the warmth from its fireplaces when the odd winter day turned cool.

The Spanish Flu took both of Art's parents while he was in service during the Great War. He had no siblings, and the thought of selling land that had been in his family for generations was beyond endurance, so Art abandoned his young man's dream of being an actor to take up farming. In the end, it had been for the best. He had dreamed of taking the stage before the horrors of the trenches. War has a way of changing a man and what he wants out of life. Art had come home from France wanting peace, security, and a place to heal. The farm represented all of that. He had risen to the task of returning the farm to productivity with unexpected grace and ability.

Della glanced at her husband. Art worked so hard to make the farm profitable, but with agricultural prices at an ebb, life was not easy. Still, they were happy and very much in love. She would not exchange what they had for all the riches of the Vanderbilts, Rockefellers, and Carnegies combined.

As the lights of Hialeah rose and then mingled with those of Miami proper, a salt-laced Atlantic breeze kissed her cheeks. The oppressive heat of the day had dissipated, leaving the night perfect for dancing and meeting new people.

The notes of a popular jazz tune floated to them while they were still several blocks from Villa Lucca. Della's feet automatically moved in rhythm to the tune.

Giving herself a mental hug, she stretched her arms wide above her head. "This is going to be a glorious evening."

Art chuckled and grabbed her hand, drawing it to his lips. "I'm glad you're looking forward to the party. Just remember . . . when all the guys crowd around you asking you to dance, you're my girl."

Della giggled. "But, sir, I'm a happily married lady. I have no need of other dance partners. I hope you're ready to show me a good time."

"You betcha, baby." Art's idea of how gangsters talked always made her laugh. Neither of them knew, nor had they ever spoken with, anyone even remotely connected to organized crime. They were much too conventional, ordinary, and unsophisticated for such.

However, with luck, their fortunes might be about to change. Art was on the cusp of something important. He had hinted that their income would increase greatly if this evening went as planned. While he would not say what this new venture was—didn't want to jinx it or disappoint her if he failed—still, it was exciting to play her small part in his future success.

The car rounded a curve, and the headlamps flashed against a stucco wall about ten feet in height. The road followed the wall for three or four blocks until the villa's open gates bade them follow the long, winding driveway down to the bay.

# CHAPTER 2

Della placed her hand in the valet's and stepped from the roadster. She never dreamed of being allowed inside the iron gates, much less invited to one of Mr. Aldridge's famous parties. While she waited for Art to get his claim ticket, Della examined her surroundings.

Villa Lucca's enormous ironwork and glass doors stood wide open, giving a view into the palazzo all the way to matching doors at the opposite end of a grand hall. Ornate iron chandeliers and wall sconces cast a warm, electric glow over marble floors, antique commodes, and a credenza of pecky cypress that, while beautifully carved, looked oddly out of place. Through the open rear doors, formal gardens with a stone path led down to the bay. A Venetian-style bridge allowed guests to cross about twenty yards of water to a huge dance pavilion created in the style of an Italian plaza.

Della sucked in a long breath and let it out slowly. It would be very easy to become overwhelmed by the opulence and the unwelcome reminder of what she had lost. Papa had always promised her a trip to Italy after college graduation, but his big, kind heart had failed them both. She'd graduated from Wesleyan in June 1921, but the trip had to be postponed.

Papa had been the manager of a bank where land development loans were booming. He could not get away just yet, but he had promised they would go one day soon, maybe in '22 or '23. When he died in 1923 of a massive coronary, Mama had returned to her childhood home on an isolated farm near Thomasville, Georgia. Uncle John, Mama's brother, would have given Della a safe home and security, too, but she could not bear leaving Miami. It was the only home she had ever known.

Della gave herself a mental shake. Just stop that right now. This was not the night for maudlin ruminations. She and Art were here to enjoy the hospitality of Miami's most famous host. The food and drink would be sumptuous and the music and company grand. Even if Art's plans fell through, this would be a night to remember.

Art came to her side and cupped her elbow. "Looks like the party is in full swing. Time to see and be seen, my love."

As they neared the front steps, two men exited the house and paused in conversation at the driveway's edge. The taller man, dressed in shirt and slacks, looked out of place compared to the shorter gentleman in evening attire.

The shorter man shrugged. "Sorry, but he's told you the subject is closed."

The taller one grabbed his companion's upper arm. "Look here, Shoemaker, he's got to hear me out."

Crunching gravel and a car's engine prevented Della from hearing the rest of their argument. She glanced up at Art, who seemed uninterested in the scene playing out on the steps. Good. They did not need anything to mar their evening or shake Art's confidence.

A uniformed butler greeted them just inside the front doors and checked their invitation. "Ah, yes, Mr. and Mrs. Monroe. Mr. Aldridge asked that you be brought to him as soon as you arrived." He snapped his fingers, and a footman magically appeared. "Show these guests to Mr. Aldridge."

Della glanced up at Art and grinned. It looked like they were to be given the royal treatment. She bit her lower lip to stave off a fit of the giggles.

Within moments, they crossed the bridge to the pavilion and came to rest near a gentleman of about fifty. While he could be considered attractive in the way that aging men were, his chin protruded a little over his wing collar, and his cummerbund appeared too snug for comfort. A combination of moonlight and torchlight emphasized the silvery white at his temples and made his face and hands appear more deeply tanned than they probably were. He held court before a group of men, regaling them with a tale of his latest exploits on the golf course.

"Missed a hole in one by a quarter of an inch, I tell you. Most infuriating, but that's the game. If it were simple, anyone would play it." The footman cleared his throat, and the gentleman looked his way. "What is it, James?"

"Mr. and Mrs. Monroe, sir." James bowed and took his leave.

The gentleman smiled broadly and extended his hand to Art. "Arthur, welcome. And this must be Mrs. Monroe. You failed to mention how lovely she is." Despite a sudden case of the jitters, Della mustered what she hoped was her most winning smile.

Releasing Art's hand, their host turned to Della. When she placed her hand in his, he drew it to his lips with a slight bow. How continental of him.

"Anders Aldridge, my dear." His eyes traveled the length and breadth of her body from face to feet and back. "I hope you do not find it impertinent when I say that you are an exquisite ornament to my little soiree."

The way Mr. Aldridge looked at her and his tone did nothing to quell the butterflies that had taken possession of her midsection. Fighting nerves, Della drew what she hoped appeared to be a languid breath and met his gaze. "Thank you. Most kind, I'm sure." She was out of her depth. No doubt about it.

Mr. Aldridge smiled, nodded, and turned his attention back to Art. "Monroe, I have asked my private secretary to guide you this evening and make introductions. Get food and drink. Mingle and meet people." Aldridge gestured toward the western corner of the pavilion, where a set of steps led down to a jetty used by guests arriving by boat. "After you've been shown around, meet me at the far end where my runabout, *The Sylvia*, is docked. It is private enough for a brief discussion. I do not want to leave my guests without their host for too long, you know. Glad you and the enchanting Mrs. Monroe are here." He nodded at a man standing near the pavilion railing. "Singletary, please see that my guests are introduced as we discussed." Turning back to Art, he nodded his dismissal. "Until later."

Mr. Singletary bowed slightly. "I thought we might start with some of the local dignitaries."

Della trotted along in the men's wake, happy to be decorative rather than the center of attention. The secretary seemed just as happy to forget her existence. Once he had shaken her hand, he ignored her, leaving it to Art to introduce her to the new people they were meeting.

Within a couple of hours, Art had been introduced to the mayors of Miami and Palm Beach, a state senator, several local businessmen, a vice president of the Florida East Coast Railroad, and finally, Mr. Aldridge's business partner, Rollie Shoemaker. With a start, Della recognized him as the shorter of the two men they had passed on the way into the party. Shoemaker did not seem to recognize her. Just as well. The scene on the front steps had been unpleasant and embarrassing.

After shaking hands, Mr. Shoemaker stepped closer to Art and spoke in a near whisper, "Aldridge is headed to the jetty. We should do the same." He smiled at Della. "If you will excuse us, Mrs. Monroe. We will not detain your husband overlong. Singletary will see that you are not left to fend for yourself."

Della's spirits sank a little as she watched Art walk away. Being on her own with a bunch of strangers, many of whom were the worse for drink, was not something she had anticipated. She glanced up at the secretary. He stood at her side as stiff and unsmiling as a poker. He was obviously just as unhappy being stuck with her as she was being abandoned with him. Singletary was either a colossal snob or the rudest man she had ever met. Probably both.

He must have felt her eyes on him for he extended his hand and said, "Shall we?"

She blinked. "What?"

He smirked. "Shall we dance? You do know how to dance, don't you?"

Heat rose in Della's cheeks. She placed her hand in his and glared. "Why yes, I do. My husband and I venture out of the Glades from time to time to enjoy Miami's nightlife. Have you been to Club Lido on Miami Beach? The orchestra there is simply divine." She winced inwardly. She sounded exactly like the girls she found so distasteful during her college years, all superior snobs to the core of their beings.

Della cocked her head toward the orchestra as they began a familiar tune. "Oh, goodie. The Charleston. Do you know it?"

A pained expression filled his eyes. "Unfortunately, I was wounded during the war. It has left me less agile than one might wish. I'm afraid my dancing is limited to the foxtrot, the waltz . . . any dance that does not require much movement from the waist up."

Della blinked again. Perhaps she had misjudged him. Maybe he was in pain, which might account for his less-than-gracious demeanor. She gave him a sympathetic smile. "Let's sit this one out. My feet are aching, and I'm rather parched."

The tension went out of his shoulders and neck. "Thank you for understanding."

"Of course." As he led her toward the balustrade and a small table overlooking the bay, Della noticed that his stiff posture had returned. His injury must have been to his back. Poor guy. From what she had heard, back pain could be excruciating.

Singletary pulled out a chair and helped her into it. "Would you prefer a cocktail or champagne?"

"Champagne, I think. I've not developed a taste for the hard stuff."

Della watched the secretary negotiate his way toward the bar at the far end of the crowded pavilion. She wasn't sure why, but she was surprised at how freely the alcohol flowed. Maybe it was the presence of so many dignitaries and pillars of the community imbibing. Of course, the law only barred the production, importing, and sale of alcohol. Drinking the stuff was still legal, but everyone knew bootlegging and moonshining were going enterprises throughout South Florida. To see the products on such open display still shocked.

She had tasted her first and last champagne when she served as a friend's maid of honor in 1919. With Prohibition beginning in January 1920, the father of the bride had bought up every case of champagne he could get his hands on. Della had drunk more than she should have because she loved the bubbles. The reception had been a rousing success.

While she awaited Singletary's return, she gazed out over the bay. Moonlight danced across water that rippled in a light breeze, streaking the gentle waves with a silvery glow. Mr. Aldridge had a beautiful view at any time, day or night. It was hard not to be a little jealous of the property's position on Biscayne Bay. He could swim in its warm, clear waters whenever he chose. On second thought, he probably had a pool hidden somewhere within that magnificent mansion, so swimming in the bay might be beneath him. On hot summer days, she and Art occasionally drove to Miami Beach to cool off. How lovely to be able to swim whenever one wished.

Della's attention wandered to the dance floor where guests, young and old, twisted hands and feet in Charleston style. Her toes tapped in rhythm to the beat of the twelve-piece combo playing "Has Anybody Seen My Gal." She started to sing along, but the song drew to a close. The musicians dropped their instruments onto their stands and departed the stage, leaving only the murmur of conversation and clink of glassware. Without the roaring brass music, the sounds of the evening turned to those coming from the bay.

Water slapping against the boats tied up at the jetty created a soothing cadence that covered the growling in her stomach. Some of the guests began moving toward the house where a buffet awaited them. Joining them was tempting, but she did not want to go in without Art. It felt like he had been gone forever. Her brow creased as she strained to see where he, Mr. Aldridge, and Mr. Shoemaker were. Their upper bodies were visible above the seats of *The Sylvia*. Their heads bent toward one another in what appeared to be concentrated conversation. Whatever they discussed, it was taking longer than promised.

Mr. Singletary returned with a champagne saucer in each hand. "Sorry that took so long. Everyone wanted to grab a cocktail while the band is taking a break." After placing a glass before her, he raised his. "May I offer a toast?"

"Please do."

"Let us drink to the evening and new friends."

Somewhat puzzled by the new friends remark, Della raised her glass, but instead of rims touching, there was a sudden pop and the glass shattered in her hand. In the next few seconds, the sound of an outboard motor moving away at full throttle roared from the bay.

Singletary jumped to his feet and growled, "Get down and stay low." He raced around their table and leaned out over the balustrade.

# CHAPTER 3

Della dropped the shattered champagne stem and leapt from her chair. Ignoring the secretary's order, she joined him at the balustrade and searched the jetty below. She found Aldridge's boat at the far end. One of its three occupants lay sprawled across the back seat. The other two hovered over him.

Her hand flew to her mouth as she choked back a scream. Whirling around, she knocked over her chair and set the small table rocking. She dodged and bumped into other party guests, racing toward the jetty steps. People conversed and laughed as though no one else realized a drama played out only a few feet away on the dock below them.

When she reached the top step, a hand grabbed her upper arm. "Please don't. That's no sight for a lady." Singletary's voice was calm and low as he motioned to one of the waitstaff nearby.

She yanked herself free and glared. "Then I'm no lady. My husband may be injured. I'm going to him."

Her heels clacked against the pavilion's stone stairway. She stumbled when the heel of her right shoe became wedged between the dock's boards and the bottom step. Grabbing the handrail, she righted herself and kicked free of both shoes, then fled barefoot toward the last boat slip in the line. Footsteps pounded behind her. There were shouts from the pavilion above, but Della paid them no heed.

*The Sylvia* rocked and banged against the sides of the slip as Aldridge and Shoemaker climbed out of the boat, leaving Art slumped at an odd angle against the back seat.

Della did not stop or acknowledge the others. She jumped the gap between the dock and boat, then climbed over the front seat to the back. She knelt in the footwell beside Art. The gaping wound in his chest told her he was beyond help, but she tore fabric from her dress and covered it all the same, trying to stanch the rapidly widening stain crawling across the front of his wing collar shirt and the seat beneath him. She slid her free hand beneath his head and cradled it in the crook of her arm.

Rocking back and forth, she cried out, "Please. Please, God. Don't leave me. Don't . . . "

The boat rocked again, and a hand gripped her shoulder. Singletary spoke in low, reassuring tones. "Please let me see to him." Squatting down beside her, he took Art's wrist between his index finger and thumb. Sympathy filled his eyes. "There is nothing you can do for him. We must leave him where he is. The police will be on their way." He pushed Art from Della's arm and pulled her to her feet.

She tried to shake herself free, but the secretary held firm. She clamped her free hand against her side to prevent slapping his face. "I can't leave my husband here alone. He needs me. Why can't you see he needs help?"

Singletary shook his head. "Please. Come away. He is beyond anyone's help." With a tight grip, he pushed her forward while Shoemaker took her hands and pulled her up onto the dock.

Her whole body shook. Her knees were in danger of buckling. Singletary gripped her elbow and led her to a nearby piling. "Why don't you sit here. We will stay in these more secluded surroundings until the police direct us elsewhere."

Secluded surroundings? In the middle of a roaring party? Was the man mad? Weak with shock, Della sank onto the rough surface of the piling and looked up at the balustrades. Instead of hundreds of faces peering down at her, the guests were nowhere in sight. Not a single soul gazed down upon the murder scene. Odd, that. Perhaps Mr. Aldridge's staff had herded them back to the mainland. She shook her head. What did it matter where the other guests were when her whole world had just come crashing down?

A sense of the unreal settled over her. It was as though the world had shrunk down to the few feet of *The Sylvia*'s varnished wood decking and leather interior. There was no sound other than the men standing nearby, whispering about something she refused to comprehend. There was no light other than that coming from a single lamp high up on a wooden pole. She held her hands out before her, turning them over and back. They were smeared with blood. She glanced down at her dress. The entire front was dark and wet, just like Art's shirt.

Blood. Art's blood. Her mind would focus on nothing else until she could take no more. Della wrapped her arms over her stomach and rocked in unconscious rhythm. It was as though fog enveloped her, obliterating all around her, sinking her into a waking dream. None of this was real. They had never gone to a party. No one had been shot. It was all a horrible nightmare from which she would soon awaken. This could not be happening. They were too young and too much in love. Time itself ceased to exist.

The wail of police sirens broke through Della's befuddled state. She blinked several times and breathed heavily. Her eyes were drawn to the boat's back seat as firmly as a magnet draws nails. Nothing had changed. Reality pierced her heart and soul. One thing was devastatingly clear—Art was dead, shot by an unknown assailant for some unfathomable reason. At twenty-five, she was a widow, her husband murdered.

Boots pounded down the stone steps announcing the law's arrival. Two uniformed men and one in plain clothes approached. Della watched the youngest of the trio crawl onto the boat and place his fingers against Art's throat. He frowned and adjusted the placement of his fingers. After waiting a few more seconds, he shook his head.

The suit surveyed those on the dock, approached their host, and extended his hand. "Mr. Aldridge, sorry to meet under these circumstances." The policeman flashed his badge. "Chief of Detectives Frank Barnett, MPD. Chief Quig asked me to personally oversee this investigation. Is there somewhere more private that we can talk?" Turning to his colleagues, he said, "Watch the body. Do nothing until the coroner arrives. He will see to its removal."

An impulse to scream swept through Della. She wanted to cry out that it wasn't just any murder victim. The body, as the detective so callously put it, was her husband, her dearly beloved, her world. The cords of her throat moved, but no words formed. She swallowed hard.

Aldridge turned to Singletary. "Where are the guests?"

"They have been moved to the ballroom. Food and beverages are being served there."

Detective Barnett's head snapped back in alarm. "What have you done with the . . . er . . . beverages that were served on the pavilion?"

Without missing a beat, Singletary gave a tight smile and replied, "All have been returned to Mr. Aldridge's private cellar. As you are no doubt aware, he laid in a vast store before the Volstead Act took effect."

Aldridge nodded. "Well done. With the crowd contained, we'll use the side garden entrance and repair to my study."

The detective seemed to notice Della for the first time. "Who's this young lady?"

Singletary placed a hand under Della's elbow and lifted her to stand. "This is Mrs. Monroe, the victim's wife."

"Very well. She'll have to come with us. See if you can find her some shoes."

"But she saw nothing. She is in a state of shock. Wouldn't it be better to wait to interview her? Perhaps tomorrow?"

The detective cast an evaluative gaze over Della. "Okay. On one condition. She's got to remain on the premises under armed guard."

Della gasped. "But surely I'm not a suspect. He's my husband. I love him."

Barnett's face became a mask of irritation. "Lady, the assailant clearly wanted your husband dead, so you could well be next on his list. Until we know why your husband was killed, you should consider yourself in danger."

# CHAPTER 4

A throbbing head woke Della with a start. Massaging her temples, she gradually opened her eyes. Her back ached, and her neck slumped at a strange angle. When she tried to sit up, pain shot through her upper body. She blinked several times, trying to understand why she did not recognize the room.

When she was finally upright, the room swam for a moment, then settled into a display of opulence. Sun slanting through glass-paned doors set the gold accents on French Empire-style chairs and credenzas ablaze. Whether they were antiques or reproductions, she did not know, but one thing was sure—she was not at home. The sofa on which she had slept was built for style rather than comfort. She leaned her head against her palm, trying to ease the pounding and sort out what had happened. Bits and pieces began surfacing.

Last night's party. Jazz. Champagne. Noise. Shouts. Oh, God. Art sprawled across the boat's seat. She stuffed her fist into her mouth. She was still at Villa Lucca. The horror had been reality, not a nightmare.

Someone, probably the secretary, must have guided her away from the jetty, over the pavilion's stone floor, across the bridge to the mainland, through a shadowy garden, and into the mansion. If someone asked her to describe that journey, she would not have been able to. It must have taken place, but for the life of her, nothing of it existed. It was as though her brain had shut down, her power of observation diminished to zero.

A male voice emanated from the area of the garden doors. "You're awake. I apologize for the accommodations, but Chief

Detective Barnett wanted everyone kept under close watch and together. He and his men are interviewing the last of the party guests now." Singletary removed himself from his perch and strode across the cavernous room. Taking a seat opposite Della, he continued, "I'm afraid we had to call a doctor for you last night. You were so distraught, we feared you might do yourself harm. He gave you a pretty strong dose of barbital."

Della's midsection turned somersaults. She covered her mouth and searched for a container. Behind her fingers, she mumbled, "I'm going to be sick."

Singletary jumped up, grabbed a porcelain bowl from a nearby table, and shoved it onto her lap. "That may be the effects of the drug."

Bile and what little food she had consumed the night before reappeared in a disgusting display in the bottom of the bowl. She wiped her mouth on the handkerchief Singletary proffered. "Thank you. I'm sorry about that."

"Please. No need to apologize. May I get you something to drink? Tea or coffee perhaps?"

At the mention of coffee, Della's stomach roiled again. "No coffee. Maybe hot tea with lemon. And a bathroom. Could I have a bath?"

Singletary rang for a maid. "Mrs. Monroe will have tea delivered to the Blue Room bath. Please include lemon and plenty of sugar. The bath should be drawn warm, but not steaming." Orders given, he turned back to Della. "I'm afraid we have no lady's maids. Being a bachelor, my employer has no need of them. I could ask the parlor maid to assist you in dressing."

Della's cheeks burned as anger bubbled up. She could not put her finger on why she felt offended, but she did nonetheless. "There's no need to disturb the staff. I assure you I can take care of myself." What she did not add was "as I have been doing since I was a kid."

The secretary nodded and raised a brow. "As you wish. I will get one of the policemen to accompany us and stand guard."

"Is that really necessary?" The last thing she wanted was strange men outside the door while she bathed.

"I'm afraid Barnett will insist. Shall we?"

Della stood and glanced down at her dress. She lifted the skirt with a sinking heart. "Oh, God. I can't bear wearing this a minute longer. Surely, I can go home for a change of clothes." She did not add that the sight of the dark stains in the torn fabric and encrusted in the embroidery made her feel faint and sick. It wasn't simply blood. It was Art's blood. The dress was an awful reminder of the previous night's horror.

Singletary shook his head. "I doubt it. The chief detective has been most emphatic." His gaze ran over Della. "Mr. Aldridge has unexpected overnight guests on occasion. He keeps an assortment of garments for the ladies. I'm sure you will find something suitable in the bedroom wardrobe."

•   •   •   •   •

Della stepped out of the enormous tub with its gold faucets and wrapped herself in a towel the size of a single bed blanket. She placed her hand on the tub's rim and stood still for a moment to ensure she would remain upright. Fortunately, the bath and tea had helped restore her equilibrium. The room no longer swam at the slightest movement, and her stomach no longer roiled.

She glanced at her dress, undergarments, and stockings crumpled on the bathroom floor. Picking up a stocking, she pulled it over her hand—multiple runs from toe to thigh band. The maid sent to draw the bath had said to just leave everything, and it would be taken to the laundry. Anything that could be salvaged would be cleaned and returned better than new. Della kicked at her things. Cleaning this lot would require miracles. The only thing Della had left that wasn't stained or torn were her shoes. The only problem? She had no idea where they were.

Deciding to take the secretary at his word, Della shuffled to the bathroom door. She opened it, stuck her head out far enough to make sure she was alone, and scurried over to a huge, oak wardrobe with French provincial-carved scrollwork across its curved top. Flinging back both doors, she found a selection of women's garments in the latest designs suitable for all times of day or evening, but the sizes were limited to what would fit only the slender.

She pulled out a couple of day dresses that looked like they might fit. She glanced at the labels and gasped. A pale-yellow, sleeveless sheath with a dropped waist and layers of silk chiffon was by Chanel. A flowered green in cotton voile with short, flutter sleeves bore the name Schiaparelli. Clearly, someone with a knowledge of designers did Mr. Aldridge's shopping.

She returned the yellow to the wardrobe and closed its doors. The green was better suited to the ordeal that was coming. At some point, the policemen would have questions for her. Whether she could answer them was debatable. She knew so little of Art's plans for his new venture. Is that what got him killed? Surely not. Her chest heaved with unspent emotion.

To fight dissolving into sobs, Della concentrated on practical matters. Undergarments were needed. She spied a chest nearby and started pulling out drawers. Everything a woman could want was found within—knickers, chemises, all-in-ones, corsets, brassieres, slips, nightgowns, pajamas. She removed a brassiere, slip, and knickers and got dressed.

Looking at herself in a mirror hung by the bedroom door, warmth spread across her cheeks. No telling what the policemen would think when she showed up decked out in an expensive dress, no stockings, and bare feet. The thought of the image she would present made her giggle. The giggle became a snort that turned into howling laughter. The laughter devolved into wild tears. She grabbed a throw pillow from a chair by the chest of drawers and sank to the floor. Leaning into the pillow, she screamed until she was left gasping. Who gave a damn what anyone thought about how she was dressed?

Pounding on the door broke through her hysteria. Tossing the pillow aside and wiping her eyes with her discarded towel, she snarled, "What is it?"

Singletary's muffled voice cut through the door's heavy wood paneling. "If you are dressed, breakfast has been laid in the dining room. Once you have eaten, Chief Detective Barnett wants to interview you."

Slowly, Della rose to her feet. "Give me a minute." She returned to the bathroom and splashed cold water on her face, then ran it over her wrists. Leaning against the sink, she gazed into the mirror above it. Red, puffy eyes and blotchy skin—not a very appealing sight, but at least the water had cooled the searing heat her emotions created.

She made her way into the hall where the secretary waited. He glanced at her and quickly looked away, having the grace to not comment on her appearance.

As she padded beside him on the carpet runner, she watched him from the corner of her eye. There was no sign of stiffness in the way he moved as there had been the previous evening. Irritatingly, he looked as though he'd had a full night's sleep and was freshly turned out in an immaculate suit and tie. But then, why should she expect anything less? This was his place of employment, and an unidentified murderer had not slaughtered the person he loved most in the world.

# CHAPTER 5

They passed through a labyrinth of hallways, each one less elaborately decorated than its predecessor until attention to decor ceased altogether. If the secretary abandoned Della, she would have no idea where she was or how to find her way to the first floor.

Singletary must have sensed her growing distress for he slowed his pace and gave her a sideways glance. "I'm taking you to the dining room via the service stairs and back hall. I assumed you would rather not face the remaining guests. The last to be interviewed are waiting in the reception rooms. A very dissatisfied lot, I can tell you."

Della swallowed hard. Her throat was dry and her lips seemed incapable of forming words, so she simply nodded. Being the object of scrutiny, speculation, and perhaps pity would just about send her over the edge. The tattered seams of her emotions were ready to shred at the slightest provocation. She choked back a sob as a shudder passed through her. She would not cry, dammit. She must not give in. There would be plenty of time for tears once she was allowed the privacy of her own home. But then, would she really be able to bear going to the farmhouse so empty of Art yet still filled to the ceiling with his presence? Every corner, every room, every stick of furniture held a piece of him.

They came to a set of narrow stairs and began their descent. At the last step, Della found herself in a dimly lit hall with a large kitchen seen through open double doors on her right and rows of closed doors on her left. A few more yards brought them to a green baize door and a more formally decorated hall on the other side.

Within moments, they were in the dining room where silver chafing dishes on an enormous, mahogany sideboard awaited them.

Singletary led her to the dishes, lifting the lid on the first and looking at her inquiringly. "You should really try to eat something. I suspect this will be a long day for you." He handed her a fine china plate. "Mr. Aldridge hires only the best. His chef is no exception. This may be the best prepared breakfast you have ever tasted."

She peered into the dish. Scrambled eggs, fluffy and soft, lay in perfectly prepared mounds. Her stomach roiled at the sight. Bacon, sausage, ham, and grits had the same effect. She selected plain toast, grapefruit, and tea and went to the closest dining chair.

When the secretary did not take a seat but turned toward the door instead, a shock of panic raced through her. "Are you not eating?"

"No, I have had breakfast."

"Are you leaving?"

Puzzlement filled his eyes. He observed her for several seconds, then his expression softened. "I can stay if you prefer."

She dropped her gaze and nodded. "Yes, please." The thought of being alone in the house where Art had been murdered left her trembling. While Singletary could hardly be claimed as a friend, he had been the only person in the last twelve hours to show her any kindness. He would have to do.

He took the seat opposite her. "Add sugar to that tea. It will give you energy."

He showed consideration and discretion by allowing her to eat in silence. As she forced down the last bite of her meal, he stood. "Time to see Detective Barnett. I'm afraid we've put him off as long as possible."

Della's cup clattered when she returned it to the saucer, slopping tea over the rim and onto the white, linen tablecloth. She gasped and tabbed at the stain with her napkin. "I'm sorry." She dipped the cloth in her water glass and patted it again. "I think it will come out with a good washing."

"Mrs. Monroe, there is no need to be concerned. I assure you our laundress will take care of it." He came to her side of the table and assisted her with her chair. "We really must go. The detective has set up in the library. I'm afraid his patience is running rather thin."

They passed from the dining room into the grand hall. The double doors of the drawing room stood wide, and several pairs of eyes followed Della. She refused to look at them. Instead, she stiffened her spine and stared straight ahead. A few yards closer to the front doors, Singletary gestured toward a room lined with shelves filled with beautiful, leather-bound volumes. As she entered, Della's gaze traveled over the space. No expense had been spared in presenting their owner as a patron of the written word. Had he read them all? Judging by the pristine appearance of their spines, probably not.

A throat clearing made Della jump. Barnett sat behind a large, mahogany desk with his sergeant standing to one side. Barnett rose and gestured toward a chair. "Please take a seat, Mrs. Monroe. I hope you are feeling better."

Della sat but did not answer his question. What does one say when one may never feel better again?

Barnett resumed his seat and placed his elbows on the desk. Making a bridge of his hands, he peered at her over tapping index fingers. "I'm sure no one wants this matter resolved and the culprit apprehended more than you, so let's get straight to work." Barnett nodded dismissal to Singletary, who turned to leave.

Della swiveled and called out, "No. Don't go. Please." The thought of being left alone with strangers suddenly seemed beyond endurance. Gathering herself, she continued, "I would like for Mr. Singletary to stay."

Barnett raised a brow, but nodded. "I don't usually allow such, but given the circumstances, I suppose I can make an exception." He shot the secretary an enquiring look.

Singletary answered the unspoken question with a slight inclination of the head. "I'm happy to be of service. Mrs. Monroe has had a terrible shock and suffered a significant loss. I was with her when the . . . incident occurred. While we only met last night, I am perhaps a familiar face among strangers."

Della nodded vigorously. "Yes. That's it. I know no one here. Mr. Singletary has been very kind."

"Okay, then." Barnett gestured toward the secretary. "Take a seat."

Barnett watched Della for a moment, then nodded toward his colleague, who stood poised with notebook and pencil. "Sergeant, I believe Mrs. Monroe would feel more comfortable without you looming over her. Grab that chair by the window."

The detective returned his attention to Della. "You're almost the last to be interviewed. Wanted to give you a chance to get ahold of yourself."

Della's eyes widened. Of course the man had a job to do, but all solicitude seemed to have melted away, replaced by a brusque, down-to-business demeanor. "Thank you. I will do my best to help in any way I can."

Barnett shuffled a set of papers on the desk. Selecting one, he slid a diagram of the pavilion and dock across to her. "Can you show us where you were when your husband was shot?"

Della studied the paper and placed her finger on the place she thought was correct. She looked at Singletary for confirmation. When he nodded, she tapped the spot. "There. We were next to the balustrade, waiting for Art and Mr. Aldridge to finish their conversation."

"What were they talking about?"

"I really don't know. Art, my husband, didn't tell me their plan—only that they were going to discuss a deal of some kind."

Barnett and Singletary exchanged glances. The detective shifted in his chair. "I see. So, it's your belief that your husband came here last night to do business?"

Della felt stirrings of disquiet. "Yes. He said he was on the verge of something big."

"Did he say what?"

She shook her head. "No, he kept the actual plan a secret. He didn't want to get my hopes up in case it all came to nothing."

"So, he didn't tell you his plans? No details whatsoever?" Doubt colored Barnett's words.

"As I said, I have no idea what he had hoped to do. All I know is what he told me." Della hated the whine her rising alarm generated.

Barnett's eyes narrowed as he leaned toward her over the desk. "And that is?"

Della's eyes darted from the detective to the secretary and back. She found no comfort in either. With a shaky voice, she answered, "That we would be meeting important people, and we needed to make a good impression."

"Did he say who these important people were?" His voice was harsher with each word.

Della's hand covered her mouth to conceal a trembling lip. "I really don't know. We met so many last night. I think Mr. Aldridge and Mr. Shoemaker were the ones he wanted to impress the most." Her words tumbled over one another in her rush to explain. What was he getting at? It felt as though he was about to accuse her or Art of some crime.

"Why? What left you with that impression?" Barnett sat back and seemed to relax. He was playing some sort of game with her.

Della drew a long breath and exhaled slowly. "Well . . . because Mr. Aldridge wanted to speak to Art in private. That's why they went to the boat. To be away from other people."

Barnett's expression hardened with suspicion. The crease between his eyes deepened. "So, you don't know what they talked about?" His words held a note of disbelief.

"No. How many times must I say it?" Della's voice rose on the final words.

Barnett placed his arms on the chair's armrests, and he leaned toward Della. "Then, you would be surprised to hear that Aldridge and Shoemaker said there was to be no deal?"

Bewildered, Della felt as though the Art she knew was slipping away from her and being replaced by a stranger. "But they must have talked about working together." Her voice sounded weak and small. "Why else would Art say there was a potential deal? Why would Mr. Aldridge want to speak to him in private?"

A note of sympathy entered the detective's eyes until he quelled it with a frown. His demeanor became all business once more. "When your husband approached him about going into business together, Mr. Aldridge felt compelled to at least hear the proposal. In the end, both he and Mr. Shoemaker believed the plan was ill advised. They told your husband as much last night. They claim the purpose in seeking the privacy of the boat was to tell your husband in the least embarrassing way possible that they had no intention of going into business with him. In fact, Mr. Aldridge and Mr. Shoemaker say you and Mr. Monroe were only invited to last night's party out of courtesy to your father's memory."

Della shook her head again. None of this was making sense. "I don't understand. What does my father have to do with any of this? He died several years ago."

"Apparently, as bank manager, your father provided business loans to Mr. Aldridge when he first settled in Florida." Barnett's voice had become very matter-of-fact. "Mr. Aldridge invested the money in real estate and has done very well. Your invitation was a courtesy and nothing more, according to Aldridge."

"But then, why was my husband murdered?"

With a smile that held no warmth, Barnett said quietly, "We're hoping you might be able to shed some light on that."

# CHAPTER 6

Della blinked twice. Barnett's probing was taking a turn she had not expected. "Me? I have no earthly idea why someone wanted Art dead." Her voice quivered. Any shred of courage or calm she had left were in grave danger of deserting her. "How can you ask such a question?"

Barnett eyed her for a moment, then said, "Because we must. No one is closer to a husband than his wife. Husbands and wives often share secrets. Did he ever mention enemies or someone who might want to harm him?"

Della shook her head. "No. Never. We're dairy farmers. We live on the family farm inherited from his parents. The only people we see on a regular basis are the farmhands. They don't own boats, and they're good men with families."

"I see. Have there been arguments over pay or working conditions, maybe?"

"Of course not. Art was a good, fair landlord."

"Landlord? So, your workers are also tenant farmers?"

"Yes. Both families have been on the farm for two or three generations. Art has . . . had the utmost affection for them, and they for him."

Barnett's brow creased as he stroked his chin. "Has the farm made a profit? Given agricultural prices in recent years, your husband would have been a miracle worker to make money. A lot of farmers have given up and sold out to people like Mr. Aldridge and Mr. Shoemaker."

Della dropped her eyes and studied her hands clasped in a grip so tense, her knuckles had blanched under the pressure. "We pay our bills and don't owe anybody. We've struggled some, but we're basically okay."

"Do you think your husband had hopes of using the farm for development with Mr. Aldridge?"

"I can't believe for one minute he would consider selling our land."

Barnett's eyes narrowed. "Then what business do you think he hoped to enter into?"

"I've told you. I don't know. I really don't know what he'd planned. Why must you keep asking? My husband is dead, and I am utterly alone now." Della buried her face in her hands and shook with uncontrollable sobs.

Singletary stirred beside her. "Detective, it seems Mrs. Monroe does not know what her husband planned or at least hoped to achieve. Given what she is facing, perhaps it would be best for someone to take her home. I'm sure there are people she must notify. You know where she lives. She's not going anywhere. Give her time to grieve and start making arrangements."

Barnett harrumphed and pushed himself back from the desk. Rising, he nodded. "I suppose you're right." Looking at Della, he continued, "Don't leave the county. We'll have more questions as the case develops."

She wiped her face with the handkerchief Singletary had held out. "I don't know what else I can tell you, and there is nowhere I want to go."

"Good. We'll be in touch." To his sergeant, he said, "Make sure we have Mrs. Monroe's details, and get an officer to take her home." He paused and glanced at Singletary and then back at Della. "I understand your farm is somewhat isolated. Since you seem to have no information about why your husband was killed, you may not be in danger, but we need to be on the safe side. Is there anybody who can stay in the house with you?"

Della couldn't muster the emotional energy to speak, so she shook her head.

Barnett began straightening a stack of papers. "Maybe one of your tenants?"

Incandescent rage swept through Della, providing the fuel she needed. She gritted her teeth. "If I am in danger, do you really believe I would want to put families in danger as well? My tenants have children. Those children need their parents."

Barnett placed his fists on the desk. Leaning forward, he glared at Della. "Now see here, young lady. There's no need to go off like that." Realizing his manner had the desired effect, he continued in a less threatening tone. "Maybe you should take a place in town until this is over."

"I can't afford it." Her voice was weak and devoid of color. The cyclone of emotions generated over the past twenty-four hours had pushed Della between giddy highs and bottomless lows. She was completely drained. "May I please go? I need to let people know what's happened."

"Very well. Since your farm is in the county, the best I can do is ask the sheriff to send deputies by your place on their rounds. Do you have a telephone?" When Della nodded, Barnett withdrew a card from his pocket. He wrote on it, then handed it to Della. "The numbers on the front are my office. The one on the back is the sheriff. If you need help at home, call the sheriff. If you think of anything, even if it seems unimportant, call me."

Della rose, then her hand flew to her mouth. "I nearly forgot. What about our car?"

Barnett looked at his sergeant. "Are the boys finished going over it?"

"Yeah. Didn't find anything."

"Do you drive, Mrs. Monroe?"

"Yes."

"I'll have one of my men follow you home then."

Singletary stepped forward. "If I may, Mrs. Monroe is not in the best frame of mind to drive herself. Perhaps I might drive her car, and I'll call a cab to bring me back here?"

Della wanted to be offended. She was perfectly capable of driving, but feeling insulted required more energy than she had. Moreover, the plan provided time to prepare herself for the dreaded task that lay ahead. Her mother and Art's cousins in South Carolina must be told. Just thinking about those phone calls sucked the life out of her. Perhaps her energy would be higher at home where she had always felt safe and loved.

$$\bullet \quad \bullet \quad \bullet \quad \bullet \quad \bullet$$

Tires crunching on oyster shells snapped Della out of her waking nightmare. She straightened up in her seat and rolled her head to relieve the tension that knotted the muscles at the base of her skull.

The farmhouse front door stood open, sending a thrill of fear tingling through her. Art had closed the door when they left last night. She was sure of it. Of course, they never locked their doors. Nobody did. There had never been reason to do so. Did this mean she would forever be looking over her shoulder and locking her doors? Della wilted at the thought.

Singletary jumped down from the driver's seat and came around to her side. Opening her door, he extended his hand. "Are you always in the habit of leaving your doors open? Perhaps I should go in first."

Della sighed and pointed at the porch where the screened door had just slammed shut. "There's no need. Mrs. Adams is here. She must have opened the door."

"Is she a friend?"

"Yes. She and her husband are tenants. I wonder why she's here."

As soon as Della stepped down from the car, Mrs. Adams scurried from the porch and put an arm around her shoulders. "Oh, you poor, dear girl. A policeman came by early this morning and told us the news. He asked all kinds of strange questions, too." Mrs. Adams cast a speculative glance over Singletary, who introduced himself by name only. "Pleased to meet you. Y'all come on inside. I've got iced tea and a pound cake ready. There's chicken casserole in the frig for your dinner. All you need to do is put it in the oven."

They all trooped into the house where Della slumped down onto a kitchen chair. Singletary stood quietly beside her. Mrs. Adams dithered about, straightening a dishrag hanging on the sink's faucet and looking uncomfortable. She fixed the secretary with a meaningful expression. "Will you be staying for dinner?"

"No . . . thank you." There was a note of confusion in his voice. "I'll take my dinner at the villa this evening, as always. I would like a private word with Mrs. Monroe, then I must return to work."

When he did not elaborate, Mrs. Adams said with a flutter of her hands, "Well then, I guess I oughta be getting back home. Mr. Adams expects his dinner on the table at noon every day, come rain or shine." She stooped and gave Della a hug. "You call us if you need anything at all. We're just across the pasture. Mr. Adams can be here in a jiffy with his shotgun." She gave Singletary a stern nod and exited by the back door.

Singletary pulled out a chair. "May I?"

Della nodded. "Please forgive Mrs. Adams. She means well. Her husband's family have been tenants since long before Art was born. I think she looks on Art and me as two more children. With us, that would make twelve all together."

Singletary whistled softly. "That's quite a brood. I'm glad you have someone you can count on. She seems like a fine woman, although I think she's suspicious of me. Perhaps my confusion over what time of day dinner is served was off-putting."

"Yes, that marked you as an uppity Yankee, for sure. We country folks follow the old Southern tradition of serving the main meal in the middle of the day."

He chuckled. "I'll try to remember that in the future so as not to be marked an ignorant carpetbagger." Singletary was quiet for a moment, then asked, "Do you have anyone to help you? This all seems a lot for you to shoulder on your own."

Della drew a long breath and exhaled slowly. "Only family left are my mother, her brother, and Art's cousins. Mama has lived with her brother on their family farm in Georgia since Papa died. She refuses to travel any farther than Thomasville. Says that she can't abide the influx of strangers into South Florida. In reality, she would be of little help. She does not bear up well in a crisis. The cousins in South Carolina have no vested interest in this farm, but one of them is a lawyer. Maybe he'll come down, if I ask."

"It's good to be with family at a time like this. I'll be happy to answer any questions your cousin may have. It might also be well to have an attorney with you when Detective Barnett speaks with you again. Sounds like the cousin fills the bill on both counts."

Della's heart thumped against her rib cage. "Why do I need a lawyer? I haven't done anything wrong."

Singletary looked away and studied the pastures beyond the kitchen window as though grazing dairy cows were of extraordinary interest. When he looked at Della again, his expression was one of sympathy and kindness. "When a crime has been committed, the investigation sometimes takes unexpected turns. It's always wise to ensure one's interests are protected."

"My interests? Why?"

"Well, that's the question, isn't it?"

# CHAPTER 7

Della stood on the porch and watched Mr. Singletary's departing cab through narrowed eyes. The man was a puzzle. He could be kind, but also brutal in his words and opinions. He had implied the police might suspect her of being involved in Art's murder. Or, had he? Maybe she had misunderstood. She wrapped her arms around her midsection to control the trembling that threatened to send her to her knees. This nightmare was so heartbreakingly confusing. Art was a good man. He had no enemies. So why was he dead?

These churning thoughts and unanswerable questions had to stop. She must get a grip. There were too many things to do, and the first was to make the dreaded phone calls. Singletary had offered to stay while she made them or even make them for her, but somehow, she needed to be alone when she broke the news.

No doubt Mama would cry and say she knew Della should not have married Art in the first place. Their wedding had taken place a scant two months after they ran into each other—literally. Memories flooded her heart and mind.

They had met in what Art called a "meet cute," a term he had picked up during his brief acting days. She had been a teller in the bank Papa managed. Even with her degree from Wesleyan College, there had been few job openings for women. Teaching had not appealed. She was not qualified to be a nurse, so with nepotism providing employment, bank teller was where she landed. She had been returning from her lunch break, late as usual, and had been dashing to the bank doors.

•  •  •  •  •

With a sharp bump against her knees, Della's feet flew out from under her. She landed firmly on her bottom with her skirt up over her thighs. A guy stood over her, grinning and extending his hand. She glared up at him and hauled herself to her feet by her own power. The oaf had the effrontery to laugh.

She placed a fist on her hip and snarled, "Do you always find humor in knocking people down?"

Her assailant had the good grace to blush. "No . . . I . . . Of course not, and I'm very sorry I bumped into you, but I must say you weren't exactly looking where you were going, either."

"Really? I had my eyes straight ahead and my hand on the door when you burst through it. It seems you're the only one guilty of not paying attention. *You* should look where *you're* going, buster." Her words bounced off the buildings opposite and echoed down the street.

The man blinked twice and then guffawed. People stopped and stared. Della's mouth thinned as she crossed her arms and fixed him with a sharp glare.

When he got control of himself, he wiped his streaming eyes. "I'm sorry. I truly am. My only excuse is that securing a greatly needed loan with the bank and being in the presence of an adorable creature has made me giddy. My manners deserted me. I apologize—profusely. Please say I'm forgiven." He looked deeply into her eyes. His expression softened with pleading. "And let me take you to supper to make up for my carelessness and stupidity."

Della's foot tapped while she considered his offer. He was clearly full of himself, but he was mighty good-looking and his apology seemed sincere. In truth, she had nothing better to do since she had broken it off with her latest beau. She pursed her lips and narrowed her eyes. "When?"

"How about tonight? Do you like stone crabs?"

"I'm not sure. I haven't tasted them."

"If you like seafood, you'll love them. There's a place on Miami Beach, Joe's Stone Crab, that serves them hot, cold, anyway you want them. Pick you up here at four o'clock?"

"No, I'm usually balancing my till at that time."

"Five o'clock, then?"

She sucked on her lower lip while she debated with herself. She was not the type of girl who allowed men to pick her up on the street . . . or any other place. Men did not respect women who were easy.

Still, he looked like a movie star and was dressed in a nice, well-cut suit. And it wasn't like he was a complete stranger.

But wait. That's exactly what he was. They had exchanged maybe a dozen words in the space of about five minutes. She didn't even know his name. On the other hand, he seemed contrite and sincere in his desire to apologize. Maybe one dinner wouldn't hurt.

Finally, she nodded and was on the verge of demanding his name when Papa's assistant manager appeared in the doorway. He looked disgruntled. "Miss Williams, this is the third time this week. Even your father is losing patience. You have a line waiting at your window."

The stranger, with whom she had just agreed to have dinner, snorted. "Your father? Mr. Herbert Williams?"

Della waggled her eyebrows. "Oh, didn't I say? Papa's the bank manager." She shouted over her shoulder while she scurried after her boss, "What's your name?"

The answer, Art Monroe, drifted through the closing doors.

•　•　•　•　•

She buried her face in her hands and sobbed. *Oh, Art. Dearest love. Why did this happen to us? Why did we have to go to that damn party?* She lost track of time as she gave in to the rising tempest. When the storm finally passed, she wiped her face with the skirt of the borrowed designer frock and trudged into the living room. She dropped onto the wing chair beside the telephone table.

The call to her mother went as predicted. Della listened for as long as she could bear to the rehashing of Mama's dire warnings about marrying a virtual stranger, then ended the call abruptly. Mama was not needed in Miami.

Next, she gave the operator the Abbeville, South Carolina number for Art's cousin's law office.

A female voice answered, "Breckenridge, Porter, and Mayfield, attorneys at law."

"Mr. Breckenridge, please."

"Whom may I say is calling?"

"His cousin's wife from Miami. Tell him it's urgent. There has been a terrible accident."

"Of course, madam."

The line crackled, and Augustus—Auggie to friends and family—Breckenridge's familiar baritone sounded on the other end. "Della, what on earth has happened? The receptionist said you sounded frantic."

"Oh God, Auggie. Something horrible has happened. Art has been murdered." She gasped out the words between sobs. "I need you here. Please say you'll come."

"Of course, my dear. I will be on the first train south. I'll telegram my travel arrangements. I must go now. With luck, I will be with you by tomorrow evening."

He hung up without even asking for details. All he had to hear was that family needed him, and he was on his way.

Della had always liked Auggie, but she now saw how truly loving and kind he was. He and Art were first cousins and had spent summers and holidays together. Auggie was Art's closest living relative and the executor of his will. He and Art were as close as brothers.

Della slumped against the chairback and laid her head against its top. Calls made. Now what? She glanced at the mantel clock. 2 p.m. She hadn't eaten since early morning, but just thinking about food left her nauseated. Still, she had to eat something. She couldn't afford to take to her bed and have the nervous breakdown that beckoned from the darkest corners of her mind.

She plodded to the kitchen and shoved Mrs. Adams's casserole into the oven. One small decision made, but so many more to come. She sank onto the closest chair. Simply thinking about the future drained away her meager reserves of energy.

# CHAPTER 8

Della rolled over, rubbed her eyes, and struggled to sit up. Someone was banging on the front door. Picking up the alarm clock, she squinted at it. It couldn't be. She rubbed her eyes again. The hands had not moved. Four o'clock. It had to be afternoon because the sun was slanting through the window. She shook her head to clear it. She had slept for . . . twenty-two hours straight. Was it exhaustion or depression that had sent her into such a prolonged stupor? Probably both.

She swung her feet down to the floor and stood on wobbly legs. Grabbing her robe, she shuffled to the living room and peered through the glass in the front door. *Oh, my goodness!* She swung the door back and flung her arms around Art's cousin.

Augustus Breckenridge, attorney at law, smiled as he eased himself from her embrace and moved them both inside. "I'm glad to see you've been resting. Am I in the back bedroom, as usual?"

Della nodded, rendered mute by a sleep-fuzzed brain. When Auggie disappeared from the central hall, she went to the sofa and flopped down, trying to organize her thoughts. He would want information.

He returned quickly, sat beside her, and took her hand. "Now, tell me everything."

For the next half hour, Della stumbled through an explanation of the previous two days' events, concluding with the most alarming detail. "The police are even hinting that I might be a suspect." She looked at Auggie through tear-filled eyes. "I know nothing. I loved him. How can they suggest I would want him harmed?"

Auggie did not answer immediately. He squeezed her hand while he appeared to ponder her question. Finally, he said, "Because the spouse and those closest to the victim are always under suspicion in these cases. Rest assured, I will see that you are quickly eliminated from their list of suspects." He paused again. His brow wrinkled. "Perhaps the first thing we should attend to is making funeral arrangements. Have the police said when they will release Art's body?"

Della shook her head. "I haven't asked. I didn't think about that because I have been so upset. I've never experienced anything like this."

"Of course you haven't." He removed a notepad and pen from the breast pocket of his blue-and-white-striped seersucker suit jacket. "I took the liberty of contacting a former classmate who has his practice here. He provided guidance on how best to proceed with local officials. If you have no objections, tomorrow I will make a few phone calls on your behalf."

"Yes, please do. I would not know where to start."

•   •   •   •   •

After three weeks of Auggie asking, cajoling, and finally threatening legal action if Art's body was not released for burial, Della stood staring into the open grave. The minister was speaking. She knew that, but his words were meaningless noise. Nothing penetrated the overwhelming fog of grief.

A hand gently squeezed her elbow. Auggie leaned in and whispered, "It's time to return to the house. The neighbors have laid out food for a reception. Mrs. Adams was most insistent."

Della sniffed and dabbed at her eyes. Still in something of a daze, she muttered, "I really don't think I can bear the inevitable questions."

Auggie gave her a small smile as he waggled his eyebrows. "I took Mrs. Adams into our confidence about that. She has everyone under control. They'll be on their best behavior. I'm assured no prying will be allowed. They've all been forewarned to only speak with you briefly once we've gotten back to the house. I've found she's something of a force within the community. I think I could easily fall in love with that woman." The last sentence was issued with a Cheshire cat smile.

Despite her muddled state, Della snorted and covered her mouth. Between her fingers, she whispered, "She takes her position very seriously, sometimes to extremes, but today, she's a godsend." Being able to laugh a little with Auggie lifted the fog somewhat, bringing a greater awareness of her surroundings.

Della surveyed her friends and neighbors as they milled around, speaking to one another and casting surreptitious glances at the lurking police presence. She found no surprises, until one face caught her off guard. Mr. Singletary nodded to her from beneath the huge live oak at the edge of the cemetery.

Tugging Auggie's sleeve, she gestured toward the tree. "I wonder why he's here."

Auggie followed her line of interest. His lips curved into a smile. "Nice-looking fella. Who is he?"

Della explained the secretary's position and his involvement in the events the night of Art's murder.

Auggie's eyes narrowed. "Do you think he might hold some answers to the mystery?"

Della shrugged. "I have no idea. If he comes to the house, maybe we should ask him if he has heard anything new."

"Do you feel up to that?"

Della breathed deeply as she mulled over the question. If she allowed her grief to control her heart, mind, and soul, she would lose what little sanity she had left. Art had been murdered. No amount of crying, shouting, or wailing could change that. Did she have the strength to think straight and function with any semblance of normalcy? God only knew, for she certainly did not. There was one thing, however, that was a certainty. This whole sorry mess was probably going to get a lot worse before it got better, and she needed to have her wits about her.

As much as she loved Art, as devastated as she was, she was becoming terrified of the future. The fact that the police had watched the service in the church and then at the graveside without speaking to her or Auggie left her uneasy. The more she thought about it, the faster her heart raced and the clearer her mind became.

She looked at Auggie as tears filled her eyes. "I don't think we have another choice. I'm scared, and Detective Barnett refusing to tell you anything when you talk to him isn't helping."

"Well, then. Let's get the reception over with and see what your new friend might be willing to tell us. I'll make sure he stays until all of the other guests are gone."

For the next hour, Della greeted her guests and thanked them for attending Art's funeral. As Mrs. Adams had promised, no one mentioned the method of Art's demise, nor did they try to discuss details, at least to Della's face. In unoccupied moments, she felt eyes on her, and turning, saw people stop speaking and look away.

When the final neighbor had been shooed home by Mrs. Adams, she approached Della. "That man who brought you home after . . . well, you know. That man says he won't leave until he talks to you. I can get my man to make him leave if you don't want to see him." She looked like she was on the verge of calling for her husband and his shotgun.

Della placed a hand on Mrs. Adams's arm. "No, please don't. Mr. Breckenridge and I want to speak with him. In fact, we asked him to stay until we were able to speak in privacy." Della hoped her emphasis on the last word did not come across as harsh as it felt.

"Well, if you're sure." Taking the rather pointed hint, Mrs. Adams gathered her family and departed.

Auggie was already with Singletary at the dining room table when Della joined them. They stood as she entered the room.

Della sat in the chair Auggie pulled out for her, then directed her attention to the secretary as both men resumed their seats. "Mr.

Singletary, thank you for attending today. I must say I am rather surprised you are able to get away from work given your responsibilities, but I'm glad you're here. Mr. Breckenridge and I have some questions we hope you'll answer."

Singletary gave her a tight smile. "Attending your husband's funeral was the least we could do. I am representing not only myself, but Mr. Aldridge and Mr. Shoemaker as well. They sent their regrets and deepest condolences, but a previous engagement could not be avoided."

Della noted he had not asked what her questions might be. "That's understandable given how unexpected . . . events have been." She glanced at Auggie, who gave her a subtle nod. "I apologize if we're about to put you on the spot, but we're wondering if you might tell us what's going on at the villa—if there's new information."

The crease between Singletary's eyes deepened. "While I have no problem divulging information in the right circumstances, I wonder why you need to ask me for it."

Della bit on her lower lip while considering the best approach. Finally, she chose honesty. "The police aren't being very forthcoming. I think they're under the impression I know more than I'm telling them, or maybe I even had a part in my husband's murder. It's all pretty confusing and frightening. Your kindness on previous occasions gives me hope that you might be willing to help me now."

Singletary leaned back in his chair and folded his arms over his chest. "My employers are very particular about talk associated with them or their businesses. Precisely what do you want to know?"

Della tried to not appear too desperate. "Can you tell me why Mr. Aldridge and Mr. Shoemaker wanted to talk to Art the night of the party?"

Singletary shrugged. "I know what they told the police."

After a moment's silence, Auggie said, "I get the impression you don't necessarily believe the company line."

"I didn't say that."

This time, Della could not keep the pleading out of her voice. "So what did they say?"

Singletary fixed her, then Auggie, with a stern expression. "If I become involved in your little cabal, what assurance do I have that you are first, innocent as you claim, and second, that my own interests will be protected?"

Della shrugged. "I guess none, other than my word and that of Mr. Breckenridge. He's a lawyer, by the way, so I guess he has to be honest where crime is concerned. Is that right, Auggie?"

"Yes, as an officer of the court, I'm bound by a code of ethics and the law where criminal behavior is concerned, unless you're my client. Then you must not tell me of your guilt. I can't defend you if you tell me you committed the crime."

Singletary smirked, then chuckled. "Fair enough. I'll tell you what my employers are maintaining. Then, I will tell you what I think is closer to the truth."

Auggie's eyes narrowed. He looked at Singletary, then at Della, then back. "Not to put too fine a point on it, but why are you being so accommodating? You have no real assurances other than the words of two relative strangers."

Singletary's gaze lingered on Della. "Because I believe Mrs. Monroe deserves the truth."

# CHAPTER 9

Della closed her eyes. If she continued looking at Singletary, she would dissolve in tears. His kindness and belief in her were overwhelming. There was no real reason to offer either, but he had, nonetheless.

Her nails dug into her palms, distracting herself from a rising tide of emotion. "You give me courage, Mr. Singletary. Please tell us what you know."

"I suspect you'll find it hurtful. Are you sure you want to hear it?"

Della glanced at Auggie for support. He studied her for a moment, then said, "I believe Mrs. Monroe needs to hear what you have to say. I doubt she can be more hurt than she has been already."

Singletary ignored Auggie and focused on Della. "Are you *sure?*" When she nodded, he said, "You need to know that my employers are holding their cards very close to the vest regarding the events of that awful evening. Normally, I'm included in all of their business discussions. They often joke that I'm their memory and their conscience. With this situation, however, they've essentially locked me out."

Auggie sat forward and frowned. "And this knowledge helps us . . . how?"

Singletary's lip curled as he shot Auggie a disgruntled look. "They must be hiding something."

"Elucidate. Being cryptic is not helping. What have they told the police?"

Singletary's gaze shifted from Auggie to Della to the front parlor's arched entrance and back. He appeared to be having second thoughts. "My employers have an expectation of confidentiality where I'm concerned. Once I've broken faith with Mr. Aldridge and Mr. Shoemaker, there will be no going back for me."

Auggie slapped the table. "Oh, for the love of God, man, get on with it. You've come this far. Either you're going to help us or you aren't."

Singletary crossed his arms over his abdomen and fixed Auggie with a hard stare. "Very well. I have no desire to hurt Mrs. Monroe, but it's unavoidable if you're to know the truth. As Barnett told you, my employers have said there wasn't going to be a deal of any kind."

Della sat forward. That couldn't be right. "But Art and I were invited to the party where the deal would be finalized. Why would Art have said that if it weren't so?"

Singletary placed his arms on the table and leaned toward Della. "How much do you know about the bank's financial dealings while your father was the manager?"

"Not all that much. I worked there for a couple of years straight out of college, but Daddy never talked business at home when I was growing up. When I went to work for him, it was as a teller. Tellers aren't privy to much of the bank's business."

Singletary nodded. "I see. According to Aldridge and Shoemaker, you and your husband were supposedly invited to the party out of respect for your father's memory and nothing more. They say they told your husband there would be no deal the night of the party. Furthermore, they're claiming it was your husband who came to them with a business proposal, but I believe it was the other way around."

Della's heart rate kicked up a notch. "Do you have proof of that?"

Singletary studied his hands. "Unfortunately, no, but I know how they operate. They don't do anything unless it benefits them or fits in with their plans."

"Yes, I can believe that. Here's another thing that doesn't make sense. Mr. Aldridge has thrown big parties for years. Why think of Daddy now? Why not soon after he died or while he was still alive?"

"Good point. Why now, indeed." Irony colored Singletary's words. His eyes narrowed. "A conversation of some sort must have taken place based on the amount of time the three of them were alone in the boat. If my employers told your husband he was not getting their financial support, he certainly appeared to take it *very* calmly."

Della blinked several times. "Here's something I don't understand. If they weren't going to do the deal, why didn't they just tell him in an office or something?"

"Precisely. They claim they feared your husband's reaction."

"Afraid of Art? That's ridiculous. He never hurt anyone. He was not a violent man."

"Yes, that was my assessment." Singletary paused and fixed Della with a look containing compassion and a hint of suspicion. "What did your husband tell you about the deal he hoped to make?"

Della shrugged. "Nothing. Absolutely nothing. All he said was if everything went as planned, our financial problems would disappear. He would make money—a lot of it."

"How confident was he about his plan being accepted by Aldridge and Shoemaker?"

"He made it seem like all we needed to do was show up and make one final good impression."

"That jibes with what I observed the night of the party." Singletary looked at the window but did not seem to see the pastures beyond. He was quiet for so long, the tension in the room became palpable. Finally, he focused on Della but did not speak.

She did not press him for more immediately, in large part because she feared what he would say. Finally, the silence was unbearable. "What do you think really happened?" Her voice was quiet, almost a whisper.

"I believe my employers had every intention of going into business with Mr. Monroe but are now hiding the truth. The logical conclusion is that the three of them planned something that is not strictly legal."

Della's heart sank. "Art would never have agreed to something illegal." She turned to Auggie. "He wouldn't have, would he?"

He shook his head. "Not the Art I knew. He was a straight arrow from infancy. Never even took an extra cookie when Grandma forgot to put them away. There must be another explanation."

Singletary pursed his lips and raised a brow. "Perhaps, but why all the secrecy?"

Della looked at Auggie, imploring him to provide an answer, but he shrugged and shook his head. Reaching into his breast pocket, he withdrew a business card and pen, wrote on the back, and handed the card to Singletary.

"You've expressed the belief that Mrs. Monroe deserves to know the truth of why her husband died. As Art's cousin, I share that sentiment. As the executor of his estate, I absolutely must know the truth. The life insurance won't pay if there's doubt about why he died. Underwriters take a dim view of anything that smacks of risky or illegal behavior leading to death. Until we know what happened, Della gets nothing. The farm is mortgaged to the hilt. She's in danger of losing everything."

Della stuffed her fist in her mouth and bit down on her knuckles, stifling a cry. When she had control of herself, she grabbed Auggie's arm. "What do you mean? We've struggled, but Art said nothing about taking out another mortgage. Why?"

"My guess is he didn't want you to worry. You know what an optimist he was. He always thought things would work out, no matter the circumstances."

"Did you know about his proposal to Mr. Aldridge? Did you?" Della's words sounded shrill, but she didn't care.

Auggie refused to meet her gaze. "No. He never said a word about that or the mortgages. In fact, I had no idea he was in so deep until I started working on the probate. I'm sorry you had to find out like this."

Della's mouth thinned. "So, you've known there was trouble practically the whole time you've been here. Exactly when were you planning on telling me?"

"Once all the debts were settled. If the insurance settlement had come through as I first thought it would, the bank could have been paid off with enough left for you to live comfortably. It will be quite a large payout if and when it comes, especially given that Art was not a rich man."

Della felt as though someone had just sucked all the air from the room. She couldn't breathe. She got up and staggered into the kitchen. Yanking the cold water tap, she bent over the sink and allowed the water to flood her face until her head stopped swimming.

Auggie placed his hand on her shoulder and handed her the kitchen towel. "I'm truly sorry. I didn't think you needed to know about the mortgages and life insurance until it was absolutely necessary."

She wiped her face, then dropped the towel on the drainboard. She leaned against the counter for support while her insides roiled. "Do the police know?"

"Of course. I'm a lawyer. I can't lie about information like that. I would lose my license. They asked, and I had to tell them." He wrapped his arm around her shoulders. "Come back to the dining room. This guy seems like he wants to help us, but I think he needs you to persuade him."

Della and Auggie resumed their seats at the dining room table.

Nodding at his card in the secretary's hand, Auggie said, "You'll find the telephone number of a local attorney should you need the services of one. He's a close friend and former classmate. You can trust him implicitly. You may give him information in the event you are unable to reach me or Mrs. Monroe. The other number is the one here at the house. Will you agree to keep us informed of anything you learn?"

Singletary's eyes narrowed as he turned the card over and back again, then he looked at Della.

Auggie was right. She had to do the asking. "Please, Mr. Singletary. You can see what a mess I'm in. Please say you'll help us."

Singletary studied her for a moment, then smirked. "Yeah, I'll help you." A derisive laugh filled the room. "I've just about had enough of my employers and their business dealings anyway. It's time someone stood up to them."

Auggie grinned. "Good man. Is there a private line we can reach you on?" After receiving Singletary's card, he stood and extended his hand. "If we are going to be partners, perhaps we can risk first names?"

Singletary chuckled and stood. Grasping Auggie's hand, he said, "I think it's worth the risk, but probably best to keep it formal outside our small circle." His eyes met Della's. "Of course, if Mrs. Monroe has objections . . ."

"No. None. Please call me Della. And thank you. Thank you for all that you have done and are doing. I could not have made it without your kindness."

Singletary's expression softened. "I'm Luke to my friends. But you're wrong, you know."

Della's forehead creased. "How so?"

"You're far stronger than you realize. I saw it the night of your husband's murder, and I see it now." He glanced from Della to Auggie. "I need to get back to the villa. Don't want suspicions raised by being gone too long."

After she saw Luke to the door, Della returned to the dining room and resumed her seat.

Auggie studied Luke's card. "Would you object if I spoke to this Anders Aldridge fellow?"

Della straightened her posture. "What excuse will you use?"

"You need the insurance money. I'm trying to get it for you. Aldridge and Shoemaker will want to verify there was nothing illegal going on. They will explain Art's business proposal as proof. Unless they lie, it should give us a starting place."

"And if they lie?"

"It may still give us a place to start."

"Won't the police object to us doing our own investigation?"

"They very well may, but it's been three weeks. What progress have they made?"

"Not much, other than to imply that I had something to do with Art's murder."

"Precisely."

"I'll call Luke tomorrow and see if he can arrange an appointment."

"I'm going with you."

"I'm not sure that's advisable."

Della drew a long breath and exhaled slowly. "Maybe, but here's the thing. If I don't do something constructive to find out why Art was killed, I'll go crazy."

# CHAPTER 10

Della and Augustus sat in Art's two-seat roadster staring at Villa Lucca's long, winding driveway. Heavy chain snaked through the decorative ironwork of the double entry gates with ends fastened by a huge padlock. A guard stood behind the gates with his arms crossed over his protruding belly. He continued to glare and shake his head at them until crunching gravel behind him drew his attention.

Everyone focused on Singletary moving toward the gates. Singletary, not Luke as he had requested. Della had not said his name, either first or last, since he had asked that they be less formal. She could not think of him as Luke just yet. It was too soon. He might address her as Della, but he would be Singletary to her.

He said something to the guard, who tugged his cap and muttered, "You're the boss."

Key in hand, Singletary released the chain, opened the right gate, and stood back for the car to pass through. When it stopped, he stepped onto the running board and grabbed the windscreen. "Take the right fork and follow the drive around to the garden gate. Mr. Aldridge is waiting for you in the solarium." An ironic chuckle floated down to the passenger seat. Della glanced up to see him smirking. "Here we are in the sunniest city in the country, and my boss thinks he needs a solarium. Be forewarned. It gets pretty warm in there, even on winter days."

Della thought for a moment. "Does Mr. Aldridge know you've agreed to help us?"

Singletary gave her a gentle smile. "No. As far as he's concerned, I made the appointment for your attorney, who's tying up loose ends for the probate."

"Will he be angry or suspicious when he sees I've come too?"

"He may find it a bit unusual given his views of women, but I doubt he'll be suspicious."

"Really? How does he see us—women, that is?"

"As ornaments, if you are pretty, and easily forgotten, if homely, but always as something to be used. To him, women are objects. Of course, you could say he sees most people that way, but he's a real piece of work where women are concerned."

Della remembered the wardrobe and drawers filled with beautiful designer clothes, lacy negligees, and silk undergarments. Yes, Singletary's assessment fit with the image Aldridge had created of what he expected in his female guests. It had been both a puzzle and a relief when he sent word that the dress she had borrowed need not be returned. A puzzle, due to what that bit of silk and lace must have cost. A relief because she could not bear to look at it. The beautiful garment hung in the darkest corner of her chifforobe. It would never be worn again—too many horrible memories attached to it. She should give it away when she could bring herself to touch it.

As Auggie applied the brakes and steered the car to a stop at the edge of the gardens, Della tilted her head and tapped the secretary's arm. "Could there be a weakness in Mr. Aldridge's low opinion of us women, one that might be exploited?"

Singletary sucked his lips in over his teeth while he stepped down from the running board. "Perhaps. I know he found you damn attractive."

Auggie gasped. "Della. Don't even think of getting involved in that way."

Della shrugged. "Don't be ridiculous. It's not what you're thinking. As a widow in desperate financial straits whose husband was killed on this property and was here by invitation, perhaps Mr. Aldridge might feel obliged to give me a job."

"Here at the villa?" Both men hissed in unison.

"Where else?" Della gripped the door handle and yanked on it.

Auggie leaned across Della and grabbed the door's ledge. "Absolutely not. I've lost one cousin. I will not lose another."

"You speak as though you think someone here was involved in Art's murder."

Auggie held the door firmly while he whispered, "Maybe. Maybe not. Until we know why he was killed, you must be very careful. I forbid you to entertain such a foolish notion."

Della pushed until Auggie released the door, then she stepped down beside the secretary. Casting a disgruntled look at both men, she said, "It's just a thought, but I've got to do something. We owe the grocer, the butcher, the power company, the vet . . . everybody. Our bank account is near zero. What do you suggest I live on?"

What she did not say was that she must stay occupied, that she could not focus on her grief twenty-four hours a day and remain sane. Furthermore, she could not afford to sit at home and wait for others to solve her problems. While her grief was deep and fresh, she was approaching the stage where she could compartmentalize it as needed. When she thought about laying aside her grief even for a few moments, guilt threatened to consume her, but she was recognizing the necessity of placing Art and her heart in a box and closing the lid. There would always be the endless nights alone in her bed where she could take it out and allow it to torture her.

When Auggie did not answer her question, Singletary said, "She's got a point, you know. Let's see how the interview goes."

A quick walk among the boxwoods brought them to the solarium. Multiple double doors stood open, allowing a fresh breeze from the bay to flutter gauzy, floor-to-ceiling curtains. Their quarry sat in an unpainted, wicker throne chair. Other wicker chairs and a sofa encircled a glass-and-bamboo coffee table. A jungle of potted shrubs, flowers, and small trees were scattered about, turning their leaves and faces to the sun pouring through the glass ceiling. The space would be unbearable in high summer, but today, it presented a lovely oasis of calm—a place where she might concoct a plan while the men talked.

Aldridge stood as the trio approached. His gaze focused on Della as a broad smile brightened his features. "Mrs. Monroe, what an enchanting surprise. Under the circumstances, I did not expect you to grace this meeting, but please be seated." He snapped his fingers and a servant appeared. "Bring tea for the lady." Della noted he did not include the men. No doubt, the cart near his chair that held crystal glasses and various bottles of amber liquid were for them. What if she had wanted something stronger than tea? Would Aldridge have been shocked? Would he have permitted it? She took a seat opposite him. It allowed the best opportunity to gauge his reactions and intentions. Auggie sat on her left, but Singletary remained standing.

Looking at his secretary, Aldridge said, "That will be all, Luke. I'm sure you have work to do." To Auggie he said, "Drink? I'm guessing you're a Scotch man, but I'm afraid we're all out at the moment. Will bourbon do?"

Della had never known Auggie to drink anything other than the occasional gin and tonic, so it came as a surprise when he responded, "Of course, but with a splash or two of water, if you don't mind."

After beverages were distributed, Aldridge resumed his seat. "Mr. Breckenridge, I understand you're working toward completing the probate. I don't see how I can be of assistance. Perhaps you should explain."

Auggie swirled the liquid in his glass and took a small sip, then placed his drink on the table. "It's the matter of the life insurance. The policy is new—only taken out a few months ago. The insurance company is refusing to pay until it's proven that my cousin's business dealings had nothing to do with his murder. If you could tell us what he proposed, then perhaps it will draw this terrible business to a close."

Aldridge drained his glass and took his time fixing himself another drink. With this one, he added soda and called for more ice. Once the ice was finally added, he returned to his chair but remained standing.

"I'm not sure if this will help, but I suppose Mrs. Monroe has a right to know what her husband planned. He came to us about four months ago with a proposal for a joint venture that he asked we keep confidential until the agreement was finalized. His third of the deal would provide the land. My partner and I were to provide cash and development expertise." He nodded at Della. "Your husband intended for your farm to become an extension of Hialeah. As I explained to him on that tragic night, real estate investments reached their zenith a few months back. We are divesting ourselves as quickly as possible. Taking on a development project at this time would be, forgive me . . . foolish."

Della bit down on her tongue to keep from crying out. It couldn't be true. Art would never sell the farm.

Auggie stirred beside her. Leaning forward, he grabbed his glass and gulped down the rest of his drink. Rising, he said, "Thank you for your time, Mr. Aldridge. If it comes to it, would you be willing to testify to this in court? I fear we may have to sue to settle the insurance."

Aldridge did not answer. After taking a long swig of his drink, he fixed Auggie with a hard stare. "My partner and I would prefer to be kept out of your legal troubles."

Della could feel what little leverage they had slipping away. The tension had to be broken. She dug a handkerchief from her purse and dabbed at her eyes to wipe away nonexistent tears. "Mr. Aldridge, please help me. I'm at the end of my tether." Two pairs of eyes looked at her as though they had forgotten her presence. Hoping that surprise might work to her advantage, she continued, "Even if it works out, I won't get the insurance money for some time. I understand you don't want to develop the farm, but will you help in some other way? I need a job. Can't you see your way clear to help me? Perhaps you know someone who might hire a poor widow?"

She hated the quivering whine she used, but Aldridge had shown he underestimated anyone in a skirt. Maybe his weakness might become her strength.

Aldridge's eyes swept over Della. "What skills do you possess, my dear?"

"I've been a bank teller, but my college degree is in art history. I've noticed you have some wonderful works, by the way." She could see by his expression that she had planted a seed. Whether it would blossom was less sure.

Aldridge glanced at Auggie, then drained the last of his drink. "Thank you. I do have a nice collection, but nothing like what it will soon be. My agent has just returned from Europe, where he completed purchases on a large scale. When I'm finished, Villa Lucca will rival many museums."

Bingo. Della had hit on a point of vanity with Aldridge. Time to push it home. "My goodness. That sounds fabulous. I would love to see what you're adding to your collection."

Aldridge's eyes glowed with superiority and pride. "It will be quite a show when finished." He paused and studied Della long enough that she had to press her knees together to keep from squirming. Finally, he asked, "Did you specialize in a particular era, or are you just a generalist?"

Thank goodness she had paid attention to his walls. They held a few minor pieces by the masters, interspersed with contemporary works. She made a stab at what she thought might be on its way from Europe. "I have training in all eras, of course, but I'm most interested in the artists who are changing art as we know it—Picasso, Chagall, Matisse, Man Ray, Klee. The art world has not seen their likes before. They're changing the way we look at art and how we define it. Do you admire their work also?"

Aldridge smiled broadly. "Indeed, I do. In fact, my new imports are exclusively in the modern style." Infuriatingly, he did not elaborate but extended his hand to Auggie.

Della inhaled and exhaled slowly, then plastered on what she hoped was her most ingratiating smile. "Do you have an archivist, Mr. Aldridge?"

Aldridge blinked and swung his gaze back to Della. After studying her with an inscrutable expression, he said, "No, no archivist. You clearly have something in mind. Tell me what it is."

# CHAPTER 11

Della studied Aldridge for a moment, then adopted a businesslike demeanor.

She tilted her head as though deep in thought. "Well . . . truly serious museums have someone who catalogs, plans displays, and maintains the works in their possession. I can see you are a connoisseur." Appealing to the man's vanity might yield results. She gestured toward a Cezanne visible in the drawing room adjacent to the solarium. "That painting alone speaks of your excellent taste. With all of the new pieces arriving, having someone on staff who is knowledgeable to care for the collection seems logical, wouldn't you agree?"

One corner of Aldridge's mouth lifted while he considered Della's question. At last, he chuckled and replied, "Young lady, your flattery has worked. You're right. I'll need someone to manage my acquisitions. When can you start?"

Della felt Auggie's eyes on her, but she refused to look at him. "Mr. Breckenridge and I need to deal with some business matters before I take on anything new. I could begin in maybe three or four days. Would that be okay?"

"Of course. The first shipments are due in a couple of weeks. Will this give you enough time to catalog what I already have?"

This was better than she had hoped. "It may, but since I haven't seen all of your rooms, it's difficult to say how long cataloging your present collection will take. Based on what I *have* seen, I suspect that will be a big job in and of itself."

"Yes, my present collection is rather extensive." He paused and studied Della. "Perhaps you should move in here. There are plenty of guest rooms. That will give you total access."

Before Della could even think about it, Auggie spoke up. "I'm afraid Mrs. Monroe is needed at home in the mornings and evenings. She still has a dairy farm to manage. Driving to and from the villa will be far too costly. In addition, I need her assistance with the probate. She can't possibly take on the expense or devote the time you will require."

Aldridge frowned. He clearly did not like having his ideas rejected. "You appear to be much in demand, Mrs. Monroe. Your lawyer seems to think working for me will be an impossible burden. Have you thought about how you will manage a farm and work for me?"

Of course she hadn't, but he needed an answer. Otherwise, her plan concocted on impulse would crumble, thanks to Auggie's interference. She placed her hand on Auggie's arm and dug her nails into the tender flesh on the underside of his wrist. "My husband's cousin is being overly protective. I've decided to lease all of the land and the herd to one of my tenants. He's already asked me to consider a lease-to-purchase agreement."

Auggie cleared his throat louder than was necessary. "While Mrs. Monroe is a very capable young woman, my first priority is her welfare and best interests." He shot Della a scathing look. "Now, dear cousin, we must leave if we are to arrive at our next appointment on time." To Aldridge, he said, "If you will excuse us?"

Aldridge shot Della an inquiring look. She stood and stepped in front of Auggie. Smiling at her potential employer, she said, "I'm afraid we really must go. I will call Mr. Singletary when I have a better idea of how long my personal business will take. Is that suitable?"

Aldridge smirked at Auggie, then said to Della, "Of course. And the living-in arrangement?" As his eyes drifted from Della's face to her torso, they spoke far more loudly than his words. It appeared Mr.

Aldridge might have designs that had nothing to do with fine art and catalogs.

Della took a moment before responding. Let both men think what they wanted. It never hurt to let the male of the species dangle before committing. "I'll certainly think about it. It's a most generous offer. Thank you. We'll talk soon."

Della could hear Aldridge chuckling as she and Auggie passed from the solarium into the garden.

Once they were seated in the car, the crease between Auggie's eyes deepened. Through tight lips, he muttered, "Have you lost your mind? We're going to have a serious talk once we're out of earshot of this place."

He guided the car to the gates where Singletary met them, breathing hard and blocking their path. He placed his hands on his knees and panted.

When his breathing returned to normal, he came to Della's side of the car. "If you're going to take the job, don't say no to moving into the villa. The boss doesn't take kindly to having his invitations rejected."

Auggie glared. "That's ridiculous. In fact, this whole idea is insane. Della could well be the killer's next target."

"And you think she'll be safer in an isolated farmhouse?" Sarcasm colored Singletary's voice.

Between his teeth, Auggie spat, "I think she needs to be with family, not strangers, at a time like this."

"And how do you propose—"

"Stop it. Both of you," Della hissed. "We all know Aldridge is hiding something. What better way for us to find out what it is than by having me, a mere female, planted in his midst? He is far less likely to suspect me of covert intentions than he is either of you."

Singletary grinned. "She's right, you know. The boss is willing to give her complete access to the entire house. I'll make sure her bedroom is close enough to mine to keep her safe."

Auggie bristled. "That would be entirely unsuitable and improper. She would become the object of gossip. Do you care nothing for her reputation?"

Singletary's answer was a disgruntled sigh. "Della, do you think Villa Lucca endangers your reputation? Some of the employees, a few of them female, live in. I doubt anyone who comes to the house will bat an eye at your being in residence."

Auggie harrumphed. "With the types of guests your employer entertains, maybe they wouldn't think anything of it, but Della's friends and family definitely would."

Della had had enough. "Stop talking about me as though I'm not here. Auggie, if you're talking about those old stuffed shirts in South Carolina, I don't give a hoot what they think. Our friends here are mostly our tenants and neighbors. They will be none the wiser, unless some blabbermouth tells them. All anyone needs to know is that I've moved into town because I had to get a job."

"But what about the dairy? You can't leave the herd to fend for itself." Auggie wasn't giving up easily.

Della rolled her head and stretched her neck. "You're giving me a headache. What I said about the lease-to-buy thing is sort of true. About six months ago, Mr. Adams asked Art if he was interested in such an arrangement. Art said no, but I am. I can't keep the farm." The more the words spilled from her, the higher her emotions flew. "I can't run it alone, and I can't afford to hire help. I need to sell. There's no other choice." Della's voice broke on an uncontrolled sob.

Until that moment, the necessity of parting with their land and the house had not hit home. Dabbing at her face with the handkerchief Singletary offered, she sighed. "Stop badgering me. I'm going to take Mr. Aldridge's offer of the job and the room and board." She glared at Auggie, then at the secretary. "Both of you will just have to learn to deal with a woman who knows her own mind and follows her instincts."

Singletary raised his hands, palms out, and took a step back. "You've got no argument from me. Leave me out of your family squabble. I'm on your side, Della."

There he went again. Addressing her as Della instead of Mrs. Monroe. She had given him permission to use her Christian name in a moment of weakness. It had made her uncomfortable, but she could not admit that in the face of all his kindness to her during the dark hours after Art's murder. Why it now rankled so much she could not say, but it irritated her nonetheless.

Mustering an outward display of patience, she replied, "Thank you. I'll let you know when I'm free to move to the villa. In the meantime, I need to know how much I'll be paid, and I insist on having two days off every week and my evenings free. You'll be the one making the arrangements, I assume?" Her voice held a curtness she had not intended.

An expression somewhere between confusion and hurt feelings crossed the secretary's face. "Of course. Please call when you're ready. I'll see to everything."

She did not trust herself to speak to Singletary again. She nodded and frowned at Auggie. "We'd better be going."

The trip to the farm passed in huffy silence. Auggie stared straight ahead, while Della pretended to watch the scenery. She propped her arm atop the passenger door and rested her chin on her fist. Her mind wandered back to the last time she'd traveled from Villa Lucca to the farm. It was the day after. That is how she now thought of time. Everything was either before or after. There was no need to name the event.

One moment in time, and life had changed forever. Less than an inch one way or the other, a few seconds earlier or later, and life would have continued as usual, albeit with some consternation at the near miss. Just a fraction of space or time, and Art would still be alive. But this was after and would remain so forever. No amount of dreaming or wishing would reverse the moment or bring back the before.

The tires crunching on the farm's oyster-shell driveway broke the spell.

# CHAPTER 12

Auggie came around to Della's door and jerked it open. He had grown angrier as the miles passed between Villa Lucca and the farm. Too damn bad. Della met his glare with one of her own. She would not be bullied.

He opened his mouth, but she held up her palm. "I don't want to hear it. I've made up my mind. I need that insurance money, and I only see one way to get it."

Auggie's shoulders slumped. "Okay. You've made your point. I only want to keep you safe. Is that such a crime?"

Della did not answer. The telephone shrilled from the parlor, giving her an excuse to dash for the front door. She skidded to a halt by the instrument's table. Grabbing the candlestick base, she placed the receiver against her ear and drew the bell-shaped transmitter toward her lips. "Mrs. Monroe speaking."

"At last. Barnett here. I've been trying to reach you all day. Where've you been?"

Heat rose in Della's cheeks. Just what she needed—another demanding man telling her what to do. "Hello to you, too, detective. I wasn't aware that I'm required to report my comings and goings to you. But if you must know, Mr. Breckenridge and I had an appointment with Mr. Aldridge." No need to lie about it. He would no doubt find out anyway.

"Aldridge? What about?" Barnett seemed caught off guard and maybe a little angry.

Della scrambled for an answer. "Since my husband believed they were to be business partners, it seemed like a logical step."

"Sounds more like interfering in a police investigation to me. Speaking of investigations, you and your lawyer need to be in my office first thing in the morning. If I'd known you were in town today, I'd have had you come in this afternoon, but it's a little late for that now."

"I'm sorry to have inconvenienced you. What time should we appear?"

"8 a.m. sharp."

"Very well, 8 a.m. it is."

From over her shoulder, Auggie asked, "To whom were you speaking in that sarcastic tone, and where are you going at eight in the morning?"

She replaced the instrument on its table. "*We* are going to see Detective Barnett." Della drew her lower lip between her teeth. "He was in a foul mood. I hope it improves before tomorrow."

"It is as I feared." Auggie placed a hand on Della's shoulder. "You must be prepared to be questioned, possibly accused. Barnett has the issue of the insurance policy between his teeth like a hound chewing on a ham hock. He's not going to give it up easily. We need a plan." He stepped around her and sniffed the air. "Whatever that is smells delicious. I'm famished. We can talk about tomorrow as we eat."

They went to the kitchen where Della found a note on the counter.

*A chicken pot pie is in the oven, and a salad is in the frig. Alma Adams*

Della shook her head and smiled. "Mrs. Adams has enough mouths to feed without providing for us."

Auggie opened the oven door and removed the casserole. "I, for one, am delighted she looks on you as another daughter to feed. She's an excellent cook."

"With ten children and a farmer husband, she's had plenty of practice. I'll set the table."

Della hadn't had much appetite since Art's death, but she would force herself to eat anyway. As long as her mouth was full, she wouldn't have to talk about tomorrow.

•　•　•　•　•

When Della and Augustus arrived at Miami Police headquarters, an officer ushered them into a windowless room, invited them to be seated in wooden, straight-backed chairs, and left. Della leaned her elbows on the heavy oak table and placed her forehead against her fists. The first twinges of a headache crawled up from the tightly wound muscles at the base of her skull. Her roiling stomach told her this was going to be a trying day. Despite Auggie's entreaties, she had refused to discuss the coming interview. Perhaps that had been a mistake.

At 9 a.m., Detective Barnett made an appearance with a subordinate in tow.

Auggie stood and fixed Barnett with an expression filled with subtle challenge. "We have been here since 8 a.m. as you requested."

Barnett scowled in reply. "Sorry to inconvenience you, but crime keeps its own schedule." His sarcasm did nothing to soothe Della's nerves.

The detective dragged out a chair and sat down across the table from her. The other man, notepad and pen in hand, sat away from the group in the shadows where the single hanging light fixture's glare did not reach. The room's austerity created a sinister and foreboding atmosphere, no doubt as intended.

Barnett studied Della for so long, she finally asked, "Is there something you want to talk to me about? If not, we have other business to attend to."

Barnett harrumphed and smirked. "I'm just wondering how much you knew about the insurance policy your husband took out."

A slow boil began in the pit of Della's stomach. "Nothing whatsoever. He took out the policy without my knowledge. I don't even know when he did it or how much it's worth."

"Really? You mean Mr. Breckenridge hasn't told you its value?"

"No. He's tried several times, but I can't bear the thought of putting a price on my husband's life. I loved him. He was my world. Dealing with his death is all I've been able to process. I would gladly not receive a dime from the insurance if it meant having Art back."

"So you say." He delivered the statement with a raised brow and eyes that were emotionless, except for the doubt lurking behind their narrowed lids. "If you don't get the insurance, how long do you have before the mortgages go into default?"

"The bank is our next appointment." Just because she already knew how deeply in debt she was, there was no good reason to reveal that fact to the detective. He clearly suspected her of involvement in Art's death. Well, good luck to him finding a connection because it simply did not exist.

Barnett tapped a file he had brought with him. "I can save you the trip to the bank. You have about a month before the bank forecloses on the farm. Interesting point about the house, though. It and about an acre surrounding it aren't included in any of the mortgage agreements. Know anything about that?"

Della shook her head. She could not trust herself to form the words. The provision about the house was so like Art. It showed how much he had loved her. He was determined to provide a home for them even if they lost everything else.

When Della did not elaborate, Barnett continued, "Seems like a wife would have been told about what would come to her if the husband died. She might be tempted to arrange an early payout if the amount was big enough."

Della stiffened and started to speak, but Auggie placed his hand on her arm and leaned forward. "My cousin felt a great responsibility where his wife is concerned. The insurance and provisions for the homestead are surely evidence of this. He chose not to enlighten my client on these points. He was a protective husband, if somewhat overly and unnecessarily so, but this in no way implicates her in any wrongdoing."

"So, she's now your client, is she?"

"Of course she is. I'm the executor of my cousin's estate. That makes his widow my client since she's his sole beneficiary, but you've known that from the beginning. Now, unless you're planning to charge her, we're leaving."

Della gasped. "Charge me? With what?"

Barnett chuckled. "Seems like your lawyer thinks I want you to be guilty of a crime . . . maybe, like hiring somebody to get rid of your husband. When somebody is about to lose everything, a big ole insurance policy can be mighty tempting."

Auggie rose so fast his chair rocked, threatening to tip over. "That's quite enough. Della, you don't have to listen to this. We're leaving."

Barnett held up his hands. "Calm down. Nobody's been charged or arrested. Have a seat, and I'll tell you another theory of the crime."

Auggie looked down at Della, who nodded. As much as she would have liked to run from the room, she had to hear what the detective would say next.

Auggie plopped onto the chair as his palm hit the table. "Enlighten us."

"Looks like Mrs. Monroe's husband may have had plans for his land that had nothing to do with dairy farming." Barnett's gaze flitted between Auggie and Della.

When the detective did not continue, Della asked, "What do you mean by that?"

Barnett folded his arms on the table and leaned in. "Prohibition's created a lot of opportunities for folks who don't mind breaking the law—very risky, but highly profitable schemes."

Auggie placed his hand on Della's arm and squeezed as he mirrored the detective's posture. "And this affects Mrs. Monroe in what way?"

"Let's say you're a man on the verge of losing a farm that's been in your family for generations. That man might look for a way to make quick cash, and lots of it. He might be tempted to go into a business that carries big risks along with the big rewards . . . maybe, say, bootlegging whisky from the Bahamas. And if that man was to get crosswise with his competition in this illegal enterprise, well, who's to say what might happen? Men have been killed for far less than the huge profits the rumrunners are making."

"Are you saying that my cousin was involved in bootlegging? Do you have any proof?"

"Not anything that would hold up in court, but it makes for a good theory, doesn't it?"

Della could remain quiet no longer. "No, not where Art is concerned." Her voice shook while she struggled with the rage, terror, and grief that threatened to consume what little control she had left. "My husband would never deliberately break the law."

Auggie gripped Della's forearm tighter and pulled her to her feet. "Detective, you are clearly on a fishing expedition. When you have something constructive to share, you know where to find us."

Barnett jumped up, his expression hard and menacing. "You're free to leave, but don't go involving yourselves in police business. No good can come of it for y'all or for us."

Della could not find her voice until she was in the car headed away from the station. Swiping at the tears on her cheeks, she turned sideways in her seat for a better view of Auggie. "So, it looks like there are a couple of ways to think about Art's murder—none of them good. Did I hire a hit on my husband for the insurance? No, of course not. Did Art fall in with bootleggers and get killed for it? I can't believe that for a minute. Was he killed for some reason no one has thought of? I have no idea." The sound of her fist hitting the dashboard rebounded. "Why, why, why was he killed?" With each "why," she pounded the dashboard harder.

Auggie glanced at her, then back at the road. "I don't know, my dear, but I agree that none of this makes sense."

# CHAPTER 13

Della glanced at Auggie across the kitchen table, then dropped her gaze. "A month. That's all I've got before I lose the farm unless the insurance pays. I dread having to tell our tenants. Who knows what the bank will do about them? They very well may lose their homes and livelihoods. As for me, I can't bear the thought of crawling to my mother and uncle, begging for a home. They'll never let me forget they didn't want me to marry Art."

Auggie's eyes grew wider. "I didn't know your family objected to y'all's marriage."

"Oh, Mama is much too polite to allow her negative feelings to show, but she definitely thought we were rushing into marriage. She also thought a farmer was a step down from my father's career in banking." Della observed pain in Auggie's eyes. "I'm sorry. I never intended for y'all to know. Mama's family has always suffered from an exaggerated sense of self-importance. It comes from being a family of very big fish in a minuscule pond."

"But isn't your uncle a farmer?"

"In a manner of speaking. He's more like a feudal lord overseeing serfs who are now called sharecroppers. The days of working the soil are long over for him, if they ever existed."

Auggie studied his hands where they lay atop the table. "I see. Your choices truly are limited." He moistened his lips before asking, "Do you trust that secretary, Luke Singletary?"

Della thought about the question. What did she really know about the man? In truth, very little, but for some rather nebulous reasons, he felt like an honest, dependable person. If she had to choose one adjective to describe him, it would be trustworthy. It was a feeling, not demonstrated fact. "You know, I think I do. He had no reason to help me or be kind after Art was killed, but he has been very much so from the moment the gunshot shattered my glass on that terrible night. Why do you ask?"

Auggie shifted in his seat, met Della's gaze, then looked away. "Are you adamant about working for Aldridge and moving into his villa?"

Della ground her teeth. With a scowl, she replied, "In what way was I unclear? I haven't changed my mind. I'll move there as soon as possible, and I'm not open to more arguments."

"And I will give you none. I've stated my opinion, which you've roundly rejected. I know when I'm defeated." He made a bridge of his fingers. "Since you're determined to accept the position, we'd better have a plan. It's clear Aldridge isn't going to tell what he and Art were up to, but it's equally clear there had to be some sort of agreement. As you said, Aldridge's explanation that y'all were invited to his party to honor your father is ridiculous. Why now? Why would he suddenly feel the need to honor a man long dead? That specter of a business deal is the logical place to start in unraveling the mystery of Art's murder. With the direction Barnett is taking his investigation, I don't trust him to get to the truth in the foreseeable future, and time is running out."

"Having the run of the entire house means I will have full access to places like his office. What should I look for?"

"Look for land abstracts, surveyor's reports, contracts, loan applications . . . anything pertaining to land use, development, and sale. As much as we don't want to believe Art would sell his heritage, it's the only thing that makes sense in this whole miserable mess."

Della's heart sank. In a quiet voice, she said, "You're right. I don't want to even think about it, but Aldridge is a land speculator and developer. We've got land. It's the only logical explanation for a partnership between Aldridge and Art."

•  •  •  •  •

Della stood at her bedroom window on Villa Lucca's second floor, watching the sun rise over Biscayne Bay. Beauty and menace blended in the red glow backlighting heavy clouds hovering on the horizon. Red sky at morning, sailor take warning. She peered at the sky for a few moments, then scowled at her image in the mirror as she tugged a brush through her hair. A stormy day meant more people would stay in the house, affording her little opportunity to search for clues. Della had always hated late summer and her efforts to do her worst before she finally departed.

As the season dragged herself toward September, tropical South Florida glistened from daily afternoon showers. Air felt liquid against the skin, and merely drawing breath could feel like drowning. Breezes rolling in off the Atlantic provided little relief, for the Gulf Stream ran close to shore and was at its warmest. Like her sisters July and August, September promised to be a month of intense heat and high humidity. But unlike her siblings, she possessed an additional feature—September brought with her the possibility of hurricanes. Another reason to dislike the month. Della gave the lowering sky a last glance and made for the grand staircase.

Since her arrival at the villa, she had discovered nothing of importance, other than the size of Aldridge's art collection. It was extensive. Crates of new additions had begun arriving, but she had not completed cataloging what already hung on the villa's walls. At her employer's request, she had saved the office wing for last. He assured her it held the least valuable of his collection and the smallest number as well. Of course, it was the one room she most wanted to spend time in.

Della worked hard to contain her frustration. If Anders Aldridge and Rollie Shoemaker ever caught on to her true purpose in taking the job, she suspected she would be in real danger. She had no proof of any criminality. It was just a feeling, but it kept her cautious. She guarded her emotions and actions carefully around them.

She met Shoemaker, valise in hand, at the foot of the stairs. It was uncommonly early for him to have arrived from his Miami Beach residence. He nodded and must have noticed her confusion. "Good morning, Mrs. Monroe. I guess no one's told you. Late last night, Aldridge and I decided to meet today with some potential investors in Jacksonville, so we won't be underfoot after all. You'll have the run of the place."

"Thank you for letting me know." What an unexpected godsend. Della prayed her excitement did not show. Keeping her tone as casual as possible, she asked, "Will you be away long?"

"Maybe a week. Maybe a couple of days. All depends on how open these guys are to our proposition."

"Are you taking the train or the automobile?" Seeing his surprise at her interest, she gestured toward the windows. "The weather looks like it may make traveling difficult."

Shoemaker's gaze flicked in that direction. "We're catching Flagler's *Key West Express* within the hour, so if you'll excuse me, Anders is waiting for me." He flashed a conspiratorial grin. "And you know how he hates tardiness."

She chuckled and nodded. "Well, good luck and safe travels."

Della watched him troop away in the direction of the front door. This was an unexpected bit of luck.

She found Luke, as she now thought of Singletary, at the sideboard, scooping eggs from a chafing dish onto his plate.

He took one look at her and grinned. "Have you been informed about our bosses' departure?"

She waggled her brows. "Indeed, I have. I take it you aren't going with them."

"No, the lawyer's going instead. Want some help in the office today?"

"You bet."

# CHAPTER 14

With the bosses on their way to Jacksonville, the office wing was deserted. Luke opened the door and stood back for Della to pass into Anders Aldridge's most private space. While she had visited the office a few times in the past, it was never for very long.

She stopped in the center of the richly hewed oriental carpet covering most of the hardwood floor and studied the room. The masculine atmosphere was complete. No woman had influenced it in any way. From the dark wood paneling to the rich, red color scheme to the leather-bound volumes lining the shelves on three walls to the heavy brocade drapery, the room looked more like the smoking room of an English baronial manor than the office of a Miami land speculator. It was in complete contrast to the rest of the house's Italianate style. The odor of cigar smoke lingered despite the pristine condition of strategically placed ashtrays and open French windows.

Della eyed Luke as he stepped beside her. "Who did the decor? I feel like I've stepped into an English castle."

Luke grinned. "It's rather over the top, isn't it? For reasons known only to himself, our boss thinks this"—a sweeping gesture took in the entire room—"represents authority, knowledge, and wealth. I suppose it does in some ways, but the people he deals with don't always see it that way. Where Anders can't hear, they snigger and make fun of it. They say things like, 'He's a jumped up Yankee, thinks he's an English lord' . . . you know, things that would put him into a rage if they were said to his face."

Della tilted her head. "Does he have a bad temper? I haven't seen it."

"That's because you've done everything he's asked and done it in the way he wants." Luke raised his brows while his mouth thinned. "Remember that if you're ever temped to cross him."

A chill ran through her. "Are you saying he might be violent if crossed?"

Luke shrugged. "Not necessarily. I just wouldn't want to get on the wrong side of him. He has a way of always coming out on top." His tone was matter-of-fact, almost teasing, but his expression said he was deadly earnest.

"Thanks. I'll keep that in mind." The conversation was becoming unsettling, given her covert purpose for being in the office. "Do you think he will notice that we've searched in here?"

"Not if we are very careful. We should get it over with while the rest of the staff is busy cleaning the kitchen and bedroom wing. There are one or two little snitches who would like nothing better than to run tattling. Anders usually pays them no heed, but where his office is concerned, he will be incandescent if he thinks we went through his stuff."

Della gave him a stern look. "After we finish our search, you must tell me who among the staff I should be careful of. Where should we start looking?"

Luke sucked his lips inward and squinted. With a smack, he said, "The wall safe, I think."

He went to a large landscape hanging over the fireplace and reached behind the frame. A soft click sounded, and the entire picture swung away from the wall, revealing a safe with a combination lock. Luke twirled the dial back and forth until a final click released the safe door. The interior held a stack of files and several packets of bound currency. Taking the files, he handed them to Della. "Give me half. We'll need to make quick work of these."

Della divided the stack and passed seven or so files to Luke, then began rifling through the ones she had retained—Land Sales 1921–

1925, Villa Lucca Title and Permits, Bank Loans and Agreements, Property and Other Tax, Federal Tax. In other words, nothing that in any way mentioned or even alluded to an agreement with Art.

She turned her attention to Luke, who was closing the cover of his last file. "Anything?"

"Nope."

"Where now?"

"The desk." He returned the files to the safe in the exact order in which they had been removed, locked the safe, and pushed the picture back against the wall. Crossing to the opposite side of the room, he knelt in front of the desk's drawers and withdrew a long, thin implement from his jacket's inner breast pocket. Grinning up at Della, he said in a casual tone, "Lock picking is one of my many hidden talents."

"And where did you learn such a valuable skill?"

"Courtesy of Uncle Sam. I was in military intelligence during the war." His expression suggested he had clearly hoped to shock.

He succeeded. Della hissed, "You were a spy?"

He turned his attention to the top drawer, inserted his instrument, and started wiggling it around. "I was assigned to the military attaché's office at our legation in Copenhagen. As Denmark was neutral, I could stroll about the city with impunity, meeting with various contacts and receiving information." Something within the mechanism clicked. With a satisfied sigh, he opened the drawer. "One such meeting did not go as planned, however, and my contact and I narrowly escaped. Revealing his identity could have been fatal. My back still bothers me from the injury I sustained while jumping from a three-story window."

"Impressive. When this is all over, remind me to write my congressman praising the military for giving you such useful skills."

They went through every piece of paper, every document, every file contained within the desk drawers.

Della's spirits sank. "Nothing. I was so sure we would find at least a clue. I guess art cataloging must commence without further delay."

She felt no guilt over the sarcasm in her voice as disappointment swept through her. She had waited so long for nothing.

Della started to move away, but Luke caught her wrist. "You know, there's one place we didn't look." He carefully lifted the leather-and-felt desk blotter. Beneath it sat a small scrap of paper.

Della grabbed the little piece of torn foolscap and examined it. "This is Art's handwriting, but it makes no sense. It's just a bunch of numbers." She held it out to Luke.

His eyes narrowed as he studied the writing, then went to a library-style bookstand upon which lay a relatively thin, but tall volume.

Della followed. "What are you looking for?"

He turned pages until he stopped at one toward the back of the book. He held up the scrap of paper. "These aren't just numbers. They're coordinates on the map of Dade County."

Della peered over his shoulder and gasped. "Is that where I think it is?"

"If you're thinking the middle of the Everglades, you would be correct." Luke's brow furrowed. "Do you own property there?"

"No. What use would we have for it? You can't put dairy cows out there. The alligators would get them."

"Well, apparently, your husband had some kind of interest in the location. Are you sure this is his writing?"

"Quite sure. See how the five is almost missing its top bar? That's Art's five."

Luke was silent for a moment. Grabbing a pencil and notecard, he copied the coordinates, then replaced the scrap of paper under the blotter. "I think you should show these to your cousin. Maybe something will turn up in the probate filings or will."

"I'll call Auggie. We can't have him here. We wouldn't be able to speak freely. Would you be able to get away for drinks or dinner at the farm?"

Luke's eyes widened in surprise. "You want me to go with you?" Was there also a hint of pleasure lurking in his reaction? Maybe.

If he saw anything other than business in the dinner invitation, it must be quelled. Della kept her tone as impersonal as possible without being outright rude. "Yes, you know Mr. Aldridge better than I do. Maybe the three of us can figure out what was going on."

# CHAPTER 15

Without looking at her watch, Della knew when teatime arrived. It came promptly at four o'clock with the tropical rain showers. Another touch of English tradition Anders Aldridge insisted on aping. She placed her notebook and pen in her satchel and headed to the solarium.

Luke stood when she entered. "Did you reach your cousin?"

Della took the seat opposite at the wicker table. Nodding, she replied, "I did. He is expecting us at 6 p.m. In the meantime, he's going through every scrap of paperwork again, looking for information on why Art would have written down those coordinates and given them to Aldridge." At some point in the recent past, she had stopped thinking of their employer with the honorific Mister. The man had become only his last name to her.

Luke resumed his seat and offered her a cup and plate. "Will you be mother, as the English say?"

She began filling their cups. They had taken tea together often enough now that she did not need to ask how he liked his—two lumps and milk added after the tea was poured.

As she poured her own cup and prepared her plate with finger sandwiches and cookies, her mind wandered to their employer. The more she learned about Anders Aldridge, the less respect she had for him. There was something dodgy about him. She couldn't quite put her finger on what form it took, but intuition told her he was not totally legitimate.

The source of Aldridge's wealth was shrouded in mystery, much like his past. Some of the servants whispered he was the disgraced son of an old Boston family, whose dissipated lifestyle was filled with gambling, consumption of substantial quantities of alcohol, and liaisons of both the natural and unnatural kind. His Brahmin manner of speaking added to the mystery. Others murmured he was a gangster who just happened to be from Boston and had developed the accent by aping his betters. Then there was the rumor that he had amassed a fortune in the stock market, lost it all, only to regain it before journeying south for his health. Whether the danger had been from physical or human sources was less clear. He certainly appeared to be in vigorous good health now.

Once settled in Florida, he was said to have increased his substance many times over through land speculation. The newspaper articles at the time of Art's murder had confirmed that much. It was not the rumors that caused Della to doubt him, but rather his secretive manner. He revealed nothing about himself while insisting that all around him pass a scrupulous inspection. As the boss, that was his prerogative. Still, he was an enigma.

Della felt Luke's eyes on her. He studied her with a quizzical expression. "You seem far away, very deep in thought. Is it something I can help with?"

Roses touched her cheeks. "No, nothing in particular. I was just thinking about our employer and who he really is. Rollie Shoemaker is straightforward by comparison. He's just what he says—a Florida cracker made good. I wonder how he and Aldridge became partners. They're so different."

Luke nodded. "Yeah, they are. I've wondered, too. Their partnership seems to go back to the start of the war in Europe, 1914 or so. They had already been working together for years by the time I got the job as secretary. The only time the subject ever came up, all Rollie said was that they met through a mutual contact. Notice, he did not say friend. I've always wondered if that contact was of the strictly legitimate type. There are rumors of black-market dealings during the war, but not enough evidence for an arrest." He paused for a couple of moments and looked thoughtful, then shrugged.

"Could just be envy and nonsense put out there by rivals who aren't as successful. Who knows?"

Della took a sip of tea as she mulled the question. "I suppose jealousy could be at the bottom of it, but there are so many rumors and they've never gone away. Of course, that's usually the case with rumors, but still . . . Do you think we have anything to fear in going forward with our investigation?"

Luke's eyes darted toward her and away just as quickly. After a momentary silence, he gave her a cocky grin. "Who from? Barnett? Aldridge? Rollie? An unnamed assailant?" His face filled with mock horror.

Della's heart sank. "Take your pick. How about all of them? How about everybody?" The hand holding her cup shook, sending tea splashing onto the tablecloth. She returned the cup to its saucer with a clatter. Her hand flew to her mouth as Luke knelt beside her.

He placed an arm around her shoulders. "I'm sorry. That was a stupid thing to say."

She whispered, "I'm frightened. I really am." Her entire body trembled. "I don't think I realized just how much until right now." When his embrace tightened and his mouth drew closer to hers, she shrugged free and glared.

Luke jumped to his feet. "My apologies. I meant no impertinence. I thought you were going to faint." His voice was stiff.

Della eyed him with bubbling fury. "I'm not the fainting sort." His face grew rigid, but his eyes betrayed pain. Guilt melted her anger. "I'm sorry. I don't know why I'm angry with you. You have been nothing but kind and a gentleman. Please say you forgive me."

Luke studied the floor. "You have nothing to apologize for. I'm afraid the war left my sense of humor with a macabre streak. Soldiers either learn to laugh at danger and death or go nuts. Some of us did go crazy. Shell shock, they called it." His voice was bitter and cold. He must have sensed the effect his words were having because he gave her a weak smile, then dropped his gaze again. "Now it's my turn to beg forgiveness—again." When she didn't answer, he continued, "You're right to be cautious, but we can't let it keep us from the truth."

Della drew a long, shaky breath. "Sometimes, I feel like shutting the door on all of it, running away, and starting over in a place where no one knows me or about Art's murder. Do I really want to know the truth?"

His eyes shot up to meet hers. "Only you can decide that, but one thing you've gotta understand. Once we get far enough down that road, there may be no turning back. Are you prepared to seek the truth no matter the costs?"

Della's eyes filled with tears. "Do I have a choice?"

His expression became gentle. "I'm not sure that you do."

She broke eye contact, letting her gaze drift out to the gardens. The rain had stopped about 4:30 p.m., as it always did. Shrubs and flowers glistened while the late afternoon sun created diamonds out on the bay. The peaceful scene was in marked contrast to the turmoil raging inside her. When had life first gone so wrong, and why hadn't she noticed?

Finding no answers, she said in a flat tone, "Well then, I guess we better get on with it. Auggie may have something new for us."

•   •   •   •   •

At a little after 6 p.m., Della guided her roadster from the highway onto the road leading to the farmhouse. She glanced at the rearview mirror. Luke followed in his MG sports car, a luxury he said he had allowed himself while in England before being demobilized. He loved it so much, he couldn't bear to part with it, so the car made the long, expensive journey from the London docks to Miami aboard the first ship he could find that would bring them both. Being in the clandestine service, rather than regular army, had at least one benefit—greater freedom with travel, or so he said.

The sight of the top of his head protruding from the windscreen on the wrong side of the car made her laugh. It was an incongruous sight to behold on a white-sand road in rural Dade County. If he wasn't careful, that low-slung auto would get stuck.

She giggled to the wind. She was going home. The stress melted from her with every turn of the car's wheels. Another bend in the road, and the farmhouse's porch light glowed in greeting. Being a Friday, she had decided to pack a bag to stay for the weekend. She needed time away from the villa, away from cataloging art, away from strange people and places, and, in truth, away from Luke. He shouldn't be allowed to become too much more involved in her life. She wasn't ready for such—not nearly ready—and she did not know if she ever would be. Art was too much in her heart and mind.

A sob caught in her throat. Art. The farm. The mystery of his death. What she thought she knew against what she didn't. She suddenly felt overwhelmed and very afraid.

# CHAPTER 16

The screen door slammed, and Auggie waved from the porch. Della swiped at the tears on her cheeks. No need for either man to see she had been crying. Sympathetic glances and solicitous questions would send her straight into the abyss. As it was, her hold on the edge threatened to fail at any moment. Better to maintain the facade of a firm grip. She guided the car to a stop just short of the front steps and leapt out.

She gave Auggie a quick hug and peck on the cheek. "Do you have anything for us? I do hope so. It's been a long week. I need a little good news."

"Maybe, but first, let's eat. I'm starving. The ever-maternal Mrs. Adams was thrilled that you will be home for the entire weekend. She left a scrumptious-smelling pot roast simmering. She wants to spoil you." Auggie draped an arm across Della's shoulders and squeezed. "Unfortunately, her husband is less enthusiastic. He's asking if you've reached a decision. I've put him off the best I can, but you're going to have to let him know something soon. He's talking about moving on after the first of the year. Says he's got to look after his own family. I think he's getting tired of all the food that ends up in your kitchen."

Della frowned and sighed. "He's a good farmer and wants his own place. You can hardly blame him." She looked up at Auggie with a sinking feeling. "So, what do you think? Should I let him have a rent-to-buy option or just put the farm on the market outright?"

Auggie's eyebrows rose a fraction as his expression grew even more serious. "The question is not what I think or what your heart may want, but what you can afford. We'll discuss that this weekend."

Tires crunched on the driveway, drawing their attention. Della noticed an unexpected light enter Auggie's eyes. "Is that Luke arriving in that lovely little MG?"

Della tilted her head and watched Art's cousin in some confusion. "Yes, it is. He's here for dinner and to see what he can do to help."

"That's good. We may need him. I've found something that may prove interesting."

After the pot roast had been demolished, Auggie leaned back from the table and put his hand in his pants pocket. He withdrew it and held out his palm. In the center lay a brass key. "Do you recognize this?"

Della took the key and turned it back and forth. She shook her head. "I've never seen it before. It looks like the safe deposit box keys we had at the bank." She ran her finger over numerals engraved on one side. "In fact, I'm sure that's what it must be. Where did you find it?"

Auggie retrieved the key and examined it. Tossing it on the table, he said, "It was taped to the underside of the farm desk's middle drawer. If I hadn't dropped a file and banged my head picking it up, I would never have noticed it. I took this key to every bank in Dade County. Of course, the last one claimed it as belonging to a box in their vault."

Luke leaned forward. "Well, don't keep us in suspense. Which bank?"

"Hialeah First State." Looking at Della, Auggie asked, "Ever do business with them?"

"No, we never had the need, considering Papa's position with Miami First National. Did you check the box?"

Auggie shook his head. "No. They will only allow you, as Art's widow and now sole owner of the box, access. We have a special appointment for nine o'clock in the morning. The bank manager is being very accommodating. He understands you work during the week, and he knew your father. Apparently, they worked together before the manager went to his present position. I have already given him Art's death certificate and shown him a copy of the will. All that remains is for you to present yourself and open the box."

"What do you think we'll find?"

"I have no idea. It wasn't like Art to be secretive, but since neither of us knew about the box, it appears he kept this one thing to himself."

Della stared at the key with mixed emotions. Fear, curiosity, anger, pain circulated through her in equal measures. If Art had not told her about the secret bank box, what else had he kept from her? It was beginning to feel like she did not really know the man she had adored and planned to spend her life with. Her beloved was morphing into a stranger—one whom she wasn't sure she wanted to know.

The next morning, Della, Auggie, and Luke sat in the bank's conference room with the mystery safe deposit box on the table between them. With jerky hands, Della lifted the latch and peered inside. In the otherwise empty box lay the type of bound volume that was used as a journal or diary. She took it out and opened it.

After looking at Auggie in bewilderment, she read the first notation aloud, "CC 25 9/5, JMN IW 30 9/5. This doesn't make sense, and this isn't Art's handwriting, either."

Luke leaned in for a closer look. "You're sure this isn't in your husband's writing?"

Della cut her eyes at him in irritation. "Quite sure. I know Art's handwriting." Scanning the list to the bottom, she added, "It's all just numbers and letters. And what might be a person's initials . . . BK. Do we know anyone with those initials?"

Auggie rubbed his chin and looked like he had sucked on a lemon. He gave the table a frustrated slap. "No. Art never mentioned anyone with the initials BK or any others. I had so hoped we would find something useful in this box. Dammit."

Della spread her fingertips over her lips. "Looks like we don't know any more now than before we opened it, but this must be important. Why else would Art have hidden it in a secret bank box? Just as important, who wrote this and how did Art get it?" The whine in her voice made Della wince. She gave herself a mental shake and squared her shoulders. "Okay. So we found no help here, only another mystery to add to our list." Looking at Luke, she continued, "I gave Auggie the coordinates we found, but so far, he hasn't established a meaningful connection. Maybe we should go to their location in the Glades."

Auggie rolled his eyes. "Out among the mosquitos and alligators. Oh, joy. Makes my heart sing."

Della scowled. "No one said you had to go. You can stay here and continue to search files or whatever."

Auggie took Della's hand. "Look. Maybe there isn't going to be an answer. I've been through every scrap of paper a hundred times. I've called Barnett's office so often, his secretary has begun answering automatically that no, nothing new has been found. There are no clues whatsoever. Maybe something Art did or knew got him killed. Or maybe—just maybe—it was all a terrible accident. Maybe a duck hunter fired in the wrong direction and ran when he realized what he'd done."

Della shot him a derogatory smirk. "It's too early in the year for duck hunting. Besides, no one hunts ducks in the middle of the night."

"Oh, then shooting at fish." Frustration colored Auggie's tone. "I've seen people do it. Whatever happened, maybe we should leave the investigations to the police and cut our losses. Sell the farm. Find a job. Try to get on with your life as best you can."

Della snatched her hand from Auggie's grasp. "Give up? Is that what you want? Well, not me. The person I loved most in this world has been murdered. I will not give up until I know why."

Auggie's mouth became a thin line. "All I want is for you to be safe and secure. So far, everything we know about Art's murder indicates the danger may continue. Barnett has said as much. Why don't you leave crime solving to the professionals?"

"Because the professionals have all but accused me of killing my husband. Who presents the greater danger? Some nameless, faceless bogeyman or the cops?" Della didn't realize she had shouted until the bank manager opened the door.

"Is everything all right in here?"

Della drew a sharp breath. "Yes. Just a family quarrel. You must know how that is."

The man peered at them over his spectacles. "Of course. Bereavement does bring its own particular stresses. If I may be of assistance . . ." He let his unfinished question hang in the air like a schoolteacher's threat of meting out correction where merited.

Della mustered what she hoped was a convincing smile. "Thank you, but no. We have everything we need. We won't be much longer."

When the door closed, Auggie looked at Della with a hurt expression. "Look, I wouldn't suggest abandoning the search if I thought any good would come from continuing. There's no need for rudeness. I have only your best interests at heart." His voice held a deeply aggrieved note.

Della drew breath to respond, but Luke held up his hands, palms out. "Hold on, you two. Sniping at one another helps no one. So we didn't find what we hoped here. Maybe we should take a break and do something relaxing, like taking a boat ride. There can't be any harm in some tourists sightseeing in the Everglades. We can pack a picnic and take out Anders's new swamp boat."

"What's a swamp boat?" Auggie and Della asked in unison.

"You'll see. It can't hurt, and it may help to see what's so important about a location on a map."

# CHAPTER 17

Della stared at the contraption Luke insisted was safe. Its flat bottom and rectangular passenger cabin looked more like a houseboat floating on the Miami River than a form of transportation, but it was the thing at the back that grabbed her attention. A small airplane engine sat on struts with its propeller protruding over the water.

Luke grinned and patted the propeller. "Latest thing in travel, at least in swamps and other places with shallow water. Anders bought the boat from Glenn Curtiss when they were collaborating on development around Hialeah. Curtiss built it for hunting and fishing in the Glades. Pretty ingenious design, if you ask me. Anders took clients out not long ago. Maiden voyage was a great success."

Auggie gripped her elbow. "Come, ole girl. If millionaires ride in it, surely it's safe enough for you and me."

Della's mouth thinned. "Either that or they have a death wish no one thought to mention."

Once Luke started the engine, the boat moved into the middle of the river and turned northwest. "Better open all of the windows. Otherwise, it'll get stifling in this thing."

Auggie moved from window to window until all of the glass had been pushed aside and wind whistled through the cabin. He then took the seat closest to Luke.

Della, on a front seat, folded her arms on a window's ledge and rested her chin so that the wind created by the boat's speed cooled her face. The sensation of rushing air was refreshing, but the day itself was hot, even by September standards. They were headed into the peninsula's interior where sea breezes never reached, unless a hurricane happened along. She ran her tongue over her lips. *This trip better be worth the discomfort.*

She watched as the buildings of downtown Miami faded behind them. The scenery evolved to low banks covered with scrubby trees, mostly pines and palms, broken only by the occasional higher white-sand cliff topped with spiky grass. The river narrowed, forcing Luke to pull back on the throttle. Buildings and other signs of human habitation grew much farther apart. Only the occasional farmhouse appeared in the distance.

Luke steered the boat past a dilapidated shack with a short dock slumping into the river, then entered an area that couldn't really be called "river" anymore. Water spread out in all directions, as did trees with Spanish moss hanging from their branches, wide swaths of grasses, and low palms that looked like their fronds grew straight out of the water.

Della had been out on the edges of the Everglades with Papa, an avid fisherman, as soon as she could hold a pole, but she had never ventured farther inland. The natural beauty of the "river of grass" struck her. This was what the world must have looked like when it was newly formed.

They wove in and out between trees and little tussocks of grass where long-legged herons with blue-gray plumage and long, pointed beaks jabbed at the water, occasionally spearing a fish. They passed a log where a line of turtles lazed in the sunshine. Next to the turtles' perch, another log floated lower in the water. Its bark had a pattern that didn't match any tree. As they drew closer, eyes snapped open and blinked at the glare coming off the water. The alligator's eyes followed the boat's progress, perhaps evaluating the possibility for its next meal. A shiver ran through Della. She was South Florida born and bred, but she would never become accustomed to living in such proximity to the reptiles.

The boat passed through stands of cypress where cone-shaped knees stuck out of the water at the trees' bases. The water was black brown, but not because of dirt. It would have been crystal clear but for the acid leaching from the cypress trees.

Luke steered the boat ever deeper into the watery terrain until the swamp closed around them like some ancient world not yet disturbed by man's intrusion. Della had no idea where they were or how far they had traveled. They pushed on through much denser growth until it fell away, and an island lay before them surrounded on all sides by thick forest. A few yards from the water's edge stood a large, one-story building covered in unpainted, weathered, gray boards.

Luke guided the boat to a dock and cut the engine. "Well, this is it, the exact location of the coordinates. Want to get out and take a look?"

Della's gaze swept their surroundings. "Are you sure? Everything has looked the same since we left the river."

Luke held up two items. "Among the many useful skills gained compliments of the US Army, map reading and using a compass were high on the list for those of us in covert operations. Yes, I'm sure this is the correct location."

Auggie stood and stretched his back. "We've come this far. Might as well see what's here."

Della followed the men onto the island and to the building. Large double doors flanked by small, grimy windows filled one end of the long, rectangular structure.

Auggie rubbed the dirt from a windowpane and peered into the structure. "Looks empty, but we might as well check inside anyway. It's pretty dark in there."

Luke lifted the crossbar securing the doors and pulled one back. Sunlight flooded the cavernous interior. Other than a rat scurrying away in fright, the building was completely empty, unless one counted spiders and the hapless insects caught in their webs.

Della looked from Auggie to Luke and back. "What's so important about an abandoned building that its location was kept a secret?"

Auggie's head moved slowly from side to side. "Good question. I think the next step is to check the county title and tax records. Seeing who owns this island may shed some light on why Art and Aldridge were interested in it."

Luke closed the door and leaned against it. "Since county offices won't be open until Monday morning, maybe we should concentrate on the journal you found in the safe deposit box. If it was important enough to keep locked away in a secret place, then it may hold the key to your husband's murder."

Della stiffened at his mention of Art's death. It felt wrong that someone should so casually speak of it. Perhaps she was being unfair. Luke was trying to help with a situation in which he had nothing to gain and very possibly a lot to lose. She wiped sweat from her upper lip and swatted at a mosquito buzzing around her face. "Let's leave. There's nothing for us here." She headed toward the dock without waiting for the men to reply.

As Luke helped her into the boat, she stopped and glanced back at Auggie. "You know, we didn't think to ask how many times Art had opened the bank box or when he rented it. Do you think the bank will give us that information?"

"Of course they will. You legally own the box. There would be no reason to keep that secret from you."

Once the boat was underway, she moved close to Auggie so he could hear her over the roar of the engine. "If we know when Art rented the box and how often he visited it, we might be able to figure out what those numbers and letters mean."

Auggie shrugged. "Maybe. Maybe not. But no matter what the bank tells us, all information is important."

Della's heart beat a little faster with the question she needed to ask next. "One thing's been preying on me. We haven't told Barnett about the island or the box. Should we? Must we?"

"As your attorney, it is incumbent upon me to advise that withholding evidence from a police investigation could have serious legal repercussions. So, yes, you must tell Barnett about both.

However, there is nothing in the law about the timing of the revelations. I would say we have until about 11:00 a.m. Monday morning before time runs out."

"I guess we'd better go to work as soon as we get back to the house. I'm going to ask Luke to stay for the rest of the weekend. Can he borrow a clean shirt?"

Auggie chuckled. "It would be a pleasure for Mr. Singletary to wear one of my shirts."

Della cut her eyes at Auggie, watching him from beneath her lashes. Something felt odd in her cousin's reaction to her request. It was hard to tell whether he was being serious or sarcastic regarding the loan of a shirt. Moreover, she couldn't decide whether Auggie resented Luke or liked him.

# CHAPTER 18

Della and the two men sat at the dining room table with the mysterious journal from the safe deposit box open between them. Single columns of figures and letters marched across three pages, but there was no key or legend of any kind to explain what it all meant.

She sighed and pushed the volume away. "This is mind-numbingly confusing. Look at this first entry—CC 50 9/5. What can it possibly mean?"

The crease between Luke's eyes deepened. "May I have the journal? Reading upside down is breaking my concentration."

Della turned the book around and slid it across the table. Luke studied each column and then snapped his fingers. "I think I know what some of the numbers are." He turned the journal so that Della and Auggie could follow. He tapped the first entry. "The numbers separated by slashes . . . they must be dates. Look at the progression—9/5, 9/17, 9/25—about once per week, something is going to happen."

"But what?"

Luke shrugged. "I have no idea, but these numbers have got to be dates. That's the most logical explanation for why they're written like this."

Auggie nodded and tapped each entry. "Yes, I see what you mean. How far do the dates extend?"

Della flipped through the three pages. "The last one is December 29, two days before New Year's Eve." She met Luke's eyes. A sudden suspicion grew as she studied him. "Has Aldridge said anything to you about dates like this?" Her voice was hard and accusatory.

He leaned back and crossed his arms over his chest. "Why do you ask? Do you suspect me of something? If so, out with it." His eyes were wary.

Heat rose from Della's chest onto her cheeks. There was no reasonable explanation for why she felt as she did, but she wanted to be angry. She needed to be angry. She wanted to strangle someone—anyone. She wanted to scream and shout that it was unfair that Art was dead while other people lived. She was in pain, and she wanted everyone to hurt with her.

She jumped up so fast, her chair tipped over. Glaring down at Luke, she shouted, "You could be working against us. You could be Aldridge's plant to prevent us from finding the truth."

Luke's eyes blared. "No good deed goes unpunished with you. Is that it?" His reply rolled around the room like thunder.

The shock of his shout pierced Della. Covering her mouth, she mumbled, "I'm sorry. I can't. I just can't."

As she fled the room, she heard Luke's voice. "Of all the female histrionics . . ." He did not finish the thought, but his tone communicated his anger. "She acts like she suspects me of something and then gets mad when I ask what it is."

A chair scraped back from the table. "She's got a right to be emotional." Auggie's voice drifted through to the kitchen where Della leaned over the sink, afraid she was going to be sick.

An arm settled around her shoulders. She buried her face in Auggie's shirt front. "Oh, God, what am I going to do? We were supposed to grow old together. We had talked about having babies. I feel like the best part of me died the night Art was killed. Why has this horrible thing happened?"

Auggie patted her heaving shoulders. "It's okay. Let it out. We don't know what happened—not yet—but we will. Once we have the answers, it may be easier to start living again. For now, you cry all you need to."

The storm within her raged until she was limp and weak. She staggered to a kitchen chair, slumped into it, and placed her elbows on the table. Resting her head against her fists, she turned her face to the side.

Auggie frowned as he leaned against the sink, eyeing her with concern. "Feel better?"

She tried to smile. "Not really, but the rage is spent for the time being." She sat up. "I think I owe Luke an apology."

Auggie grinned and offered her his hand. Pulling her to her feet, he said, "Yep. You accused him of being the enemy without so much as a shred of evidence and much to the contrary."

"Ugh, I pretty much know how that feels."

After trudging back to the dining room, Della resumed her seat. She studied Luke for a moment. He still looked ruffled and angry. "Accusing you of treachery was unfair and unfounded. My only excuse is that Art's death has left my emotions at the breaking point. You have been kind and helpful. Please say you will forgive me."

He did not reply immediately. His eyes were glued to hers until it seemed they would bore into her very soul. Finally, he said, "Yeah, all is forgiven. You've got good reasons to be upset. Why don't you take Monday off? You need to go to the bank and to see Barnett. I'll cover for you with the boss. And speaking of Anders, give me that scrap of paper with the coordinates. It better be back in place before he returns."

Auggie stirred beside Della. "I've advised her to turn it over to Barnett."

Derision colored Luke's laugh. "Do you really want us to have to deal with the boss when he discovers it's gone? He hid it there for a reason, and he will expect it to be there when he returns."

Auggie stroked his chin. "I see. Perhaps that is the best course, but we need to make a copy. Did your training in covert operations happen to include forgery?"

Luke grinned. "I was never an expert, but I did my share of it good enough to fool the Germans."

Relief flooded Della as she realized how much she had come to rely on Luke's friendship and support. He was right about the paper and a lot of other things.

·    ·    ·    ·    ·

Della and Auggie passed into the bank's lobby as soon as the manager unlocked the doors.

The man ran his gaze over them with a quizzical expression. "How may I be of assistance?"

Auggie took the lead. "We have come again about the bank box Mr. Monroe rented. We would like to know when he rented it and how many times he visited."

"Is there a problem? I assure you there was nothing out of the ordinary or untoward in renting the box."

"No, no problem. We need the information for the purposes of probate."

"Oh, of course. I'll get the vault clerk to help you."

The manager disappeared down a back hall. Presently, a little gnome of a man stepped into the lobby, scowled, then beckoned to them in the manner of someone on the verge of scolding a wayward child. Della rolled her lips inward to suppress a giggle. It was clear why this particular employee was hidden away. While he was probably excellent with keeping records and the like, his manner left something to be desired when it came to interacting with customers.

Once they were all seated in the gnome's office, he pulled a ledger from the bookcase behind him. He flipped pages until he came to the one with Art's box number. "Ah, yes. I see here the box was rented on August 15th of this year." He turned the ledger toward Della and Auggie. "As you can see, it was visited only once after it was rented until Mrs. Monroe opened it last week. Yes, Mr. Monroe only came the one time, August 20th. Is there anything more?"

Della and Auggie thanked the gnome, then returned to the car. After sliding into the driver's seat, Auggie engaged the gears and pulled into traffic.

Della laid her arm on the passenger door's ledge and watched the scenery as they headed south toward Miami. "Do you think we should have let Barnett know we are coming?"

"Not necessarily. Anyone can take down the information. If he wants to talk to you, he knows where to look."

Della drummed her fingers against the door. "I don't want to see him. He has it in for me, and I don't understand why."

"Oh, I don't think he necessarily wants you to be guilty. He simply has no idea who killed Art, and you are a convenient target until a better one comes along." Auggie flashed her an encouraging grin. "If he actually thought you were guilty, he would have charged you by now."

"Gee, that really doesn't make me feel better, but thanks for trying."

When they arrived at police headquarters, Della discovered that luck was not with her. She and Auggie were ushered into Barnett's office where he and another detective were in conference.

The policemen rose, and Barnett gestured toward a chair set against the wall. To his colleague, he said, "Give Mrs. Monroe your chair and have your notepad ready. I believe these folks have something interesting to tell us."

Della felt uneasy. It seemed like Barnett already knew what they had come to share.

After she was seated, he wasted no time. Barnett fixed Della with an intimidating expression. "So, you've been busy. A boat trip into the Glades, and then a visit to a bank where you don't have an account. What did you find?"

Della blinked in surprise. "Do you have someone following me?"

Barnett gave her a grimace of a smile. "Of course. We put tails on all suspects in a murder investigation. That's how we solve crimes."

Della wanted to scream and slap his insolent face, but Auggie's hand squeezing her arm sent a warning. Instead of assaulting the detective, she drew a deep breath and willed herself to speak calmly. Raising a brow and fixing her mouth in a firm line, she asked, "Do you think I would have come here to give you information if I had played a part in murdering the man I loved?"

Barnett met her glare with one of his own. After a couple of seconds of stalemate, he chuckled. "No, I don't guess you would. So, what do you have for us?"

For the next few minutes, she and Auggie outlined what they had discovered at the island and the bank in Hialeah, ending by sliding the mysterious journal across the desk.

Barnett flipped through the pages. "Thanks for bringing this in. We'll log it in as evidence." He tapped the journal. "Do you recognize the handwriting?" Della shook her head. "And you can't tell us what these figures and letters mean?"

With a sinking feeling, Della shook her head again. "No, I can't, at least not for the majority." This was feeling too much like an interrogation. "The best we can make of them is the numbers separated by slashes could be dates. Other than that, we're clueless."

The detective's eyes narrowed. "What drew you out into the Glades? It's hardly a resort area."

Della's heart jerked. Tell the truth or lie? She cut her eyes at Auggie, who nodded, leaned forward, and passed a piece of paper to the detective. "We found what looked like map coordinates on this piece of paper. Going to the location seemed the logical next step."

Veins in Barnett's neck bulged. "Before you thought to mention this to us?"

Della held her breath and prayed the detective would not ask where they found the paper. What she had given him was a copy of the one Luke would return to Aldridge's desk.

Auggie spread his hands in supplication. "We didn't know what we would find or if it was pertinent to your investigation."

Barnett hit the desk with a fist, rattling his nameplate, an ashtray, and bouncing a pen to the floor. "Counselor, everything is pertinent, as I think you surely know." Barnett's sneer took in Della as well. "I will not remind either of you again that interference with a police investigation is a punishable crime, as is withholding evidence. Don't do it again. It makes us think you have something to hide—maybe a lot."

Auggie looked contrite. "Please accept my apologies. It will not happen again."

Barnett stood. "It better not." Looking at Della, he barked, "Where will you be staying? Farm or villa?"

Della swallowed hard. "I'm returning to the villa this afternoon. I still have a lot of work to complete for Mr. Aldridge."

"Okay. Make sure you let us know where you are at all times, and don't even think about leaving Miami. Now, unless you have something else you've been withholding, I'm late for a meeting with the captain."

Della found that she had not been breathing fully until they were driving away from the police building. She gasped for air as her body spasmed and shook.

Auggie glanced at her. "You're not going to be sick or pass out on me, are you?"

She could not stop gales of laughter that suddenly took control. She bent double. She laughed. She howled. She gasped. When the storm finally passed, she wiped her eyes with a handkerchief Auggie offered. "I'm sorry for the hysterics. I couldn't help it."

"No need to apologize. You've had a very trying time, and it looks like it may get worse before it gets better."

Della hiccupped and sighed. "Do you think Barnett will eventually ask where we found the coordinates?"

Auggie tilted his head and pursed his lips. "With luck, no. He probably assumed it was in the box with the journal. It would be the logical conclusion. There is no good reason to disabuse him of that notion, and we can't be held accountable for questions he doesn't think to ask."

Della smirked. "Slick. Very slick. I see Luke is not the only one with a shady side. And all this time, I thought you were just a mild-mannered, country lawyer who handled wills and real estate transfers."

"Oh, I do plenty of that, but I've also handled my share of criminal cases. Rural areas are not immune to the vagaries of human nature. We have our share of murders and robberies whose perpetrators deserve legal counsel."

"You know, I wish we hadn't given Barnett the journal. Now, we can't continue to work on what it all means."

"Don't be so ready to despair. Look in my briefcase."

Della tugged the case from the space behind his seat. Opening the flap, she withdrew several loose pieces of paper. Shuffling through them, she gave a shout. "Hallelujah! You thought to make a copy. I've been so busy feeling sorry for myself, I've left the thinking to you and Luke."

Auggie gave her a sympathetic smile. "Well, I'm not so sure about the feeling sorry for yourself bit. I'd say grieving, and all that goes with it, is a natural state with what you've experienced."

"When did you make this?"

"After you went to bed last night. Luke and I agreed that, although the journal and the coordinates had to be turned over to the cops, we should keep a copy of the information. Since he's a secretary, I left the job to him. His handwriting is rather nice, wouldn't you say?"

Della focused on the numbers and letters. "Yes, it is. I'm so glad he made the copies. Something else I need to thank him for."

As the car pulled up to a stop sign, Auggie asked, "Which way do we go? Do you want to take the rest of the day and return to the farm or go back to the villa?"

Della wrinkled her nose and curled a lip. "As much as I dread returning to the villa, I told Barnett that's where I'm going. I guess I'd better do what I said. He already thinks I killed Art. Better not give him evidence that I'm a liar as well."

"Okay. To the villa it is. I'll visit the county records office after I drop you off."

# CHAPTER 19

Della paused at the door to Aldridge's office and casually glanced in both directions to make sure she was alone. Even though she had a legitimate reason to be there, she had no desire for a maid or the butler to walk in on her with what she was about to do.

She entered the office, went to the desk, and sneaked a peek under the blotter. Yep, the coordinates paper was in place where she and Luke had found it. Or was it? She replaced the blotter and closed her eyes, trying to visualize how the desk had looked. Her eyes flew open as her heart skipped a beat. She was not sure. She simply did not remember. A nightmare scenario of her boss demanding to know who had messed with his desk raced through her mind.

Shaking her head to clear her mind, she moved to the window overlooking the bay. The view was beautiful, and she needed some beauty to calm her jangling nerves. Would Aldridge notice if the scrap was out of place a fraction of an inch? The very thought made her ill. Every instinct told her that there was something nefarious connected with the building on the island in the Everglades. Why else would Aldridge have hidden the scrap of paper?

Movement in the open doorway made her whip around. Luke stood, watching her. "You seem very pensive. Sorry to disturb, but we've just received notice that the final shipment will be arriving this week. How much longer do you think we have before your job is complete?"

"It depends on how many items are in this last shipment. Do you have the bill of lading?"

"Not yet." He would have said more, but the telephone rang at a jarring volume. Luke grabbed the base and placed the receiver against his ear. "Villa Lucca, Singletary speaking. Yes, she is present in the house. One moment. I'll see if she is available." Luke set the telephone on the desk, covered the transmitter with one hand, and pressed his index finger against his lips. He motioned for her to move closer. Once she stood by his side, he whispered, "Some guy asking for you. Are you expecting a call?"

Della shook her head and matched his whisper. "Is it Auggie?"

"No. I don't recognize the voice." He leaned in. "Wait here, keep the transmitter covered, but put the receiver against your ear. Give me a couple of minutes. When you hear me shout that you have a call, answer it. I'll be listening in on the extension in my office just down the hall."

She did as he asked, and within a minute or so, his voice rolled down the hallway. Picking up the transmitter, she said, "Hello. Mrs. Monroe here."

"You and your friends need to stop snooping in stuff that don't concern you." The voice was gruff and uncultured.

"Who is this? What are you talking about?"

"Stay away from the island if you know what's good for you. Gators are always hungry."

A click on the other end of the line signaled the conversation had ended. Della returned the telephone to its place on the desk. Numbed by shock, she waited, frozen in place, for Luke's return.

He rushed into the office and gave her the once-over. Placing an arm around her shoulders, he asked, "Are you okay? Did you recognize the voice?"

She shook her head. "No. I've never heard it before." Her voice was barely above a whisper.

Luke became pensive and his eyes narrowed. "Someone must be watching the island, but where on earth are they hiding? The barn looked like nobody had been near it recently. Of course, we didn't see the other side of the island, but the trees and undergrowth are so thick, it would be hard to keep a lookout unless you were close by." His voice was calm, and the pressure of his embrace was steady.

Borrowing some of his strength, she asked in a fuller voice, "Do you think someone could have followed us?"

"I think I would have seen them when we passed through the areas of open water. There was absolutely no one but us in that part of the Glades that day."

"But the rigging at the back blocks the view from the back of the boat, and the island is surrounded by thick growth. Couldn't someone have followed?"

"Maybe, but you forget my training. Out of habit, I watch for being followed. Makes me seem uncommonly suspicious, I know, but extreme caution kept me alive during the war. No, I think there must be another shelter of some sort on the island, a place from which someone can keep an eye on the barn. Whoever this man is or these men are and whatever is planned, one thing is sure—danger lurks out there for anyone who crosses them. The caller made that clear."

A spasm of trembling passed through Della. Instinctively, she laid her head on Luke's shoulder. "Oh, Luke, I'm afraid. So very afraid."

He wrapped his other arm around her and pulled her even closer. "You'll be safe as long as I have breath. I promise."

Della jerked from his embrace. What was she doing? What was she allowing him to think? She avoided looking at him by staring at the floor. "I'm sorry. I was overcome by being threatened. Please forgive me." When she dared to meet his gaze, she saw frustration and acceptance mixed with a touch of emotional pain.

Luke stepped back several paces. "You have nothing to apologize for. You were upset, and I made a clumsy attempt at comforting you. It is I who should apologize."

They stood in the center of the room staring at one another for several seconds. Finally, Luke broke eye contact. He sauntered to the desk and began shuffling papers. "Anders and Rollie will be home by tomorrow. I know the boss will want to see progress on the cataloging. Better get back to it."

All she could muster was a quiet "yes."

•   •   •   •   •

The next afternoon, a commotion in the front of the house told Della that her boss and his partner had returned. Hard-soled shoes sounded in the office hallway, and within moments, Anders Aldridge burst through the door.

He took no time in demanding, "Well, how far have you gotten? I understand you spent the weekend elsewhere."

Della opened the ledger she used for the cataloging and passed it to him. He thumbed through to the last entry and smiled. "Very good. You're a fast worker. By this account, all that remains is for you to catalog the new shipment. What are your plans when this job is finished?"

Della's chin snapped up. The question caught her off guard. "I've been so caught up in the cataloging that I haven't given the future much thought."

"I see." Aldridge studied her for a moment. Della could almost see his mind working. Finally, he said, "I've been thinking about your predicament and one of my own. I may have a solution that will serve both of our needs. Are you interested?"

Della cocked her head to one side and tried to keep her excitement from showing. Perhaps he would ask her to stay on at the villa in some capacity, which would suit her own purposes beautifully. Making her voice and expression as casual as possible, she replied, "I may be. What do you have in mind?"

"As you know, I entertain often and lavishly. My parties are famous far beyond Miami, and my guests number among the cream of society. But the evenings have always lacked something. I need someone to act as my hostess, someone who would be an ornament to the evening. She must be beautiful, charming, witty, and intelligent. I believe you possess those qualities in abundance, my dear."

Heat played across Della's cheeks. "My goodness. That is certainly flattering. What are you expecting of your hostess?" Would he expect more of her than she was willing to give? His reputation said he might.

"We can work out the particulars once you have said you will accept the position."

"May I have some time to think about it?"

"Of course, but not too long. Let's say you will give me your answer once the cataloging of my last shipment is completed. Would that give you sufficient time?"

"I believe so. Thank you for considering me."

An unsettling gleam entered his eyes. "Believe me, the pleasure is all mine."

Della broke eye contact. Something needed to be done to deflect his attention and give her time away from the villa. With his coy remark about pleasure, living-in seven days a week, as she had done since taking the job, took on an oppressive, maybe even dangerous quality. On impulse, she said, "Mr. Aldridge, my husband's estate is proving more difficult to settle than anticipated. My cousin, Mr. Breckenridge, has asked that I spend more time with him in pursuit of various details that require my attention. I need to spend two days per week at home, and one of them must be a business day. Perhaps I might start taking Fridays and Saturdays off?"

He watched her for a moment with a neutral expression. Finally, he smiled. "You may take two days, but let's make them Sunday and Monday, or Monday and Tuesday, if you prefer."

"Thank you. Monday and Tuesday would be perfect." Feeling rather wistful, she hunched her shoulders and added, "Who knew death would be so complicated?"

Aldridge became somber. "Death, my dear, is never easy or without complications."

# CHAPTER 20

That evening, Luke guided his car into place beside Art's roadster and applied the brakes. Neither he nor Della spoke as he came around the car and opened her door. She accepted his proffered hand and stepped from the vehicle but did not look at him. Since their encounter right after the wretched phone call, a cautious tension had developed between them. They had gone from being relaxed around one another to being stiff, formal, and polite to the point of absurdity.

A more honest woman would just admit that she had felt safe and comfortable in Luke's arms, but she would not—could not—allow that. She was a recent widow. She had no right to feel anything other than friendship for any man. It was fear that made her feel as she had when they embraced. Of course, it was. She was still in love with Art and probably always would be. Stiff . . . well, maybe not stiff, but formal and polite was as it should be between Luke and her. Della was relieved that the roadster was in the yard because it meant Auggie was in the house.

When she and Luke entered the parlor, Auggie looked up from his newspaper in surprise. "Well, hello. I didn't expect you back so soon." Eyeing Luke, he continued, "Has something happened?"

Della plopped down on the sofa. "Yeah, you might say something has happened. Luke, why don't you sit instead of looming over us like a bird of prey?" She winced inwardly at her rudeness. Just because she was upset didn't mean she had the right to be mean to others, especially not Luke.

Before she could apologize, he replied, "No thanks. My back injury is acting up. I'm more comfortable standing right now, if it's all the same to you."

Shame washed over Della. "I'm sorry. You've been a good friend, and I'm acting like an ungrateful jerk. I don't know what comes over me sometimes. Thank you for driving me out here."

Luke barely glanced at her. "It was my pleasure." His tone was devoid of emotion. Was he angry, hurt, insulted? It was hard to tell.

Auggie eyed the two for a moment. "Well, children, now that you've gotten that out of your systems, perhaps you can tell me what's going on."

Della sought a distraction—anything to keep her mind off her conflicted emotions. A stack of envelopes lay on the coffee table. She scooped them up. While flipping through the unopened mail, she explained about the new work arrangement, meaning that she now had the next day, Tuesday, to herself.

Auggie nodded. "Very good. We need you to be available during business hours. We still have some probate issues to resolve, among other things." He gave Luke and her a meaningful look. "Is there anything else? By the looks on your faces, I sense there is."

The threatening phone call hung in Della's mind like a reaper's scythe, something she didn't want to think about but which she had to acknowledge.

She reached the last envelope. Bills, bills, and more bills, save for one intriguing letter, which she placed in her lap. Tossing the rest of the mail back onto the coffee table, she tried to adopt a casual tone. "I had a rather disturbing phone call this afternoon. Someone must be watching me."

She described what the caller had said and how he sounded, ending with, "I didn't recognize the voice. I think I would remember if I'd ever met him, but he must be following me. Otherwise, how would he know I'm at the villa and that we went to the island?"

Auggie directed his attention to Luke. "What do you think? Did you recognize the voice?"

Luke shook his head. "No. I've met some of his sort around Miami, but the voice was not familiar."

She opened the final envelope, removed a single piece of notepaper, and skimmed words pasted together from newspaper cuttings. Her heart skipped a beat, then thumped hard. She placed the note on the coffee table. Her throat was dry, and her tongue seemed frozen.

Luke glanced at her, then looked away quickly, apparently unaware of or choosing to ignore her distress. "Whoever the caller is, he either has access to the villa or has an informant on the inside. My guess is the latter. Whatever the case, having Della remain in residence seems better than having her stuck out here. Besides, she'll have the run of the place, and that may prove useful."

Auggie studied Luke through narrowed eyes. "I agree that having her continue at Villa Lucca could be useful, but it makes me uneasy. Can you guarantee her safety? The threatening phone call should be taken seriously. My former classmate has a successful criminal law practice in Miami. One of his operatives has done a little snooping into Aldridge for me. There is every possibility that your boss is not totally legitimate in his business dealings and may even have ties to underworld figures. What do you know about this?" The question rang with accusation.

Luke leaned against the wall and crossed his arms over his chest. If he took offense at Auggie's tone, he chose not to reveal it. "Well, I haven't seen anything that would interest the local cops or Federal agents, but when you have as much money as he does with no explanation of how you got it, rumors fly." He eyed Della. "I suppose you've figured out that the story about your dad loaning all of the start-up money for their real estate speculation is mostly malarky?"

Finally able to form words, Della blinked and drew a quick breath. "We certainly questioned it." With a casual air, she turned the note face down. She needed time to think about what its words meant and whether she should reveal them to Luke. Was she being warned against him along with everyone else at the villa? Surely not, but how could she be certain?

Luke continued, "They did actually get a loan from your dad, but it's not where the bulk of the start-up money came from. I suspect they secured the loan to stop questions about the source of their funding. Nobody knows how Anders got his start, and he isn't telling."

Auggie harrumphed. "That brings us back to my original question. Will Della be safe continuing at the villa?"

Luke's lips rolled inward while his expression became thoughtful. "Unless you have military training, she will be safer under my protection than here at the farm. We don't know who we're dealing with, but Anders will hardly allow criminals free rein in his home. My work keeps me pretty much confined to the house, as does Della's."

Auggie's eyes narrowed. "And when the cataloging is finished, how will Aldridge expect her to fill her time? Even someone who entertains so often rarely does it every night."

Although Della had asked that question of herself, she was beginning to resent being spoken of as though she was not present. If she hadn't wanted to hear Luke's response, she would have told them as much right then. She watched Luke through lowered lashes. What would he say? Would their boss have desires beyond what she was willing to give?

Luke inhaled and exhaled slowly, as though he was exercising supreme control. "She will, by necessity and definition, take on the hosting responsibilities I have so far performed. With the number of parties Anders gives, the planning has become a full-time job. The boss had already talked about hiring someone for the role before Della ever came to the villa."

He sidestepped the issue, damn him.

Auggie's face developed a rosy glow. "But his reputation is . . ."

Della's shout cut his raised voice short. "Oh, my God, stop it! Y'all are making me crazy. I'm right here, you know. Neither of you seems to have considered that maybe I'm smart enough to see the risks I'll be taking. Anders Aldridge is a man who gets what he wants, but I doubt he takes women against their will. He may even be repulsed by a grieving widow who can talk only about her murdered husband with whom she is clearly still in love."

Cutting her eyes at Luke, she continued, "It's not our boss I fear. It's this afternoon's nameless caller. It's the fact that a murderer is still at large. And if that's not enough, one minute Barnett thinks I killed Art, and the next, he thinks I will be the next victim." Glancing at the note on the coffee table, she reached a decision. Luke had done nothing to earn her distrust. In fact, quite the opposite. She grabbed the note and threw it at him. "And now, this."

The sheet of paper fluttered to the floor near his feet. After he retrieved it, his eyes flicked over the pasted words, then jerked toward Della. "Any idea who might have sent this?"

Auggie marched across the room and snatched the paper from Luke's hand. He turned to Della with brows nearly meeting his hairline. "This is strange, indeed."

Auggie held the note out and read aloud. "Do not believe everything people will say. Your husband did not deserve what happened. I am very sorry." He rubbed his chin and frowned. "Why on earth would someone write this and not reveal his or her identity? It's a simple note of condolence. Why all the subterfuge?"

Della slumped lower in her seat. "Why is any of this happening? Damned if I know." A bitter laugh escaped before she could stop it. Slapping her thighs, she continued, "What I do know is that sitting here thinking about my problems is a waste of time. We can't do anything about any of it tonight. I'm not really hungry, but I guess we have to eat. Anything in the icebox?"

Auggie shook his head with a guilty expression. "I fear I've eaten the leftovers from the weekend. What say we go out? My treat."

Della grabbed her handbag from the sofa and trotted to the front door. "Sounds good. The drugstore lunch counter in Hialeah serves a great veal cutlet and mashed potatoes. Really sticks to your ribs."

Without waiting for the men to comment, she turned on her heel and headed out the door.

# CHAPTER 21

When the waitress put her supper on the counter, Della found she was actually hungry. Breaded veal cutlets, mashed potatoes, and English peas reminded her of the Sunday dinners she and her parents enjoyed at the hotel restaurant around the corner from their church. She, Mama, and Papa would walk from First Methodist to the hotel after the service for an hour of good food and family time interrupted only by friends stopping by the table to say hello. No problems were spoken of—only happy talk was allowed. It was one of her favorite memories, so different from tonight's conversation.

She sat sandwiched between Auggie and Luke, allowing her to talk to both. Auggie had promised to do some research, but he had not yet revealed his findings. The note in the mail had pushed everything else from her mind. Fortified by food, the subject of his research rose to the surface.

Placing her fork on her plate, she turned to Auggie. "Did you go to the county records office today?"

She caught him mid-bite. Chewing and swallowing took a few seconds. Finally, he said, "I did, but you will not like the results."

"Has there been anything about this whole mess I *have* liked?"

"I suppose not."

"Okay, then tell me what you found out."

Auggie looked around her at Luke, apparently seeking support. Luke nodded while moving a little closer to Della.

Auggie drew a quick breath and sighed. "Well, you see, the matter is that I had forgotten about the island." Infuriatingly, he stopped speaking and forked another bite into his mouth.

Della shot him a look filled with irritation and confusion. "How could you have forgotten something we so recently discovered?"

After making sure his food was properly, painstakingly masticated, he said, "I don't mean our trip. I mean I had completely forgotten that Art's grandfather bought the island back around 1890. He'd planned to use it for fishing trips, thus the lodge he started but never finished. I forgot it because I had not visited it before we went out there. So, the fact is, Art inherited it, and you are now the legal owner."

Stunned hardly described how Della felt. She blinked and jerked around to face him. Her lips moved, but no sound came out. After swallowing hard, she whispered, "If that's so, why would someone warn me to stay away from my own property?"

Auggie leaned forward and waved his fork in Luke's direction. "Care to make a guess?"

Della turned to Luke, tilting her head in silent question.

He took a sip of water, then wiped his lips with a paper napkin. His eyes sought Della's, mouthing the words, I'm sorry. "If we're to answer that question, I'm afraid we've got to consider some upsetting possibilities. The most obvious is that someone has plans for the island that aren't legal. Why else would they want to keep people away?"

Della held out her palm to stop the men from continuing. Her head swiveled from one to the other and back. "Y'all are dancing around the real issue. Just say it. Was Art involved in something illegal with Aldridge? Is that why he was murdered?"

Auggie put his hand on her shoulder. "Now, see here. We can't say that based on what little we know. Art may have been an innocent victim caught up in a situation beyond his understanding. Here's what we do know." He held up a hand and began ticking off items on his fingers. "One, Art had hopes of some kind of lucrative deal with Aldridge and Shoemaker. Two, he was killed by a person or persons unknown. Three, someone wants you to stay away from your own property. Four, Aldridge may not be above board in some of his dealings. That's all we know with any certainty."

Della put her elbows on the counter and leaned her head against her fists. "A couple of months ago, Art and I were living a normal life. We had our home and farm. We weren't getting rich, but we were making ends meet. Then came Anders Aldridge and his damn party. If he hadn't lured Art with promises of money, Art would still be alive and we wouldn't be talking about criminals making threats." Her voice cracked as her shoulders heaved.

Auggie's stool creaked as he shifted his weight, turning to face her fully. He attempted to put an arm around her shoulders, but she shrugged him off and peeked at him from beneath her lashes. His expression was guarded and cautious. He clearly had something more to share.

Della gritted her teeth. "You might as well say whatever it is you've held back. It can hardly make me feel any worse than I already do."

With an audible intake of breath, Auggie replied, "I think I know what the letters BK stand for."

"Well, don't stop there. What? What?" Della's voice rang through the store. Other customers paused in their conversations to stare.

Auggie squirmed and made a shushing sound, then leaned in so that he would not be overheard. "The county records refer to the island only once by this name, but I think it is significant. Boggs Key—BK. I think Boggs Key must be the BK noted in the journal we found in the secret bank box."

Luke moved in closer as well. "Yes, that makes sense, but what do the letters and other numbers mean? Aside from what we think are dates, nothing else makes sense, unless . . ." He stopped and eyed Della.

"Oh, go ahead. Y'all are acting like I'm some delicate flower who will be crushed by new revelations." She straightened up on her stool. "I may be crushed by Art's death, but I'm determined to find out why he was killed, no matter what Barnett says."

Luke nodded. "Okay. You deserve to know the truth. Here's what I think. Tomorrow is 9/5, September 5—the first date entered in the secret journal. I think we should go to the island and see for ourselves what the letters and numbers might mean. I think the island may hold the key to solving our mystery."

Auggie shook his head and frowned. "While I see your point, what if the guy who warned Della to stay away is there? I cannot support putting her life at risk . . . or mine, as far as that goes. Perhaps we should turn this over to the police. Let them figure out what the island has to do with anything."

Luke smirked. "You trust the police, do you? What if someone in the department is on the take?"

"What do you mean?" Della gasped. "Do you have proof?"

"No proof, just a feeling based on personal experience with covert operations. Something feels off in the way the police are investigating Mr. Monroe's murder. It's like they're dragging their feet, like they don't want to solve it."

Della sucked on her lower lip while she reviewed what she knew of the police investigation. Luke was right. Unless Barnett was keeping information from her, the police weren't doing very much, other than accusing her of being involved in Art's murder. "I agree, Luke. I think we should continue our own investigation, starting with a trip to the island tomorrow. Will you be able to take us out there?"

"I think I can manage it. Since I'm basically on call seven days a week, I take the occasional day for myself. I also have free use of Anders's boats, so I'll arrange to use the swamp boat tomorrow. He'll be in Palm Beach all day at a fancy society thing, so it shouldn't be a problem."

# CHAPTER 22

Tuesday morning dawned warm and humid, nothing out of the ordinary for September in South Florida. By 9 a.m., the thermometer read 90 and climbing. Della sat in her employer's swamp boat, using a very inadequate handkerchief to dab at the sweat trickling down her face. The little scrap of white linen and lace was already soaked to the point she could probably wring moisture from it.

Once Auggie had opened all of the windows and settled beside her, Luke adjusted the knobs in preparation for starting the engine but did not press the ignition. "We're taking a different route to the island today. I'm going to stay in open water as much as possible to ensure we aren't being followed. We'll go on the western side of the island first and then completely circle it before landing at the dock. The island isn't very big, so we should be able to see if there are other structures on it or people skulking around."

Della stuck her head out of a window and breathed deeply. The water looked inviting, but it was too far below her to be reached without squeezing the whole of her body through the window. Not an appealing option. Instead, she called over her shoulder, "Please get this tub underway before we all pass out from heat prostration."

Luke guided the boat into the river and onto the open waters of the Glades. Instead of taking the most direct route, he zigzagged across the open water, occasionally pulling back on the throttle and idling in place while searching in all directions. Satisfied that no prying eyes followed, he returned the craft to cruising speed. After an eternity, he slowed as they approached the forested area surrounding the island. Within minutes, they were creeping along between the cypress trees and solid land.

Over the roar of the engine, Luke shouted, "This is it. Watch for a shack or anywhere a person might hide."

Della scooted to the other side of the boat and searched as they slowly began their circumnavigation of the island, whose interior was concealed by thick vegetation. Near the middle, the undergrowth at the water's edge had been hacked away.

She pointed and shouted, "There. Can you see that? It looks like a path has been cut in the forest."

Slowing the engine, Luke guided the boat to the bank. "This may be what we're looking for."

Della swiveled to face the stern. "Let's get out and see where the path leads."

Luke cut the engine. "I bet it will lead straight to the building on the other side of the island. Yeah, let's give it a look."

Auggie held up his hand. "Now, hold on. We'll have to wade ashore. There are all manner of creatures in and out of the water."

Luke raised a brow and grinned. "You would prefer to sail around the island and straight into whoever is warning you away from it?"

"I suppose not, but how do you know they'll be here?"

"How do you know they won't? This crate makes enough noise to wake the dead. If someone is at the building, with luck, they will think our noise was only a passing craft that slowed and then moved on." Luke waggled his brows. "With that settled, how about jumping out and tying the bowline to a tree?"

"I wasn't aware anything had been settled, but I guess I see your point." After removing his shoes and rolling up his pants legs, Auggie eased himself from the boat into the knee-deep water. He grabbed the line and secured it to a palm leaning over the water.

Luke jumped into the water, then assisted a barefoot Della down beside him. The trio slogged onto the bank where she spied a convenient fallen log. Taking a seat, she donned her canvas, rubber-soled sneakers, glad she had thought to wear them instead of leather shoes. She eyed Auggie with a grin as he put on his oxfords, muttering to himself about the possibility of permanent damage to his trousers. Like Della, Luke had thought to wear beach shoes.

He strode to the path's narrow mouth and peered into the forest. "The island isn't very wide. We should be able to reach the other side in about twenty minutes. Ready?"

They marched single file through brush so thick that one could not see the ground beyond the white sand of the path. The uneven nature of the ground and fresh-cut marks on the palmettos and other shrubs showed the path had been recently opened. After fifteen minutes of trudging, they came to a clearing, out of which loomed several small cabins of sorts on stilts. By the looks of them, they had stood in place for a long time, probably much longer than the building that was their destination.

Luke held up a hand and the party stopped. "Well, would you look at that. It must be an old Seminole camp. During the Seminole Wars, the tribe hid out here in the Glades to avoid federal troops. This camp must have been built while they still owned the island. That ladder by the closest one looks new, though. Let's check it out."

Without waiting for a reply, Luke dashed to the hut and climbed the ladder, then disappeared inside. After only a few seconds, his head appeared in the doorway. "Someone's been camping here, and recently, too. There's a cot and some canned food." Climbing down the ladder, he continued, "My guess is the guy using the hut is the same guy as the caller who warned you to stay away."

Della ducked her head in thought. "Uh-huh, that would make sense." She thought for a moment more, then snapped her fingers. "And you know who else warned me away? Barnett. Could they be one and the same?"

"Maybe, but you said you didn't recognize the caller's voice."

"Okay, then someone who works with Barnett?"

Auggie, mopping his face with a handkerchief, interjected, "My dears, I suspect there will be any number of criminals involved in whatever it is that makes secrecy so important with this confounded island. Let's move on so we can leave and return to civilization."

Another fifteen minutes brought them to the edge of the clearing with the large building and dock. Luke, in the lead, held his hand up. Della and Auggie stopped and tried to peer around him. He turned to them with his finger pressed against his lips. With a jerk of his head, he stepped aside so they could see what had made him so cautious. Della moved forward a few inches and covered her mouth to prevent gasping aloud.

A boat, piled with crates, was tied to the dock. Two men had one crate each hoisted upon their shoulders. They went into the building and returned empty-handed. The process was repeated until the boat's entire cargo had been stowed inside the building. One of the men placed the crossbar over the double doors, then threaded a heavy chain through the large, U-shaped bolt on each and joined the ends with a padlock. He gave the lock a swift yank. Apparently satisfied with his work, he motioned his comrade to the boat. Within moments, they were out of sight.

Della started to dash into the clearing, but Luke grabbed her arm. "Wait until we can't hear their motor. Only then can we be sure they're truly gone." His whisper was warm and moist against her ear, creating an unexpected shiver.

Shame washed through Della. Luke was an attractive man, but Art held her heart. It was Art whom she loved, whose honor and reputation she had come to realize were at stake. She must fight to defend his reputation. She would not—could not—dishonor his memory with a foolish dalliance that was no doubt instigated by grief, loneliness, and fear of the future.

When the roar of the intruders' boat finally disappeared, Della flew from the forest and ran until she reached one of the grubby windows beside the building's double doors. Wiping a spot as best she could, she cupped her hands around her eyes and pressed against the glass. A stack of crates sat near the doors. She could just make out their labels—Canadian Club Blended Canadian Whiskey and

John Jameson & Sons Dublin Whiskey . . . CC and JMN. The puzzle of the journal entries was solved.

Her knees turned to jelly. She sank into the dirt, her fist stuffed into her mouth. Bootleg whiskey stored in a building that belonged to Art—no, wait, a building that now belonged to her. What did Art have to do with illegal alcohol? Surely nothing, but this certainly explained why she was being warned away.

Luke stepped back from the window and let out a low whistle. "Well, I'll be damned. There must be at least fifty cases with more to come, if the journal is to be believed. These alone are worth more money than most of us will ever see. This much booze would be worth killing for."

# CHAPTER 23

The sound of a boat's motor in the distance caught Della's attention. "Do y'all hear that? Are those men coming back?"

Luke cocked his head toward the sound. "Maybe. Let's hide under some cover to wait and see."

Auggie held out his hand to Della, helping her to her feet. "Absolutely not. We must leave at once. You said yourself that those cases of booze are worth a fortune. I, for one, have no intention of being caught here." He gave Della and Luke a hard stare before marching toward the path.

Della shrugged and wrinkled her nose. "I guess we'd better follow him. When Auggie gets his mind set on something, he isn't easily dissuaded. Besides, I think he's right. We don't want to be caught by bootleggers."

The trip back to the swamp boat took half the time of the original since the trio now knew where they were going and what to watch out for. Auggie gave Della a boost into the boat while Luke fiddled with knobs and switches.

She chose a seat in the middle of the craft where the air circulated best. It could be the humidity or perhaps the fear of being discovered by criminals, but the day felt unbearably warm. Fanning herself with her limp handkerchief, she glanced at the stern. "Are you having trouble starting the engine?"

Luke frowned and muttered, "Blasted thing won't turn over. It's always been a little dicey."

Della craned through the window. "I don't see another boat, but the sound is getting louder. Please hurry."

After several more attempts, the engine caught. Luke guided the swamp boat away from the landing spot, but it would be several minutes before they gained open water. Thick cypress and mangrove forests on all sides guarded the narrow channel surrounding the island.

Della laid her arm on the window ledge and rested her chin against it. The slight breeze created by movement gave a little relief from the heat of midday. When she glanced behind them, her heart jerked. A motorboat filled the spot they had just vacated. The sole occupant tossed an anchor overboard, then jumped down into the water. The man paused and leaned against his boat, following the swamp boat's progress. Della jerked her head back, her heart thumping.

Auggie slid over next to her and pointed toward the new arrival. "Man, look at that. We just missed him, and he appears to be very interested in us. Any idea who he is?"

Della caught her lip between her teeth as she thought. "He looks familiar. I swear he's a guy I've seen several times talking to the villa's security guard." She scooted out of her seat and sidled up to Luke. Pointing, she asked, "Do you know that man? I think I've seen him at the villa."

Luke did not even glance where she indicated. With a grim expression, he replied, "I saw him behind us as we launched. Yeah, he comes to the villa. I asked Rollie once who he is but got an answer I don't believe. Whatever his business, Rollie, and maybe Anders, don't want it disclosed."

Della squinted at the figure now disappearing into the forest. "The most logical explanation is he has something to do with the liquor crates we saw in the building. Do you think he's the one sleeping in the hut?"

Luke shrugged. "Maybe. It's hard to know."

The boat lurched sideways as Luke maneuvered around a half-submerged log. Della braced herself against a wall. "I wonder why he didn't use the dock."

Luke gave her a quick glance. "Maybe he doesn't want to be seen by anyone watching the building. These cypress and mangrove forests are thick enough for a boat to hide in and allow someone to watch the dock. A better question is, why isn't he following us?"

"I'm glad he isn't. If he's been to the villa so many times, do you think he recognizes this boat?"

Luke smirked. "I would be surprised if he doesn't. It's a one-of-a-kind original. There was a front-page article in the newspaper when Anders bought it from Glenn Curtiss."

Della's shoulders slumped with a heavy sigh. "Great. Just great. A nameless man who probably recognizes us and knows about the island, but we don't know who he is or why he's here. One more thing to add to our growing list of mysteries. All we seem to have are questions and no answers."

Luke nodded but did not reply. Instead, he turned his attention to guiding the boat through the last of the forest and out into open water, where he shoved the throttle forward.

Della returned to her seat beside Auggie. He gave her a sidewise glance and put his arm around her shoulders. "Are you okay?"

Della's voice caught on a rising tide of emotion. She swallowed hard to prevent the quiver that threatened. "I . . . feel . . . I . . . " Giving up, she let the words tumble out in a trembling rush. "Everything feels so messed up, like my life will never be normal again. As much as I love Art, I'm furious with him, too. Why did he have to become involved with Anders Aldridge? We were doing okay until the get-rich-quick scheme came along—whatever it was supposed to be. Do you think Art knew about the booze? I'm so confused and sad and very angry, all at the same time." Tears streamed beyond her control.

Auggie hugged her so that her head rested on his shoulder. "I wish I had the answers. I would like to say that Art could not have been involved in anything remotely illegal, but given what we saw today . . ." His words ebbed away on a wave of resignation.

Della dabbed at her cheeks and shifted out of his embrace. She turned to face him. He needed to see that she was in earnest. "I have to know what Art was up to. That's got to be the key to everything." She paused for a moment to think. "What kind of law does your old school buddy practice?"

Auggie's eyes narrowed. "He's built quite a reputation in criminal defense. Why do you ask?"

"We need someone with connections, someone who can put out feelers to the bootleggers without raising suspicion. He helped us once before. Will you ask him to help again?"

Auggie studied her for several seconds. "I suppose I can, but are you sure about this?"

"Absolutely. The doubt and not knowing are killing me."

"And you're willing to risk being charged with interfering with a police investigation? Because that's what you're proposing. Barnett has warned us off once. He'll take a very dim view of future involvement. And don't forget. He's only hinted that he believes you're guilty. My impression is that it's only a ploy to shake free whatever information he thinks you might be withholding."

Della hit the seat with her fist. "If being charged is what it takes, then so be it. Barnett isn't making progress, so he's looking for the most convenient explanation. If he's going to settle on me as his chief suspect, I need to be ready to defend myself. I need to know what's going on in the bootlegging trade and what Art's part in it could have been."

Auggie held up a hand. "Now, hold on. You don't know if Art was involved. Moreover, by stomping around Barnett's territory, you may do yourself more harm than good."

"That's a chance I'll have to take. Do I have to talk to your lawyer friend, or will you do it?"

Auggie huffed. "No, I'll do it. Making overtures to bootleggers is against my better judgment, but I can see you won't be dissuaded."

"Damn right."

# CHAPTER 24

The telephone was jangling when Della, Auggie, and Luke arrived back at the farmhouse. Della rushed in and scooped up the base and earpiece. The voice on the other end of the line startled her.

"Mrs. Monroe, how many times do I need to tell you to stay out of my investigation? Do I need to lock you up?" Detective Barnett's displeasure sent a sliver of anxiety through Della.

She drew a deep breath, then motioned Auggie to her side, tilting the earpiece so he could hear the conversation as well. "Detective, it's so nice to hear from you. I deeply appreciate your concern." A sharp elbow in the ribs made her gasp. Meeting the policeman's anger with sarcasm felt good but perhaps was unwise.

She cut her eyes at Auggie, who was giving her a look of doom and destruction with a finger drawn across his throat. Without asking, he snatched the telephone's transmitting stem from her hand. "Breckenridge speaking. What can we do for you, Detective Barnett?"

"You can damn well keep your noses out of police business."

Auggie took the earpiece from Della, held his index finger against his lips, and blared his eyes at Della. Having made sure she got his message, he continued, "And what gives you the impression we are involving ourselves in your business?"

"I told y'all not to go back to the island. Did you listen? No. There you were again today. Did you like what you found? Does it ease Mrs. Monroe's grief to know that her husband was a bootlegger?"

Della could not stop a little anguished cry. She shook her head vehemently. Auggie glared and turned his back to her. "May I ask how you know we returned to the island?" She tapped Auggie's shoulder, but he shrugged her off.

"No, you may not." Della could hear Barnett's shout even without the earpiece near her ear. "It would serve y'all right if I charged her with her husband's murder and locked her up. Kill two birds with one stone. Keep her safe and keep her out of my business." His anger apparently ebbing, Barnett lowered his volume to a rumble.

After listening for several seconds, Auggie turned back to Della with a raised brow in clear warning that she should remain silent. "I see. I cannot promise to stop our own investigation. Let me remind you that a rather sizable insurance settlement rests on the outcome. I can, however, assure you we will turn over all information we may uncover. As to putting Mrs. Monroe into protective custody, that is wholly un . . ." Auggie stopped speaking and rolled his eyes. Della could hear Barnett's tone, even though she could not understand his actual words.

When the noise from the earpiece ended, Auggie continued, "As I was about to say, that will be wholly unnecessary. It may interest you to know that Mrs. Monroe's employment at the villa continues. She is to be Mr. Aldridge's social secretary. She will have access to all guest lists, etc. Having a reliable source embedded within Villa Lucca may be useful, don't you agree?" After another moment of silence, Auggie added, "No, we will not hold you or the Miami Police Department responsible. Now, if there is nothing else . . ."

Auggie placed the earpiece on its hook and returned the candlestick instrument to its place on the table, his expression grim. "As you probably surmised, Barnett refused to divulge how the police are keeping tabs on the island. I don't think he was serious about arresting you, but we must not make him any angrier than he is now." He fixed Della with a firm expression. "Being a sassy smart aleck with him doesn't help."

Della nodded. "Okay, okay. Sorry. I'll keep it civil and cooperative with him." She put her fist on her hip. "But I'd like to know how on earth he knew we'd been back to the island."

Luke, who had been hovering nearby, cleared his throat. "It's possible the guy we saw arriving as we were leaving is a police informant or even a cop. If he left the island not long after we did, he could have reached a phone to call Barnett before we arrived here at the farm. The timing would have been tight, but achievable."

Della pulled her lower lip between her teeth as she processed Barnett's accusation against Art. It was inconceivable that her honest, hardworking husband had become involved with criminals, and yet, everything they had discovered seemed to point that way. With a sinking heart, she said, "It looks like Barnett thinks Art was up to no good, but I can't bring myself to believe it. There's got to be another explanation for why the liquor is stored on his island and why he was killed. There's just got to be." She could not control her quivering lip or the welling tears.

Luke's eyes filled with sympathy. "If another explanation exists, I promise you we will find it." He glanced at his wristwatch. "I think we need to head back to the villa. Anders mentioned something about wanting to get started on some plans with you sooner rather than later. I believe he's expecting us for dinner this evening."

Della frowned. "He didn't say anything to me about it."

"No? I'm sorry. I thought you knew. I'll get the car started." Luke nodded at Auggie and headed for the yard.

Della hugged Auggie and whispered, "Have you asked your lawyer friend to help us contact people who know the bootlegging business? I have to know whether or not Art was involved."

Auggie pushed her back and held her at arm's length. "As I've said before, I'm uncomfortable with the danger this may mean for you, but I'll keep my promise. I'll talk to him tomorrow."

Della gave him a damp smile, then kissed his cheek. "By the way, you never told me his name."

"I haven't? How remiss of me. It's Jacob Berkowitz."

•   •   •   •   •

Della finished organizing her notes from her meeting with Aldridge and started thumbing through his address book when the phone on her desk rang. "Villa Lucca, Mrs. Monroe speaking."

"Good afternoon, cousin. I see you are settling nicely into your new roll." Auggie's voice came over the wires with a chuckle.

"I'm happy to say I am. In fact, Mr. Aldridge and I are working on plans for his next party. Would you like an invitation?"

"My goodness, that would be lovely. From what the society columns describe, everyone who is anyone will be there. I might even find a reason to stay in Miami. I've grown rather fond of the area."

Della's forehead wrinkled in surprise. "I never thought I would hear that from you. Leave the family estate in South Carolina and move to the South's most notorious sin city? What brought this on?"

"Lately, I've been feeling the need for a change—a big one. Living in the same place all one's life can become stifling. Miami has opened my eyes to new . . . possibilities."

"Well, okay. If you decide to make the move, you are always welcome to stay at the farm until you find a place of your own."

"Thanks. I hope you mean that because I just might take you up on the offer."

Della was not sure what to say next. This was so unexpected, so unlike the Auggie she knew. He had always been the rock in Art's family, so for him to suggest he might up and move away on short notice was a shock. There had to be more to his sudden announcement, but she sensed he had said all he was willing to for the moment. He had always been someone who would not be pressed for details about his personal life. He claimed to be a confirmed bachelor and that the subject was closed beyond that. When the time was right, maybe he would tell her what was really on his mind.

"Della? You still there?"

"Oh, yes. Sorry. I'm afraid I am sort of distracted today." A change of subject was needed. "Has your friend, Mr. Berkowitz, made any headway? I want to clear Art's name, if I can. I feel like I can't move forward until I know what happened to him—and why."

"That's actually the purpose of my call. We have an appointment this evening at 6:30, if you can get away. Think your boss will give you the time off?"

"My workday is 9–5. What I do with my evenings is none of his, or anyone's, business."

"Unlike Luke's day, I gather?"

"Yes. He's on call, but then I assume he is paid a great deal more than I am. What time will you pick me up?"

Having written the address for their rendezvous and agreed that Auggie would arrive at 5 p.m., Della returned the telephone to its place on her desk.

Movement at the office door made her jump. She glanced up to see Luke leaning against the jamb. "News from your cousin Augustus? And why were you discussing our relative pay scales?"

Della's eyes narrowed. "Eavesdropping is an unattractive habit. Auggie asked if I could get the evening off, if you must know. That was what prompted my comments on the difference in our salaries. You are paid more than I am, aren't you?"

"Of course. As you so correctly stated, I am virtually on call all the time, and I have seniority. Why are you leaving the villa?"

"My goodness, you are inquisitive." His questioning and tone were getting under her skin. "Why do you want to know?"

"Because I suspect you're going to meet with a bootlegger, and I want to go with you. You have no concept of how dangerous those people are."

"And you do?" She couldn't keep the sarcasm from her voice.

"I absolutely do." He opened his suit coat, displaying a shoulder holster and pistol.

Della swallowed hard. "Good Lord! When did you start carrying that?"

"Since I got this in the mail this morning." He walked over to the desk and threw an envelope on it.

She pulled out a card and read aloud, "Keep away from Boggs Key if you and your girlfriend want to stay healthy."

Della wasn't sure whether the threat or the word girlfriend upset her more. She dropped the card on the desk as she weighed Luke's demand against the possibility that he might be getting too close to her and the situation. It was ridiculous to take the implication from an unsigned card seriously, but it gave her pause all the same. Did he think of her as a potential girlfriend? Did Auggie? Surely not. She was a grieving widow, for God's sake. But, still . . . In the end, wisdom won out.

"If you can get away this evening without raising suspicion, I would very much appreciate your going with us to meet our contact."

"You got it." Luke's smile suggested he was a little too pleased at being invited to the meeting. Please don't let him be getting the wrong idea.

# CHAPTER 25

At 5:00 p.m., Della slipped out from a side entrance onto the gravel driveway and hopped into the roadster beside Auggie. Glancing up at the house, she saw Luke standing in his second-floor office window. He raised a finger in farewell and nodded slowly.

She leaned toward Auggie and whispered, "Luke said to turn left on Ingram, go until we are out of sight of the villa's entrance, and pull over to wait for him. He'll leave in fifteen minutes, take a different route, and circle back to us."

Auggie put the car in gear and guided it toward the front gate. "Seems like overkill, but okay. Looks like our Mr. Singletary wants to keep his connection to us private from y'all's employer. How much do you think Aldridge knows or at least suspects?"

Della thought for a moment. "He knows Luke has driven me to the farm on several occasions because he mentioned it when we had our meeting. I explained that you must have my car, so Luke is my only source of transportation. Aldridge asked how much longer you plan to be here, which surprised me. I don't know why he's interested."

Auggie made the left onto Ingram. "Maybe he was just making conversation."

"Perhaps, but he doesn't seem the type. I've gotten the impression he never does or says anything without a reason. I told him you'll work on the estate until the insurance is settled and I have decided what to do with the farm."

Auggie glanced at her with a raised brow. "Did that satisfy his curiosity?"

Della shrugged. "I guess. He isn't the easiest guy to read."

"Did you mention my invitation to the party?"

"I did." Della chuckled and tapped Auggie's arm so he would look at her. She straightened up into a prim pose. "He said, and I quote, 'Please tell Mr. Breckenridge he is welcome at any and all of Villa Lucca's gatherings. I have certain friends who would be very happy to make his acquaintance.' Sounds like you made a good impression."

Auggie downshifted and extended his arm, pointing right over the top of the car. He applied the brakes, and the car rolled to a stop on the grassy shoulder. "I can't think why. I only met him the one time. Perhaps it's you whom he wishes to impress by being hospitable to your cousin."

"Ugh. Please don't say that."

"Well, it is a possibility, one that you should keep in mind."

Della tilted her head in thought. She had never gotten the impression her boss had any designs on her, other than completing the art catalog as quickly as possible. "I don't think he sees me as someone he needs to impress. What do you think he meant by certain friends of his?" She could have sworn Auggie turned pale at her question, but it must have been the way the lowering sun flashed off the side mirror.

He stared straight ahead. "I'm sure I don't know, but then, from what you've said, he knows all types of people. Where is Luke? It's been over fifteen minutes." Irritation colored his voice, something out of character for the usually even-tempered Auggie.

Della ran her tongue over her lips in concentration, trying to decide if she should apologize for some unrealized offense or ask if something was troubling her cousin-in-law, but movement on the road ahead interrupted her train of thought. Thank goodness. Distraction from the sudden tension between them was on the way.

She pointed at a car approaching from the opposite direction. "That's Luke's MG. He'll circle in front of us so he can lead the way.

He knows the area better than either of us and offered to help find the place."

Luke U-turned and pulled in front of them.

Auggie guided the roadster back onto the pavement and followed as Luke led them south along Ingram Boulevard. "If we are to be accurate, I know nothing about South Dade County. It's a good idea having him along."

"Yeah, even more than you know." Della described the note Luke received and his shoulder pistol.

Auggie whistled. "This is getting truly serious if Luke thinks he needs to be armed. If it weren't for the insurance payout, I would have put a stop to this long ago. I only support you because I know you need the money."

"And to clear Art's name." Her voice was harsher than she intended.

Auggie cut his eyes at her. "I understand your desire. I share it, but I fear the evidence is beginning to point in an unhappy direction. You must be prepared to accept that. Tonight's meeting may not yield any information. In that case, I insist you give up the search. No amount of money is worth your life. Agreed?"

Della turned so that her back rested against the door. She weighed the evidence they had gathered so far against the danger presented by the threats they were getting. "No, I'm not ready to make any promises. You said Jacob Berkowitz's investigators have all sorts of nefarious connections. Is he actually a good source?"

Auggie nodded. "Comes with the territory being the top criminal defense attorney in South Florida. As crime is rampant in these parts, Jacob has a thriving practice and employs top-notch operatives."

"Then surely we'll learn something useful tonight."

•　　•　　•　　•　　•

The sky glowed red and orange by the time the two cars pulled off the paved highway onto a white-sand single track heading into the wetlands south of Florida City. The way the trees crowded and hung over the lane reminded Della of the road leading to the farmhouse, but instead of finding comfort in that, anxiety slithered through her. She dreaded what she might learn and longed for it all the same.

Within minutes, the trees parted, and they came to an open area with a lake in its center. Beside the lake, a rambling, white, clapboard structure stood, surrounded by wooden fencing. At the gate post, a large sign stated that Royal Palm Rod and Gun Club was private property, trespassers beware. Auggie followed Luke through the gate and parked behind him on the circular driveway.

Della studied the two-story lodge where a single, first-floor window glowed with lamplight. Piers elevated the building about four feet off the ground, no doubt in anticipation of flooding from tropical weather. Screening enclosed a long, deep porch, and she could just make out a row of rockers running its length. Bahama shutters on each second-floor window angled out to its fullest. While the lodge was not grand or elegant, a considerable amount of money must have been spent to construct such a large building in the middle of nowhere. Other than crickets and a gator bellowing in the distance, the place was steeped in silence.

Auggie opened her door and assisted her from the car. Della squared her shoulders and drew a long breath as she followed him toward the front steps where Luke waited for them. She clasped her hands at her waist to stop their shaking. She could not afford to appear weak or to display nervousness during this interview. Before they departed this place, she might very well know why Art was killed. Pray the answer would not kill her as well.

Before the three of them got to the lodge's front entrance, the door swung back, revealing a tall man in shirtsleeves. His dignified persona and proprietorial air spoke of being in service, perhaps as a butler or club manager.

The man ran his gaze over them. "Mr. Guthrie is expecting you. Please follow me."

Their guide stepped aside for them to enter the club's foyer. The space was grand in its rustic simplicity. Varnished, cypress-wood walls and floors gleamed in the low light of kerosene lamps placed on antique chests and credenzas. Clearly, electricity had not yet reached this remote area. The reception desk and curved staircase behind it were also made of cypress.

The club's members must have kept local taxidermists busy for years for tarpon, bone fish, sailfish, deer heads, and a complete alligator carcass were mounted on walls that soared at least twenty feet to the darkened, upper-story balcony. Sofas in faded chintz sat in strategic locations, adding a feminine touch to the otherwise masculine atmosphere.

The manservant led Della, Auggie, and Luke across the foyer to a door marked office, opened it, announced them, and departed.

The man behind a large, mahogany desk rose and motioned them into the office. "Mr. Berkowitz failed to mention there would be three visitors." Looking at Luke, he gestured toward a wall and continued, "Would you mind getting another chair?"

"Not at all."

As Luke returned with a chair for himself, Guthrie replied, "Good man." He then turned his attention to Della and Auggie. He extended his hand first to Della and then Auggie. "Aldo Guthrie. A pleasure to meet you. Please be seated. I have instructed my man to bring refreshments presently." Eyeing Della, he said, "Now, tell me, to what do I owe the pleasure of your visit?"

Aldo Guthrie was nothing she had expected. Rather than being a backwoods yokel, he was suave, impeccably dressed, and spoke with a cultured, East Coast accent.

Auggie stirred beside Della as he did when he was about to speak. She placed her hand on his arm to stop him. This was her investigation, her need for information, her murdered husband. She would ask the questions. Clearing her throat loudly, she leaned forward. "Thank you for seeing us. I must admit I'm at a bit of a loss. Did Mr. Berkowitz not mention why we wished to see you?"

Guthrie gave her an oblique smile. "He indicated you have an interest in certain business concerns of which I may have knowledge." A knock at the door drew his attention. He nodded and tapped his desk. "Place it here, and then you may be dismissed for the night." The servant brought in a tray with four glasses, a decanter filled with amber liquid, a soda dispenser, and a bottle of sherry.

Guthrie gestured at the tray. "Whiskey, gentlemen? Perhaps sherry for the lady?"

Della did not want their minds muddled by alcohol, but refusing to imbibe might be taken as an insult by their host, a man whom she had no wish to offend. She glanced at Luke, who nodded ever so slightly. Della smiled. "Yes, thank you. A small sherry would be delightful." Just because she accepted the glass, it did not follow that she had to consume all of its contents.

Once the drinks had been distributed, she took a sip and placed her glass on the desk. "First, please let me express my sincere gratitude for your agreeing to see me. If we could have discovered the information we seek in another way, we would not have inconvenienced you. I hope we aren't imposing on you. It's most gracious of you to agree to meet with us." She was rambling. She knew it but could not bring herself to get to the point.

Guthrie chuckled and held up a hand. "Mrs. Monroe, you are both charming and a vision of loveliness, but I have another engagement this evening. Please ask your questions, and I will endeavor to be of assistance."

Della sighed. "I just don't know where to start."

"Why not at the beginning?"

Della thought for a moment. She sensed Guthrie might not help her unless she was completely forthcoming. Starting with the night of the party, she painted a picture of what her life had been since Art was killed, moving forward in time through finding the journal in the bank box, until she came to their most recent visit to Boggs Key. She told him about the insurance and the mortgages. She held nothing back.

"So you see, not only do I desperately want to clear my husband's name, I must do so in order for his life insurance to pay. If he was involved in illegal activity and it got him killed, then I lose everything—my home, the farm, my livelihood. Can you tell us if my husband was killed because of bootlegging?"

Guthrie stiffened at the word bootlegging. Apparently, he had no problem taking part in the importing and sale of illegal alcohol but objected to calling it by name. He stroked his chin while he studied Della. Instead of answering her question, he directed his attention to Auggie. "Our mutual friend, Jacob Berkowitz, tells me your cousin was not the type to become involved in, shall we say, activities that are not strictly legal. Is he speaking correctly?"

Auggie nodded. "He is. I certainly have a hard time picturing Art breaking the law."

"But this journal . . . might it indicate otherwise?"

Irritation swelled as Della realized Guthrie intended to conduct the conversation with a man rather than a woman. She squeezed Auggie's arm and said, "We're not sure what to think. The journal is not in Art's handwriting, and we have no idea how he came by it. Is having it in his possession what got him killed?"

"In certain circumstances, that would be a definite possibility." Guthrie placed his hands on the desk and pushed himself up. "As it is, I cannot confirm or contradict any theory of Mr. Monroe's untimely passing. What I can say is, while he may have been on the verge of becoming peripherally involved in my chosen profession, he was not part of the . . . um . . . community. I had not heard his name until Jacob asked me to help you, and believe me, I know everyone of interest in the business, from the biggest sharks to the smallest minnows.

"Because Jacob asked, I put out feelers. No information came back. No one knew of your husband or of this pending deal with Mr. Aldridge. If your husband was killed because of the journal or what you found at Boggs Key, I would have heard of it." He stopped and fixed Della, Auggie, and Luke with a stern expression. "You understand, of course, that how you came by this information must be held in strictest confidence? It would prove unhealthy for all of us if certain people thought someone was talking to the police."

When she reluctantly nodded, he extended his hand. "Now, you must excuse me. My next appointment will be arriving shortly."

Della followed Auggie and Luke from the office with conflicting emotions. She did not know whether to be happy, relieved, disappointed, or angry. All the worry and stress over getting information had not brought the satisfaction she hoped. She could take comfort in the fact that Art hadn't fallen into bootlegging, but where did that leave her? She couldn't prove it to the people who mattered because she couldn't divulge the source of her certainty.

As Della, Auggie, and Luke trooped down the front steps, a car pulled to a stop behind her roadster. The passenger door opened, and a beautiful platinum blonde emerged, leaned in, and spoke to the driver, then started toward the lodge. If Della hadn't known better, she would have thought the girl was a movie star. The blonde eyed Luke and smiled, then walked by them without a word. Della watched Luke as his eyes followed the blonde ascending the front steps.

She tapped his shoulder. "Do you know that girl?"

He turned back while shaking his head. "I wouldn't say *know* exactly, but she comes to Anders's parties. You'll find her name on his guest list—Lila Gardner, I believe she calls herself."

"Is that not her real name?"

"Maybe. One never knows with Anders's women friends. They come from all over, some of them with pretty shady backgrounds and undetermined sources of income."

Della blushed. "Do you mean to say she's a . . . ?" She could not bring herself to say the word.

Luke crammed his hands in his pants pockets and rocked back on his heels. "You guys hungry? I know a nice little diner in Florida City. Great chicken and dumplings. Can't beat the lemon meringue pie. We could get a bite and decide where we go from here with the investigation."

Despite Luke's failure to answer her question, the tension of the last couple of hours melted a little at the thought of a homey, comforting meal. Her appetite had disappeared the night Art was killed but had slowly begun to return. "That sounds good. I could use some plain, solid food. It'll help me think better about our next step."

# CHAPTER 26

The diner and food were as Luke promised. Della savored the chicken and dumplings to the last morsel. She dabbed her mouth with a napkin and realized she must have gobbled her food because Auggie and Luke had not finished eating. It was a little embarrassing, but she had actually been hungry for the first time in longer than she could remember. Being able to consume a normal meal gave a sense of well-being that had been missing since . . . since . . . that horrible night.

Her thoughts tumbled over one another. The scene came rushing back—the gunshot from out of the dark, the blood spreading over Art's white dress shirt, Art crumpled in death. How could she allow herself to enjoy anything? Art's murder marked time itself. Every event in her life was now either before or after. But she had to go on living, didn't she? Shouldn't she? Mustn't she?

The muscles at the base of her skull twisted in knots, portending a serious headache if the racing thoughts weren't stopped. She gripped the edge of the table hard and gave herself a mental shake. Allowing her mind to wander like this brought only heartache, but it had been like this since Art was killed. One minute, she was thinking about something ordinary, and the next, her mind bounded out of control. Morbid musings were ruining the food's positive effect. Focusing on anything other than her pain and loss was the only way to stop the mental churning. She picked up a fork and turned her attention to dessert.

Poking at the lemon pie's meringue topping without much enthusiasm, she came to a decision. "I'm going to call Barnett and try to steer him in the right direction without divulging why I'm sure Art wasn't involved in bootlegging. If he can be convinced of Art's innocence, then the insurance company will be forced to pay." With a sinking feeling, she added, "I'm beginning to think we will never know why Art was killed. Maybe it will have to be enough just knowing we've proven he was really the man I knew and loved."

Auggie stopped mid-chew and swallowed. "Securing Barnett's cooperation will be difficult. He needs a culprit to take the blame so he can close the case. We must be very careful he doesn't decide to try to see you convicted. Circumstantial evidence has sent more than one man to prison. And, of course, insurance doesn't pay if the beneficiary of the policy is convicted of killing the insured."

Heat crept onto Della's cheeks. "The only thing that Barnett could possibly see as evidence against me is the insurance policy. Surely, that alone isn't enough."

The space between Auggie's eyes creased. "Some DAs might see a policy in that amount as sufficient. They might cobble together just enough other details to secure a conviction."

"Other details? Such as?" Della's volume rose on the second question.

Auggie studied Luke, who shook his head as though he had a premonition of what was coming.

Auggie drew a deep breath and released it with a sigh. "Forgive me for what I am about to say. I would not speak if I did not feel it absolutely necessary." He took Della's hand and held it firmly. "Dearest, anyone who has observed you and Luke together will have noticed a certain attraction between you two. Although you have both behaved impeccably, the attraction is there for anyone who cares to see it. Della, you may not even be aware of it because you are still grieving, but in time, I think you will come to realize it yourself. It exists in the way you look at one another. It is there in the way you have come to rely on Luke when it is not strictly necessary. It is apparent in the way he wishes to help and protect you, even at the cost of his career and danger to himself. All these things might raise suspicions."

Della's stomach roiled. "That's ridiculous. Luke and I didn't meet until the night of the party."

A couple nearby craned at Della's raised voice.

Auggie shushed her, then whispered, "As true as that may be, a jury might be convinced you were tired of your husband and your circumstances. The contrast between life at the farm and that at the villa, coupled with a sizable insurance policy, could lead some people to believe you were ready to move on with the first man who showed interest."

Della's temples pounded. "But I was nowhere near Art when he was shot. Doesn't that count for something?"

"Not necessarily. There are men willing to kill for a few dollars. Finding the actual shooter might become secondary if Barnett thinks there is enough circumstantial evidence to make an arrest."

Della stared at Auggie. Shock hardly described her reaction. It was as if he had set her ablaze, then doused the flames with ice. She would not dignify his theory, because that is all it could be, by acknowledging it. "If Barnett arrests me," she hissed, "I'll get Jacob Berkowitz to defend me. You said he's the best, didn't you?" She tugged her hand from Auggie's grip.

He dropped his gaze as though trying to control himself, then looked up, a somber expression darkening his eyes. "Jacob *is* the best, but let's see if we can avoid having to hire him. Please do not call Barnett. He has warned us often enough not to involve ourselves in police matters. It can do no good to say Art was innocent of bootlegging without offering proof. Furthermore, you two must be circumspect in your association from now on." He fixed Della with stern eyes and a hard mouth. "I need your promise that you understand and will follow the advice of your attorney."

When she failed to respond, Auggie continued, "Della, do you understand?"

She dropped her eyes and nodded. "Okay, okay. I get what you're saying."

Auggie signaled their waitress. "Very well then, I think we're finished here."

Luke put some bills on the table and stood while Auggie was waiting for the waitress to bring his change. "Breckenridge, you've given us something to think about. Della and I will take extra care to keep our relationship strictly professional starting with not arriving back at the villa together. Good evening." With a stiff nod, he departed.

The ride back to the villa was tense and quiet. Auggie had embarrassed her, and she suspected Luke as well. No matter what Auggie thought he saw between them, she was in mourning and would be so for a very long time. Art had been—no, still was—her only love. She might never get over losing him. How dare Auggie, of all people, think she could even look at another man so soon after Art's death? The more she ruminated, the angrier she got. Her hands twisted around one another in a frantic attempt to keep themselves off his throat.

After forty-five minutes of silence, Auggie shot her a disgruntled look, his lips pursed in irritation. "You can pout all you want, but at some point, for your own good, you've got to face reality."

"I'm not pouting. I'm furious that you said what you did. I will never stop loving Art."

"Of course you won't. I never said or implied anything else. But you are a young woman. At some point, you will need to start living a normal life again. You can't be in a state of deep, perpetual grief forever. Art wouldn't want or expect it, and you shouldn't, either."

Della buried her face in her hands. "Stop. It's too soon. I can't deal with this." She dissolved in tears.

Auggie patted her shoulder. "And I wouldn't ask you to if it weren't for Barnett. All I'm saying is to be cautious in your words and actions with Luke. Believe me. Others are watching."

"How would you know?"

"Because people are always watching. One can never get away from it unless one chooses to live in complete isolation."

"I see." But she didn't, not totally. Something told her there was more to Auggie's words than a desire to forewarn her. His tone had been wistful, as though he was speaking as much for himself as for her. Guilt at her self-centeredness pricked her conscience. Auggie might have troubles she knew nothing about.

The anger began to melt as she glanced at him from beneath her lashes. He appeared troubled, but what did he have to dread in the scrutiny of others? The scion of an old South Carolina family, he had wealthy friends who entertained him in style. He rode with them to the Aiken Hounds and spent time at their cabins on the Savannah River. They ensured his law practice was successful. As far as she knew, he was respected and loved by all.

They fell silent again and continued so until the villa's gates came into view. Auggie turned onto the gravel driveway and guided the car to the parking area. "Promise you won't call Barnett."

"I already said I won't, but I promise again if it makes you feel better."

"It does. And please remember what I said about the other thing. We can't ignore danger where it lies. We can't give Barnett any excuse to settle on you as the culprit. You're family. I couldn't bear losing you as well."

All remaining anger disappeared. She leaned over and kissed his cheek. "Thank you for that."

"For what?"

"For saying I'm still family."

"Of course you are. I loved Art like a brother. That makes you my sister." He unfolded himself from the driver's seat and came around to her door.

Della crawled out of the roadster. "I'll be careful. I promise." She kissed his cheek again and turned toward the house.

Once inside, she slipped to the service stairs hoping to go to her bedroom without seeing anyone. At the top of the stairs, she came face-to-face with Anders Aldridge. She jumped with a small gasp.

He ran his gaze over her. "I'm sorry. I didn't mean to startle you. I saw you entering by the side entrance and wanted to speak with you. Did you enjoy your outing with your cousin?"

Caught off guard and a little frightened, Della fumbled for words. "Yes, I suppose I did. We had dinner together."

"That's good." His eyes narrowed. "By chance, was Singletary with you?"

Della plastered on what she hoped was a convincingly confused smile. "Luke? Why, no. Is he not here?"

"Both of you apparently disappeared within minutes of one another." He shrugged. "Oh, well. Coincidences do happen, don't they?"

"Yes, they certainly do. What was it you wanted of me?"

Aldridge gave her a conspiratorial smile. "We have some planning to do. Please make yourself available after breakfast tomorrow. Bring your calendar and notepad to my office around 9:00."

"Of course. Is there anything else?"

His eyes bored into her like a bear sizing up its next meal. "Not for the time being."

"In that case, I have a splitting headache and thought I would have an early night."

"Please do." He did not move but continued to stare at her without blinking.

"Well, good night."

"Good night," he spoke quietly with a slight inclination of the head.

She left him at the top of the stairs. As she made her way toward her room, she had the distinct feeling his eyes followed her until she had closed and locked her door.

# CHAPTER 27

Della's alarm went off at its usual 7:00 a.m. She opened her eyes and noticed a thumping in her temples. Raising up on one elbow, it became clear her feigned headache of the evening before had become reality. What a damn nuisance. She put the back of her hand on her forehead. At least there was no fever. Hopefully, a couple of aspirin would save her from a morning of pain.

Swinging her legs to the floor, she pushed herself to standing. Best get the day started. Aldridge expected her at 9:00. She went to the bathroom and leaned over the sink, studying her reflection in the medicine cabinet mirror. She didn't look ill. Perhaps the fact that one nightmare after another had awakened her until she finally fell into a proper sleep about 5 a.m. accounted for the throbbing in her head.

In the cabinet, she found aspirin and Phillip's Milk of Magnesia. She opted for both. First, she swilled down two aspirin and then the recommended dose of Phillip's. Before she closed the cabinet door, the memory of the previous evening's interview with her boss played in her mind. She grabbed the aspirin bottle and choked down two more tablets.

After a restorative bath, she dressed and made her way to the dining room, where she found Luke serving himself at the sideboard. The butler, serving dish in hand, was just disappearing into the hall in the direction of the service area.

She slipped up beside Luke and whispered, "Do we dare eat at the same end of the table? Someone might get the wrong idea." Rather than an embarrassed awkwardness resulting from Auggie's admonition of the previous evening, joking sarcasm seemed the better choice.

Luke chuckled quietly and whispered from the corner of his mouth without looking at her, "I think we can risk it, as long as you sit in mournful silence and I keep my eyes trained on the morning paper." Della hid a grin behind a fake sneeze. He had caught on with his usual quickness.

He scooped eggs onto his plate and paused over the bacon. "On second thought, people will be suspicious if our manners fail. We should make polite small talk. Exchange a few banal comments. You should say good morning, now, but not in an overly friendly way."

Catching sight of the returning butler, she said in a normal volume, "Good morning, Mr. Singletary."

Good to his word, Luke casually perused the newspaper, remarking on the weather and the stock market report. Della replied with single words as though his conversation bored her. She felt the butler's eyes on them. No doubt he would report to the boss as soon as she and Luke left the dining room. They finished eating at different times and departed by different doors.

Della collected her notepad and calendar from her room and headed to Aldridge's office. When she arrived, she found it empty, so she sat in a chair by the window to wait. The day was warm and humid, but the thick, stone walls of Villa Lucca provided a cool retreat from South Florida's tropical climate. Della had to admit she would miss this aspect of her job when it ended, for end it would. She had no intention of remaining in Anders Aldridge's employ forever. No matter what the outcome with the insurance, starting a new life in a new place was beginning to have tremendous appeal.

As she thought about a future without Art, Miami held nothing but sadness and grief. Mr. Adams wanted the farm, and selling to him seemed the most logical thing to do. Common sense said she could not keep it going by herself, even if she wanted to. She had neither the training nor the skill.

Where she would go and what she would do was still very nebulous, but there had to be something somewhere for her. She'd be damned if she would crawl to Mama and Uncle John in Thomasville, begging for a home. They would be kind, but invariably, they would sigh and say something along the lines of how they knew marriage to Art would come to no good end. Mama would pat her hand as Uncle John expounded to anyone who would listen how it was really a blessing in disguise that Della was no longer tied to a dairy farmer in South Florida. At that point, Della would have to sit on her hands to prevent them strangling her mother's brother. No, ma'am. That would not be her fate.

A throat clearing brought her back to the present. Aldridge settled behind his desk and took out a leather-bound book. "Please join me. You looked very far away when I entered. Has some additional misfortune befallen you?"

Della took the seat opposite him and put her calendar on the desk's edge. "No, nothing in particular."

His raised brow said he expected a more detailed answer. Della settled on the truth, just not all of it. "Sometimes I feel overwhelmed by all that has happened in such a brief period. My life is nothing like I thought it would be. Please forgive me if I have been distant."

Aldridge's expression relaxed. "You have nothing for which to apologize, my dear. You have every reason to feel as you do. Now, if you are ready, we have a soiree to plan for the 16th. It will be the biggest I've hosted." He tapped the book on the desk. "This is my address book. Once we have the details nailed down, you will send an invitation to everyone within it. Time is of the essence. My trip to Jacksonville has caused an unfortunate, but necessary, delay with the planning. This book also contains the addresses and telephone numbers of any suppliers you will need. The chef already has the menu for the evening and has ordered accordingly. The invitations, music, and decor for the evening are your purview."

Della took the book and thumbed through it. "Your guest list is extensive. I'm afraid mailing may not provide adequate time for your guests to respond."

"I don't expect RSVPs. We always plan for large crowds." He chuckled and winked. "No one refuses an invitation to Villa Lucca. The guests with stars by their names should have their invitations either hand delivered or phone calls made to insure they know they are invited. Perhaps Singletary should help with the most important invitations, unless you prefer he is not involved."

Della glanced up in surprise. "Sir?"

"It's just that I've had reports of a certain coolness between you. I rather thought he was developing an attraction to you. I must have been mistaken. I hardly expected my secretary to take offense at sharing his workload, but perhaps he has?"

Della adopted as neutral an expression as she could muster. "I couldn't say. We really don't know one another all that well. We are work colleagues—no more than that."

"But it is my understanding that he has been to your home several times."

Aldridge's probing was making Della's pulse race. "Yes, he's been out to the farm occasionally. Mr. Breckenridge, my husband's executor, needs my car to conduct estate business. Mr. Singletary has generously given me a ride home a few times. He also represented you and Mr. Shoemaker at my husband's funeral, which we appreciated. Other than those times, he and I have had little to say to one another, unless discussing Villa business."

Had she overdone the denial? Della searched her memory for occasions where other staff might have been present when she and Luke were together. Nothing alarming came to mind, but then she had not thought any of their interactions were worth noting for the future. Dear Lord, what did Aldridge know or suspect?

"Hmm, I see." He studied her for a few seconds. "Did you enjoy the boat trips into the Everglades?"

Della's heart jerked. She breathed slowly to keep her reactions in check. "Mr. Breckenridge discovered a property the family had forgotten about. Mr. Singletary kindly offered to take us out a couple of times so we could ascertain its value and decide what to do with it."

"And did you?"

"Pardon?"

Aldridge tilted his head like a schoolmaster demanding an answer. "Have you decided what to do with the property?"

His tone was casual, but Della sensed an underlying urgency in his question. He was far too interested in a small island in the middle of a swamp that just happened to have a building filled with crates of illegal booze.

She scrambled for a reply. "No. It's of little importance. I have no interest in what happens with it. I may let it go for the taxes. I can't see anyone wanting to buy it."

Instead of speaking, he studied Della until her cheeks glowed. Unable to trust herself, she broke eye contact and let her gaze drift to the window and bay beyond.

Apparently satisfied, he said, "I see." He began shuffling through a folder on the desk. "I've decided you need a space of your own in which to work. I left orders for the staff to prepare an office for you at the end of this hall. Has anyone shown you the room?"

"No, but thank you for being so thoughtful. I've worried about being in your way if I continued to use your office."

"Excellent. I'm glad the plan meets with your approval. There are other rooms available closer to this one, but I thought a view over the bay might be something you would like. A desk and supplies are being delivered as we speak. Later today, telephones will be installed in your bedroom and the office. I hope these changes meet with your approval."

"How wonderful. You've thought of everything. The bay is beautiful, and I'll enjoy the view tremendously. Thank you so much."

"Very good. That will be all for now. Please get back to me before dinner with your plans for the soiree."

Della left the office and headed to the kitchen. Knowing what the chef planned to serve would help in planning the other details of the evening. She learned the meal would be lavish with plenty of champagne, other French wines, Maine lobster, caviar, foie gras, and other expensive delicacies. The chef mentioned their boss threw the same extravagant end-of-summer party each year, but this one was intended to top them all. With a knowing smile, he suggested Della plan accordingly. The pressure to make good on her first big event was on.

# CHAPTER 28

Since Auggie's warning and Aldridge's implications, Della had made a point of appearing strictly professional where Luke was concerned. If her sudden withdrawal hurt or insulted him, he said nothing about it. He seemed to understand without discussion what was at stake. He, too, adopted a businesslike demeanor.

Della made an effort to see that they were never alone in the villa. This new phase in their relationship created tension and stress, but it could not be helped. She neither wanted nor needed the gossip that would grow if others thought there was something between her and Luke. Auggie was right. Other people were always watching.

A maid appeared at her office door carrying several boxes that looked like they would topple at any moment. Della jumped up from her desk chair and rushed to help.

The girl grinned as she handed off some of the boxes. "Thank you, miss. The printer's boy just brought these."

"Hallelujah. I was afraid he wouldn't get the invitations done in time. Let's put them on the floor by the desk."

After the maid departed, Della returned to her desk and opened the first box. Inscribing names and addresses for so many guests would take hours. She started with the starred names. Those absolutely had to go out in a timely manner.

By noon, she had made her way to the "Gs." As she turned the first page in that section of the address book, one entry jumped out at her—Lila Gardner, the woman who had arrived at Aldo Guthrie's as she, Auggie, and Luke were leaving. So, it looked like Luke had not exaggerated the woman's connection to their boss. In fact, it seems he might have underestimated her importance.

Lila's Miami Beach address was in the recently constructed Riviera Plaza Apartments, two blocks from the beach and a very desirable location. How could a young, single woman afford such a chichi residence? A rich daddy? It seemed unlikely, given Luke's implications regarding their boss's lady friends. Although he had not used the word, it appeared most likely Miss Gardner was a high-class prostitute.

Flipping through the book, she found several other names preceded by Miss and a star, all living at affluent addresses. How many of them shared Lila Gardner's profession? If Aldridge employed the services of such women for his male guests, it would certainly account for the assortment of beautiful garments she had found in the wardrobe the morning after Art's murder.

Della pushed back in her chair, a sick feeling growing in her midsection. With his tremendous success in real estate and great wealth, why would Anders Aldridge feel it necessary to become involved in bootlegging and promoting prostitution? Did it follow that Rollie Shoemaker and Luke were involved in those activities as well?

For the first time since taking the job at the villa, genuine fear of her boss curled through Della. Every instinct said she was getting entangled with gangsters. In a way, this was Art's fault. It was agonizing to admit, but it seemed he had either been surprisingly naive or had turned a blind eye to Aldridge's plans for Boggs Key. Given the way Aldridge questioned her about the island, he had to know about the crates of liquor in the barn. Otherwise, his interest in an unnamed scrap of land in a swamp made no sense.

Della pressed her fist against her mouth. Reality was crashing in on her like a poorly built wall, teetering at first, then losing a stone or two and finally crumbling in a heap. Anyone in its path risked being crushed beneath its weight.

Luke rapped once and walked through the open door. His forehead wrinkled. "What's happened to upset you?"

She glared up at him and snarled, "I want an answer."

His eyes widened with surprise. He hesitated, then closed the door. "If we're going to fight, it should be in private." Frowning, he asked, "What's your question?"

Between clenched teeth she hissed, "Are you involved in our boss's bootlegging and prostitution racket?"

He stopped halfway to the desk, the color draining from his face. "What makes you think he's involved in such?"

Della held up her hand. "Not so fast. Answer my question. Are you a gangster?" Anger and a sense of betrayal propelled her harsh whisper.

Luke eyed her as he reached the desk. Placing his fists on it, he leaned in and spoke quietly. "Far from it, but that's all I can tell you. Please believe I'm one of the good guys. If I could tell you more, I would, but I can't. And for pity's sake, keep your voice down." He came around and knelt by her chair. When he tried to put his arm around her, she shook him off. He placed a hand on each of her shoulders and forced her to look at him. "I know you're confused and frightened. You have every right to be, but I won't let any harm come to you. I only want to protect you, and since you asked, no, I'm not a criminal."

Common sense screamed Della was a fool to believe him. She had no earthly reason to accept his promise, yet his eyes said he spoke the truth. Or maybe she simply wanted to believe him. Maybe Auggie was right about the attraction between them and its influence on her. On the other hand, Luke had not given her any actual reasons to doubt him, but there was so much she could only guess at. She put her finger under his chin, studying him while turning his face left and right. She had to make a decision.

Dear Lord, she needed someone she could trust. It might as well be Luke.

Della shoved the address book at him. "I may be young and unworldly, but I'm not stupid." She outlined details as she saw them, including Aldridge's questions about the island and how everything fit together. "Can you give me a logical explanation for all of this, other than Aldridge being a bootlegger and a high-class pimp?"

Luke covered her mouth with his hand. "Never say that out loud again. It would jeopardize everything and be very dangerous."

She jerked his hand away. "Do you agree that he's involved in these rackets?"

"You must never talk about this to anyone." Luke's whisper held a frantic note. "Not even your cousin." He grabbed her wrist. "Promise me you'll forget about sticking your nose into Anders's business."

"No, I won't . . . not if it has anything to do with my husband's murder."

"Aldo Guthrie pretty much confirmed that it didn't. How much more proof do you need?"

"I don't know," Della snapped, yanking her wrist free. "If he wasn't killed over the booze at Boggs Key, then why did he have to die?"

"If I had the answer, I would've told you long ago. For now, let's concentrate on keeping Aldridge pacified and believing you are ignorant of his operations."

Della rolled her lips inward in thought. Her eyes drifted from the desk to the window and back. Finally, she met Luke's gaze. "What I don't understand is why a man with all his money needs to bootleg."

Luke stood and loomed over her. "I can see you're not going to stop interfering unless you know a little more. Against my better judgment, I'll say this. Consider the most likely reason a man like Anders would involve himself in illegal activities."

Della grimaced. "That's not . . . Wait. Are you saying he's not as rich as he makes people believe?"

Luke's answer was a cryptic smile.

# CHAPTER 29

Della stood at her bedroom window, taking a last look east over Biscayne Bay before she turned in for the night. She and Luke had worked late getting the final details for the party in hand, but no matter how tired she was, she always spent a few moments before bed gazing at this view. It was a source of peace and calm amid her otherwise chaotic, stressful existence.

The moon bathed the bay and gardens with a silvery glow that highlighted prominent objects and cast lesser ones into shadows. The effect always reminded Della of the fairyland described in her favorite childhood storybook. Given Villa Lucca's beautiful gardens, the scene really was rather magical. Tomorrow night, the moon would be at its fullest and perfect for Aldridge's soiree. With luck, the weather would hold fair as it had for most of September. The soiree. Oh, Lord. The thought of it made her stomach roil.

She pressed her forehead against the glass. Although Luke and the household staff were a tremendous help, the reality that she had never planned a society event weighed on her far more than she had anticipated. If her efforts disappointed, or, worse yet, were an utter failure, Aldridge would no doubt send her packing.

As much as she hated it, Della needed her salary. If he fired her, where would she be? Debts mounting, the mortgages on the farm in arrears, Art murdered for no reason she could see, Barnett insinuating she had him killed, life insurance refusing to pay—could life get any worse? Terrifyingly, the answer was yes. Life could get much worse. Barnett could make good on his threat to charge her with Art's murder. Racing thoughts tormented her.

Tears trickled down her cheeks. She dashed them away with an angry sweep of her hand. She had to get a grip, starting with these maudlin ruminations. If worrying and crying would change things, she would bury her face in a pillow and sob until she had no tears left. But stewing on what ifs and crying solved nothing. It was late, and she needed to get some sleep if she was going to function in the morning.

Della stretched her shoulders and rolled her neck. The tension eased a little, but a headache lurked beneath her knotted muscles. She padded to the bathroom where she filled a glass with water and shook two aspirin tablets from the bottle found in the medicine cabinet. After washing the aspirin down, she returned to the bedroom and crawled between the sheets.

Despite her best efforts, she tossed and turned until the sheets were a tangled mess. It seemed like it was going to be one of those nights—light sleep and wake cycles that did not provide true rest. This problem was a recent phenomenon in an otherwise ordinary life, but then, until now, she had never been a widow threatened with arrest for her husband's murder. All the sordid business surrounding Art's death was certainly taking a toll. As much as she wished to hold on to the things that represented Art and their life together, letting them go would mean that she might resume a more normal life away from the villa and Miami itself. A black fog of heartache and horror pervaded every thought of remaining in the city of her birth.

Della sat up and straightened the bed linens, then stretched out again. A little self-hypnosis was in order. She concentrated on her toes while silently chanting the word relax. When those digits had followed the directive, she moved to her feet, ankles, legs, and so on, until her entire body was under the spell. Sleep followed.

•   •   •   •   •

Della sat straight up out of a deep dream. Something wasn't right. She strained to see if someone had entered her room, but all was quiet. She was alone. It might have been an unfamiliar sound that had awakened her, but she couldn't be sure. Rubbing her eyes, she glanced at the bedside clock. It was 5:00 a.m. Sunrise was not far off because the full moon had disappeared and the night was at its darkest. She got up and pulled on her robe.

She went to the windows. Nothing moved. Even the bay looked still. She was on the verge of returning to bed when a shadow on the dock caught her attention. As she watched, a human form crept into the boathouse. Someone was out there. It was a little early, but perhaps he was a groundskeeper fetching a tool or one of the guards checking on the boathouse.

The longer she stared at the dock, waiting for the form to reappear, the more she suspected he was up to no good. It didn't take that long to do a security check or find a gardening tool. Growing fear coiled through her. The figure was absolutely an intruder up to no good. The knowledge came to her as surely as she knew her own name. She turned and raced for the hall.

Thank goodness Luke's bedroom was nearby and he was an early riser. With luck, he would already be up. She flew to his door and pounded. "A stranger is in the boathouse. I saw him from my window."

The door flew open. Luke, already dressed in shirt and trousers, held a pistol. "Yeah, I heard a boat arrive and saw the guy go into the boathouse. It's much too early for a visitor arriving by boat or any other form of transportation. Wake the butler. Tell him to alert Anders, then call the police."

Della stepped back for Luke to enter the hall. As he raced for the stairs, she called, "Be careful. We all need you to be safe."

If he heard her, he gave no indication. His feet pounded on the grand staircase's stone risers. By the time she reached the service wing, the butler was already in his robe and heading to meet her.

Interestingly, the butler also held a pistol. "Mrs. Monroe, please use the phone in my pantry to summon the authorities. I will assist Mr. Singletary."

Della sped after him. "Should I awaken Mr. Aldridge?"

"Yes, please do." He disappeared into the garden through the dining room doors.

Instead of returning to the service hall, Della went straight to the foyer, where a phone sat discreetly behind a potted palm. She depressed and released the earpiece cradle in rapid succession until an operator came on the line. "Put me through to the police. This is an emergency."

With a few clicks, the connection was completed. "Desk Sergeant."

"Send officers immediately." Della's voice trembled as she explained the situation. She finished with, "And you better alert Detective Barnett."

With shaking hands, she returned the telephone to its nook. Movement at the green baize service door made her jump. Wheeling around, she found the housekeeper huddled with a maid, their eyes wide with fright.

"We heard the commotion. Are we being robbed?"

A male voice boomed from the top of the stairs. "Perhaps. Go to your rooms. Lock your doors and windows. That includes you, Mrs. Monroe." Anderson Aldridge, armed with a pistol and dressed in robe and pajamas, descended the steps, two at a time.

He paused at the bottom of the stairs. "Where is Singletary?"

Della pointed toward the dock. "I saw a man sneaking into the boathouse."

Aldridge nodded and left to join Luke and the butler. Instead of going to her room, Della sat down on a nearby chair to wait for the police. Within moments, shots rang from the area of the boathouse. She rushed to the garden room doors in time to see a boat speeding away toward the Atlantic. Luke, Aldridge, and the butler fired at the fleeing intruder, but it was unclear whether they hit their mark.

Another fifteen minutes brought police sirens, followed by driveway gravel crunching under tires.

Della answered the pounding on the front door. Barnett pushed in. "Anyone hurt?"

Della shook her head. "No, but the villa's men are out there. Please don't shoot them by mistake. I think the intruder is already gone."

Barnett glared but did not acknowledge her sarcasm. He motioned to the men standing just inside the entry. "Go down to the dock but be careful. These fool civilians are trying to get themselves killed."

By the time they determined the intruder had indeed fled, the sun was turning the bay into liquid gold. Della watched from the villa as policemen swarmed over the grounds. The butler returned to the service hall via the kitchen door, but Luke and Aldridge remained on the dock with Barnett.

A shout went up from within the boathouse, and an officer emerged on the run. He approached Barnett, who immediately pointed him toward the house. Barnett then shouted to his men, saying what sounded like, "Bomb, get back."

Luke, Aldridge, and Barnett moved on to the pavilion with Luke gesturing, shouting, and looking very angry. As they reached the garden room doors, Della could finally hear what he was saying. "Look, Barnett, my training during the war makes me the only person you can trust to disarm a bomb. You said there's no one on your staff who has the experience. I've disarmed bombs made by German spies. They were the best in the world. At least let me take a look at it."

Aldridge interjected, "Damn right. You want to blow up my boathouse with a sixty-thousand-dollar yacht inside? By God, that's not going to happen." He turned to Luke. "Go see what you can do."

Barnett grabbed Luke's sleeve as he turned to leave. "Hold on, Singletary. I'm not going to be held responsible for a civilian getting blown up. I've got a guy who went to the training. I'll send for him."

Luke snatched his sleeve from Barnett's grasp. "Is he married?"

"Yeah, wife and two kids."

"I have neither. Use your head, man."

Barnett rubbed his chin as he cast a wary eye over Luke. "Okay, do what you can. But if you can't disarm it for sure, get the hell out of there and we'll take care of it like I said."

Della gasped. "Luke, no! Don't."

He looked at her as though he just realized she was present. The fire in his eyes died. He watched her for a moment, seeming to gauge her words. Perhaps for a hidden meaning? With a tight smile, he shook his head and left.

The next twenty minutes were as tense as any Della had experienced. No one spoke. She and the two men sat in the solarium with their eyes trained on the boathouse. At the point when Della thought she would run screaming from the room, a grinning Luke walked out of the boathouse holding a bucket. Giving a thumbs-up, he handed the bucket to an officer who had rushed from behind the rock garden wall.

Luke trudged toward them, looking like a man who had just won a marathon. Sweat soaked his shirt and grease streaked his face and hands, but his smile was that of the victor.

He paused in the doorway and accepted a towel from the butler. Running it over his face, he grinned through a nervous laugh. "I need a drink."

Aldridge hoisted himself from the wicker throne chair. "Sit here." To the butler, he shouted, "You heard the man. Bring ice, water, and a large whiskey."

Once Luke was seated, Barnett took charge. "Good job with the bomb. How was it constructed?"

"Your typical homemade device—dynamite, fuse, trigger set to go off when the boat's motor was started. Nothing sophisticated. It took more time to figure that out than to disarm it. Your officer has the device."

"Anything about it that will help identify the bomber?"

"I doubt it. The parts are available at any farm supply or hardware store."

As Della watched their back-and-forth, a tide of resentment rose until she could no longer remain silent. "Detective, do you still think I had something to do with my husband's murder? Do I look like someone who would try to kill her employer or who knows the type of people who could build a bomb?"

Barnett's expression hardened, then he laughed. "No, I guess not. I suppose I'll have to take you off the suspect list." His eyes narrowed. "In fact, I'm wondering if we're dealing with two separate crimes or if they're related. Related makes more sense, wouldn't you agree?" He waited for his audience to nod in agreement. "Mrs. Monroe, I'm also wondering if your husband was the only target the night he was killed. Maybe our killer didn't have time to get off a second shot. Mr. Aldridge, given the bomb was in your boat, it looks like you're the one in danger. Anybody have a grudge against you?"

Aldridge looked disgruntled. "Until today, I would have thought not." Something in his eyes told Della he was not being honest. He sort of bowed up like an angry rooster. "No, I'm afraid I have no explanation for Mr. Monroe's killing or the bomb, other than a madman is on the loose."

"I suppose that could be, but madman or not, he seems to have his sights fixed on people here at the villa. There's got to be a reason for that."

"I assure you, there is none. As I said, some madman must have become fixated on Villa Lucca for a reason known only to himself."

Barnett stood and shoved a hand in his pants pocket. "Okay. If you think of something, call me. In the meantime, I understand you have a big party planned for this evening."

"We do." Aldridge's voice held a note of surprise.

"There's a possibility one of your guests will be the guy we're looking for. I'll send over a list of my men who will attend. Tell no one they're officers. Let them blend in with your other guests. They'll be armed if anybody tries anything."

"But, Detective, I protest most strenuously." Alarm tinged Aldridge's tone. "My guests will be formally dressed. Your men can't possibly blend in. They'll stick out like the policemen they are. My guests expect a pleasant evening among their own kind—their equals, if you will. There must be another way. Can they perhaps be concealed around the grounds? Nearby, but out of sight?"

As Della watched the exchange grow ever more continuous, Luke's hint about Aldridge not being as rich as he appeared got her thinking. On at least two occasions, she had come to Aldridge's office and heard him on the telephone, speaking in an angry and aggressive tone with someone he called Saunders. She had not thought much of it at the time. Aldridge tended to act like that when told something he didn't want to hear. Should she interrupt and mention this? In reality, what did she actually know? Not enough to accuse her employer of lying.

Barnett fixed Aldridge with a hard stare. "No, and this is an official police order, unless you'd rather cancel your little get-together. While we're on the subject, my men aren't your equal. They're your betters."

"You, sir, are as rude as you are uncouth."

Della's head jerked in surprise. Aldridge seemed to have no worry about antagonizing Barnett.

The detective's face flushed crimson. Through clenched teeth, he replied, "I may be what you say, but I'm in charge of a murder investigation and an attempted murder. Cancel your party or have my men mingling with your guests. Your choice."

"By all means, then, send over your list. Mrs. Monroe will make the arrangements. Please see that your men are properly dressed for the occasion if they are to remain incognito. The evening is black tie. You do know what black tie entails, I hope."

Barnett gave an angry nod. "Don't be a jackass. I'll see that my men are dressed to blend in."

Aldridge rose and extended his hand, which the policeman ignored. "Very well. Now, you must excuse me. Business calls. Singletary, please see Detective Barnett out."

Della was on the verge of leaving for her office when Aldridge waylaid her. "Are we ready for the soiree? Is all in hand?"

"We've seen to every detail. I believe this evening will be one of your best." Della prayed she told the truth, but showing self-doubt served no purpose. She scanned her notes and tapped her pad with a pen. "You haven't said. Will any of your guests be staying overnight? Should the maids prepare the bedrooms?"

Aldridge's eyes widened with surprise. He cleared his throat before replying, "Several of the young ladies may wish to. They usually stay until 3:00 or 4:00 a.m. and are uncomfortable leaving at such a late hour. Have the north wing rooms made up."

"Yes, sir. Will do."

The north wing. The room she had used the day after Art's murder was in that wing. Were all of the wardrobes in those rooms filled with designer clothes? She made a mental note to find out.

# CHAPTER 30

The first thing Della wanted to do after Barnett permitted all of them to return to their normal activities was call Auggie. She grabbed the telephone, summoned an operator, and gave the number for the farm. Please let it be early enough for him to still be there. On several occasions, she had called thinking Auggie should be at the house due to the time, and no one answered. It was odd that he had not answered at 7:00 a.m. last week. Perhaps he was a very sound sleeper. He answered on the second ring. Thank goodness.

Della explained the situation at the villa and Barnett's latest theory, which excluded her as a suspect in Art's murder. "So, it looks like the insurance will have to pay after all." Without warning, her future had suddenly become clear. Her voice caught on the pain of what she was about to say. "Once that's settled, I'm going to sell the farm to Mr. Adams and leave Miami for good."

Auggie was silent for a moment. "I see. Leaving Miami makes sense. There is nothing here to hold you." He paused again, then spoke like the lawyer he was. "The insurance, however, is another matter altogether. Just because Aldridge looks like a target, it does not necessarily follow that Art's murder was an accident. The proposed business deal may have put both of them in danger. Until we know what they'd planned, the insurance company will probably try to use the boathouse bomb to maintain that Art was engaged in activities that got him killed."

"How can they say that? They have no proof."

"Barnett has already said he thinks the events are connected. The insurance adjustor will take that into account to deny or at least delay paying the claim."

"But Aldridge has declared they had no deal."

"True, but you have said Art told you there was. Guess who the adjustor would prefer to believe?"

Della wanted to scream. Instead, she held her temper in check by furiously tapping her foot. "This is all so unfair. It's damned if you do and damned if you don't. I knew my husband better than anyone. He would not have gotten caught up in something illegal." Until proven otherwise, she would cling to this belief, all evidence be damned.

A deep sigh came over the line before Auggie replied, "While you and I believe that, it may come down to proving his innocence. If that's the case, I'll do all in my power to convince everyone he was the man you and I knew him to be."

Della's voice caught in her throat, strangled by rage, frustration, and welling tears. She swallowed hard. "I don't know what I would do without you," she choked out. "You keep me sane."

Auggie cleared his throat as though he, too, was fighting to control his emotions. "I am happy to be of service." The line fell silent for several seconds. His intake of breath was audible. Finally, he continued, "Dearest, I've delayed having to tell you this, but I can't stay in Florida much longer. I have a major client who is demanding attention. He's determined to file a suit with only a marginal chance of winning. I have told him this, but he insists. I am needed at home."

Della's spirits sank even lower. Having Auggie at the farm had provided a sense of security, but soon, her champion and advocate would be several hundred miles away. She summoned as much courage as she could muster. "I understand. You've been here far longer than I'm sure you expected. I will forever be grateful for all you've done." Her voice trembled and broke on a sob.

"Oh, my dear, I'm not deserting you or giving up on getting the insurance settled. I'll just have to work on it from Abbeville for a while. Once I've got things settled in South Carolina, I'll return to Miami, if need be."

"I'm sorry. I'm trying to stay strong, I really am, but it's just so hard sometimes." She dashed away tears and drew a deep breath to regain control. "You aren't leaving before the party tonight, are you? I need all the support I can get. You and Luke will be my only friends there." She tried to laugh, but it came out more like she had choked on her own saliva.

"I doubt you need my presence, but I'm not departing until the 17th." Auggie's voice was calm and reassuring. "I'm looking forward to the evening, and I'm sure it will be a great success."

"Thank goodness. Aldridge specifically invited you, and I think he'll wonder if you don't show up."

That settled, Della returned to the party plans. With difficulty, she forced herself to concentrate while she reviewed the details for the umpteenth time. Nothing was out of order. There was now little to do until later in the day when the rented linens, tables and chairs, florist, and caterer arrived. She needed to be on hand to direct them. She glanced at the desk clock. She had just enough time for a quick sponge bath and to grab a bite of breakfast. The intruder and his damn bomb had thrown everything off schedule.

•　•　•　•　•

After a late lunch, Della headed to the north wing ostensibly to check on the condition of the bedrooms. When the housekeeper had objected, Della persuaded the woman to let her take on this burden since there was nothing to do until the rental vans arrived. It was a big house, and they really should have added additional staff for this event. In the end, the housekeeper smiled and gave her blessing.

Della wandered through the first room, ran a finger over the wooden surfaces, checked the bed corners, and slipped over to the chifforobe. Sure enough, a collection of gowns and dresses stood at the ready, the styles and sizes suitable only for the young and slender. Each room contained a similar assortment, except for the last two rooms at the end of the hall. Instead of women's clothing, they contained gentlemen's suits, shirts, ties, and the like. Aldridge had said nothing about male guests staying the night, but apparently, he believed in being prepared regardless of gender.

She entered the hall ready to return to her office. Luke strode toward her from the other end. When he reached her side, he gripped her arm. "I need to talk to you." He pulled her into the bedroom and locked the door.

Della tugged her arm free, placed her hand on his chest, and gave him a shove. "What on earth has gotten into you?"

A muscle in Luke's jaw twitched while his eyes bored into her. "I may not be at the villa much longer. I think I'm about to be fired."

Della blinked in surprise. "I don't understand. How? Why?"

"Anders is freezing me out. I think he no longer trusts me." The edge in Luke's voice was tinged with anxiety.

Della's lips thinned. "Really? You saved his boathouse and yacht for him this morning. Aldridge appeared plenty happy with you then."

"Most good businessmen are also good actors, and our boss is a consummate businessman." Luke emphasized the word "consummate."

"I still don't understand. What about Rollie Shoemaker? Does he give you the same impression?"

Luke's expression became grim. "Anders Aldridge is my only employer. I may have attended business meetings with both of them, but Anders pays my salary. If I'm going to be fired, he's the one who will do it."

"But what makes you think he's going to fire you? I still don't understand."

"It began subtly after Anders and Rollie returned from Jacksonville. It was little things at first. Writing a letter himself rather than having me type it up. Sending me out of a meeting before it ended. Making phone calls I was not asked to listen in on to take notes. Getting me out of the villa on errands, only to see Rollie leaving as I returned. Stuff like that. Today, I'm not included in a meeting with a new client—one with a dubious reputation. Anders made an excuse about the guy not wanting anyone other than him and Rollie in the room. Given that Anders Aldridge always gets precisely what he wants, the excuse doesn't ring true."

He put a hand on her shoulder and stepped closer. "When I'm gone, promise me you'll quit this job and get out. I'm not sure what he has planned, but you don't need to be part of it."

Della's forehead creased. "I can't afford to quit. I *need* the money."

Luke jammed his hands in his pockets. After a moment, he replied, "Your life is worth more than any salary. Please." Removing his hands from his pockets, he turned her to face him with one hand. Placing his free hand on her other shoulder, he gave her a gentle shake. "Promise you will not stay."

She rested her forehead against his chest. Warmth spread through her. She felt safe in his embrace. "Only if you promise to go before things get dangerous for you." Her voice was small, filled with pleading.

"I would if I could, but I've got to stay as long as I'm allowed."

She jerked herself from his grasp, appalled and confused by her reaction to his touch. Taking a step back, she tried to muster anger to replace her confusion. "Why must you continue to work for a man you so clearly dislike and distrust? Who are you, really?"

"I can't tell you. You simply have to trust me."

For the second time, he asked her to trust him without a reason to do so. Della tilted her head while she considered his demand. After a moment, she nodded. "Will you let me know if you're about to leave?"

"Yes. If I can't see you myself, I'll get word to you. I promise." His nod and expression communicated more than agreement. If she would allow it, he would have kissed her. Della saw it in his eyes. She moved back a step and shook her head.

Luke clearly got the message. He squared his shoulders, and his face settled into full business mode. He stepped to the door and unlocked it. "We'd better get back downstairs. We shouldn't go together. I'll take the service stairs. You go by the grand staircase."

•　•　•　•　•

Promptly at 4 p.m., trucks and vans arrived, disgorging men who swarmed over the estate toting tables, chairs, flower arrangements and the like to the pavilion. The caterer and barmen arrived at 5:00. The kitchen filled with the caterer's staff, and soon a delicious fragrance wafted through the house. At 6:00, Della surveyed their work and gave herself a mental hug. Everything was in place. The evening would be fabulous if she did say so herself. The guests would not start arriving until 9 p.m., so she could get ready with time to spare. She trudged to her bedroom, exhausted but confident.

The bedroom hall was empty when she arrived at her door, but a maid was placing a large box on the bed.

The girl turned to Della with a knowing smile. "Mr. Aldridge asked me to bring this up. It's from a fancy store in New York. The boss must like you a lot."

Della smiled, despite her irritation at the maid's impertinence. Making an enemy of the staff would only do harm. "Thank you. Now, if you will excuse me, I need a bath."

The girl giggled on her way to the hall. "Yes, miss."

Slapping the silly creature's face would have felt so good. Instead, Della stuck out her tongue to the girl's back. Turning on her heel, she strode to the bed and snatched the lid from the box. Atop the tissue was an envelope with her name on it. She pulled out a folded note with Aldridge's initials embossed on the front.

*Della,*

*I took the liberty of ascertaining your size based on the garments in your wardrobe. I hope you are not offended, but I wanted this to be what I hope is a pleasant surprise. Please wear this dress tonight, but do not bother with stockings. The outline of the garters would disrupt the lines of the dress. My hostess must be the most beautiful, best-dressed woman at our soiree.*

*Until this evening,*
*Anders*

A chill slithered down Della's spine. Oh, Lord. Anders Aldridge had been in her bedroom. He had been through her things. Worse yet, the tone of his note implied he had certain expectations where she was concerned.

She tore back the tissue to reveal an exquisite evening gown with a first-class designer label. She held it up and blushed at the thought of having to wear it. Over a cream-colored, silk underslip, a gown of tulle in the same shade draped in folds light as air. White, silver, gold, and transparent beads and sequins covered the entire dress.

The fabric was beyond beautiful, but the garment would be very revealing once she put it on. The straps connecting front and back were very thin, which would have been fine if the front and back were constructed differently. The back was nonexistent. Only a tightly fitted waist and the shoulder straps attached to the bodice running under her arms would keep the thing on her body. The front plunged to just above her navel. Fortunately, three thin straps connected the strips of cloth, covering her breasts. She ran her hand under what passed for the bodice. *Thank goodness.* With luck, light padding over the breasts would conceal her nipples. Her forehead creased. No matter, really. She would still look like one of Aldridge's high-class harlots.

Della turned the dress back and forth, trying to figure out what type of undergarments she had that would not show under such a gown. Nothing. She didn't own a single thing that the dress would cover. She dropped the blasted dress onto the bed. She grabbed the box, ready to put it in the hall for a maid to discard, when the briefest piece of silk fluttered to the floor. She stooped down and retrieved it. She held the briefest pair of panties she had ever seen. That was it. Nothing more. In a couple of hours, she would appear before the largest crowd she had ever been part of in a dress that made her feel naked.

She stared at the pile of fabric spread over the bed. Her heart sank, along with her confidence. What had she gotten herself into?

# CHAPTER 31

Della slipped on the harlot's gown, as she now thought of it, and minced her way over to the cheval mirror, the dress's train slithering behind her. She ran her hands over her hips and thighs, adjusting the fabric's drape. The dress was truly beautiful, the embroidery exquisite. She gazed at her reflection, pleased that the beading concealed more than she had thought possible with such delicate tulle and fluid silk beneath. When she swished from side to side, the fabric glided over her body in a glittering stream, the beads tapping against one another in a delicate symphony. If she were a different type of girl, she might enjoy wearing this lovely confection. As it was, she hated it, even though it was the most beautiful thing she had ever worn.

She returned to the chifforobe and pulled out a cream-colored, silk shawl that she wore over spring dresses when the weather was still cool. She held it up to a bedside lamp. The light shone through, gauzy and muted. Draping it about her shoulders, she tied the ends in a loose knot over her breasts. Another glance in the mirror revealed a more modest appearance. It would have to do.

She slipped on the shoes that had magically appeared in her chifforobe yesterday with a note that simply said "For the soiree." There had been no hint then of what would arrive today. She checked her lipstick, pinched her cheeks, and dusted her nose with a final dip in the Coty box. She was as ready as she would ever be.

Della went to the windows to take a last look at the pavilion before heading downstairs. Strings of lights suspended above the pathway down to the pavilion and around its perimeter, and uplights at ground level, set the whole area aglow. Crisp, white cloths beneath aqua table toppers were in perfect contrast, while the coral-pink accents in the table arrangements completed the tropical theme for the evening. By morning, it would look like a swarm of locusts had descended, but at the moment, the setting was glorious.

On impulse, she had selected the colors of Biscayne Bay glowing with the setting sun because they reminded her of Miami, the only home she had ever known, the home she would flee as soon as she was able. She stood, staring out over her creation until she was sure every detail would stay with her. She had done this. She had made this magical scene. Despite her worries, a sense of pride and accomplishment accompanied her as she headed for the hall. The moment was now etched in her memory. It might well be the only happy memory she would carry with her from Villa Lucca.

She reached the top of the grand staircase to see Aldridge awaiting her at its foot. He held out his hand and called, "Come, my dear. Our guests will be arriving any moment. We should be on the pavilion to greet them. I hope you are good at remembering names. Some of these people are very important to my business. Others are socially or politically prominent and, therefore, equally important to my success." When she reached him, his gaze drifted over her until heat rose from her throat onto her cheeks. He smiled and continued, "Radiant, simply radiant. I see the gown fits perfectly, but the shawl must go. Please take it off."

"But I feel so . . ."

Anger flooded his eyes. He grasped her upper arm and tightened his grip until pain shot to her shoulder. "I said, take it off. I did not buy that exquisite gown to have it marred by a frumpy scrap of fabric. Leave it—now."

Della realized she either did as he said or faced his continued anger. The pressure on her arm indicated he was not above using force, or maybe even violence, to get what he wanted. She shrugged the shawl from her shoulders and dropped it on a nearby table. He smiled condescendingly and placed her hand in the crook of his elbow. Della smiled in return but boiled inside. If being at the villa wasn't her best hope of finding out why Art was killed, she would gather her things and leave without giving it another thought. As it was, she needed to stay. She had to know what killed Art if she was to ever find any peace.

At 9:00 p.m., the great, the good, and those of dubious reputation began arriving to the riffs of a jazz band playing the latest tunes. State senators mixed with alleged bootleggers masquerading as businessmen. Society matrons chatted with rumored gangsters. Aldo Guthrie arrived with Lila Gardner on his arm, giving Della a moment of fright. Fortunately, Guthrie had the good grace to act like he was meeting Della for the first time. If Lila recognized her from their passing at the Royal Palm Rod and Gun Club's entry, she did not show it.

Aldridge stepped away to speak to a newcomer, leaving Della on her own in a sea of strangers. As she surveyed the growing crowd, her spirits lifted. Auggie pushed toward her bearing two glasses of champagne, which he held aloft in greeting. Handing her one of them, his eyes widened as he took in her gown. He leaned in, gave her a brief kiss on the cheek, and whispered, "My dear, what *are* you wearing? It's lovely, but I mean really, it is rather . . . how should I put it? Revealing?"

Although his lighthearted teasing and accompanying grin did nothing to improve Della's confidence regarding the dress, she could not help giggling. "Oh, shut up. Don't you say another word." With a gesture that swept the length of the gown, she muttered, "This is apparently the latest fashion for party hostesses."

Before they could continue their conversation, a man Della did not know whisked her cousin away. She watched Auggie disappear with a sinking feeling. This must have been how Titanic survivors felt watching the great ship split and sink beneath the Atlantic, leaving them alone on the vast ocean. She scanned the pavilion for Luke. He was nowhere in sight. She was abandoned to Aldridge and the crowd.

Returning to her side, Aldridge placed her hand in the crook of his elbow and tugged with his arm. When she failed to move, he shot her a stern look. She gave him an apologetic smile in reply and trailed off with him to greet some dignitary holding court by the bandstand. The charade was in full swing.

Della spent the next two hours being squired about as Aldridge introduced her to his most important guests. Many of them could not hide wide eyes, surreptitious glances, and generally shocked expressions as they took in her scandalous attire. Luke was right. She needed to get away from Villa Lucca and Anders Aldridge as fast as she could, but for tonight, she had to play the part assigned to her.

She studied each honored guest for a unique feature to create an association. The names were familiar since she had gone through the address book many times, so matching faces with them became a sort of game for her. When she was introduced to a particular society matron, a Mrs. Butts, the association was immediately obvious. Curvaceous was a generous description of the lady's posterior. Della bit the inside of her cheek to keep from giggling in the poor woman's face.

After being glued to Aldridge for what seemed an eternity, he finally deserted her to join a group of men huddled around a table, puffing on cigars. She scanned the pavilion for Luke. Still no sign of him.

A shot of false courage might be helpful, so she grabbed a glass of champagne from a passing tray. Finding an isolated corner of the balustrade, she sat on its edge and rolled her shoulders. She had not realized how tense she had become. Maybe the champagne would help. Over the rim of her glass, Della saw Lila Gardner pushing through the crowd with glass and bottle held firmly in her hands. Her eyes were fixed on Della.

Lila reached Della and did a little shimmy to straighten her gown. From her expression, the woman clearly had something on her mind.

Lila held up the bottle. "Need a refill?"

Della replied, "Yes, please. Won't you sit down?"

Lila grabbed Della's glass and poured, then sat beside her. "Nice to get a load off. My feet are killing me." She held out her feet, displaying gold evening shoes with delicate straps and heels higher than Della had ever seen. "This is the last time I wear these puppies without plenty of places to sit down. Anders really should limit his invitation list or put tables and chairs all over the gardens."

Della's face flushed. "I'm sorry about the seating, but I was instructed to keep all of the party on the pavilion. The house is open, so there is more seating inside."

Lila smirked. "Sorry, kid. I didn't realize you were in charge. It's a lovely evening. I'm just grumpy from too little sleep. Had a big date last night"—Lila took a swig and giggled—"if you catch my drift."

Della had no idea what to say to this woman. Ladies of the evening were beyond anything in her experience. "I worked really hard to make it everything Mr. Aldridge wanted. I hope he is pleased."

"Oh, sweetie, he's more than pleased. He's bragging about what a find you are. Taking care of his art collection and his social engagements. I'd say you're a hit."

Della smiled and gulped champagne to keep from having to think of something to say.

After glasses were filled again, Lila scooted closer. "Look. I know we don't know one another, but I only want the best for you."

Della choked in surprise and spluttered, "Thank you." After wiping her mouth with a napkin, she glanced at Lila from beneath her lashes. "I don't know what to say, but I appreciate the goodwill."

A soft laugh floated from Lila. "I see Art never mentioned me."

Della's heart beat faster while her stomach roiled. "No, he didn't. Were you his . . . special friend?" Thinking of Art having a mistress who was also a prostitute brought bile up from the pit of her stomach.

Lila's smile became wistful. "In a way I was, but not how you're thinking. I can tell you know what I do for a living." Lila reached out and took Della's hand. "You can rest easy. Art was not one of my clients. He was just my friend. He was probably the best friend a girl like me will ever have."

"I see." But Della didn't. She could not fathom why Lila was telling her this. After tonight, they would never see one another again.

Lila leaned in and whispered, "Did you get my note?"

Della drew back and shook her head. "No. When did you send it?"

"A couple weeks back. I said not to believe everything people told you about Art."

Della searched her memory. It came to her in a flash—the anonymous note. "You wrote that?" Lila nodded. "I couldn't figure out why anyone would write such a note without signing it. Why did you send it?" Della's volume drew the attention of nearby guests.

She moved to rise, but Lila grabbed her arm and pulled her back. "I'm not finished. And for God's sake, keep your voice and your ass down. What I'm about to tell you could get both of us killed."

Della's heart raced. "Perhaps we should go somewhere more private?"

"No, that would only draw attention. Laugh every so often and pretend that I'm telling you a funny story. We'll be two girls together sharing naughty tales. Now giggle like I just said something shocking."

Della covered her mouth, adopted a scandalized expression, and shook with fake mirth. Lila grinned. "That's it. Now look at me and say tell me more."

Della did as instructed, but added, "Now tell me what this is really about."

Lila tilted her head and her smile faded. "What you need to know is that Art and I go way back. We were kids together on your farm. My daddy was one of his daddy's tenants. Even though Art was a couple of years older, we played together when we were little. We were pretty much best friends until high school, then we went in different directions. He was the football captain and dated the popular girls. I was drawn to the wild boys, the ones who smoked and drank and beat up other kids for their pocket money.

"Because we were so close when we were younger, I think Art looked on me like a little sister he needed to look out for. He never let those wild boys go too far with me. A girl who grew up as fast as I did needed someone like Art as a friend." She poked Della's arm and laughed as though she had just told a hilarious joke.

Taking the hint, Della held her sides and laughed along with Lila.

Wiping imaginary tears from her eyes, Lila picked up the thread of her history with Art. "After high school, we drifted apart. Art went to Clemson and I . . . well, let's just say I didn't go to college. I got an education of a different sort. I started dating older men and soon discovered that some of them were willing to provide me with the kind of life I had always dreamed of having. Everything was great until I got pregnant."

Just when the story was getting truly interesting, a couple of gentlemen planted themselves before Della and Lila.

Holding out his hand to Della, the taller of the two said, "Lovely ladies should not be left unattended. Would you care to dance?"

Della looked at the man's hand and then at his face. He seemed genuinely nice, but she had no desire to dance with anyone. "Thank you, but no. I haven't seen my friend here in a very long time. We are catching up on all we've missed."

"Aw, come on, sweetheart. You can talk to this broad anytime. Give a guy a break." It seemed the guy wasn't so nice after all.

Della shook her head and glared. "No thank you."

Before Della could comment further, Lila growled, "Can't you see we're having a private conversation? Beat it."

The two men looked at each other and shrugged. As they shuffled off, the shorter one muttered something that sounded a lot like stupid bitch whores.

Della swallowed hard to fight back a gasp. Her experience of men like these was limited, so she did not have the thick skin Lila seemed to possess. Lila, for her part, appeared unfazed by the encounter. Della whispered, "Thanks for getting rid of them."

Lila smirked. "Being polite doesn't work with some guys. They think every woman owes them a piece of her time . . . and more. What bastards."

"Indeed. You were telling me about your friendship with my husband?"

"Yeah, about the time I got pregnant. The baby's father arranged for me to go to a back alley butcher who took care of our problem. After that, the bastard cut me off without a penny."

Lila became wistful and quiet for several moments, then she laughed again and poked Della as though she had said something funny. "Art was home from college for the summer, working on the farm. One night, I started bleeding real bad. I certainly couldn't tell my parents. Daddy was a hard man. He would have skinned me alive, hemorrhage or no, so I ran to Art." Lila raised her eyes and looked into the distance. "You know, he never once asked me who the father was or why I allowed myself to get into trouble. He just asked how he could help."

Lila fell silent. She shivered as though she was reliving a terrible event.

Della cast her a sideways glance. "And did he? Help, I mean?"

"Yeah, he saved my life. He put me in the farm truck and drove me to a hospital in Palm Beach. It was far enough away from home that he figured no one would know us. He took off his high school graduation ring and put it on my finger. When we got to the hospital, he told them he was my husband and I had miscarried at home. I never knew whether the doctor believed him or not, but I was given a blood transfusion and the hemorrhage was stopped with a procedure. Art paid the hospital bill with the money he was going to use for his fall semester at Clemson. He got a job to pay for school once he was back to South Carolina and never told a soul what had happened. Yeah, I owe Art Monroe my life. That's why I've tried to look out for him, and now you. Now, let's giggle together."

With a fake giggle, Della asked, through an equally false smile, "And what form does this protection take?" Giggle, snigger, ha-ha-ha.

Lila laughed and replied, "Funny you should ask." Spying an empty chair, she snagged it and drew it up to the right side of Della so that their knees touched and their faces were hidden from the other guests. "That's better. The forced laughter was getting old." She massaged her cheeks. "One more fake ha-ha, and I think my face would have cracked."

A light breeze ruffled Della's hair. She pushed loose strands from her face and said, "You were about to tell me how you are protecting me. Please. If there is danger, I need to know who it's from."

Lila's brow creased. "Oh, honey. You're in danger from almost everybody you know."

# CHAPTER 32

Della's heart leapt into her throat. She strangled on a gasp, then tried to catch her breath. Between coughs, she spluttered, "You can't mean my cousin or Luke."

Lila toyed with a lock of her bobbed hair. "No, I suppose not, except both of them are hiding something."

"What can they be hiding?" Della's head swam with possibilities, none of which made sense. This woman must either be deluded, or she had ulterior motives. Della spat, "Auggie is my husband's cousin and the closest thing he had to a brother. Luke has been very kind and helpful. Exactly why do you think they are hiding something?"

Lila's mouth turned down at the corners, then she made a smacking sound. "Well, call it intuition based on keeping my eyes and ears open." Lila cut her eyes at Della. She apparently sensed she had crossed a line in accusing Auggie and Luke. "Oh, never mind what I said. It isn't really related to what I want to ask."

"Which is?" Della coughed again.

"Have you found a journal in Art's stuff?"

Before she could think, Della hissed, "What do you know about it?"

Lila smirked, lifted her brows, and tilted her head so that her chin tucked into her throat. "Hmm . . . I see you've found it. Do you have any idea what it contains and why it's important?"

"You tell me what you know about it first." Della's whisper was sharp. "How do you even know it exists?"

Lila winked and leaned closer. "Because I'm the one who gave it to Art. I asked him to hide it."

Della could hardly control herself. If they had not been within sight of Aldridge's several hundred guests, she would have grabbed Lila Gardner by the shoulders and shaken her until every morsel of truth came tumbling out of her red-painted mouth. "Is the journal what got my husband killed?"

Unfazed by Della's anger, Lila shrugged. "The man who wrote the original list had no idea who Art was. Aldridge only told the guy where to take the booze. He never said anything about Art or that he owned the island."

"Who wrote the list, then? It wasn't Aldridge or Rollie Shoemaker. I know their handwriting."

"A guy who makes regular runs between Miami and the Bahamas." Lila opened her evening purse, withdrew a cigarette packet, and offered it to Della, who shook her head. With a nonchalant shrug, Lila pulled out a cigarette for herself and lit it with a match. After a couple of puffs, she removed a bit of tobacco from between her teeth and flicked it over the balustrade.

Della glared at Lila in frustration. "Don't stop there. What got Aldridge interested in Boggs Key to start with? Was it because of the isolation and the barn?"

"No, that came later." Lila took a drag on her cigarette and released the smoke in a long, steady stream. She tapped ash from the tip before continuing. "In the beginning, Anders wanted to develop the Key as a legitimate fishing club, make it a place where members could stay and go out with fishing guides into the deepest parts of the Glades. Art would put up the land. Anders would finance building a lodge, buying boats, and hiring guides. They would be equal partners. Then Anders and Rollie lost millions on a land deal. So did other people. Some of them lost everything." Lila squinted at Della through the smoke from her cigarette. "That's when Anders and Rollie decided the island could serve as a legit place to launder bootlegging money. Build the lodge and buy the boats with their ill-gotten gains, turning them into a legal investment. When Rollie discovered there was an old building on the property, they decided there was a good use for it as well."

"Hold on. Art would never have agreed to anything illegal. Are you trying to tell me he did?"

Pity flooded Lila's eyes. "Well, no, not exactly. He thought he could keep things legal on his end, regardless of what Anders and Rollie were doing. Art sometimes saw what he wanted to see. He'd been like that from childhood . . . always the optimist, always thinking things would work out if he worked hard enough. I warned him not to do business with those two, but he wouldn't listen. He was pretty desperate by then and saw the deal as a way to save the farm."

Della's voice broke in a whisper. "So how do you know all of this?"

"I was at Villa Lucca one night when Rollie was there. In my line of work, eavesdropping on clients' conversations can come in handy, provide a kind of security. I overheard Anders talking to Rollie about Art and the plans for your island, including using the barn to store booze. Anders mentioned having a list of shipments coming in from the Bahamas. That's when I started snooping. I found the list and put two and two together. I discovered an unused journal in Anders's office and copied the list. I gave it to Art to hide in case he ever needed leverage."

"Wait." Della pressed her fingers to her temples. "I'm confused. Did Art know what the journal meant?"

"I told him what the numbers and letters meant, but like I said, Art was desperate to save the farm. He thought he could talk Aldridge out of getting the island involved in bootlegging. Then he was killed, and I'm guessing the booze started arriving at the island not long after. True?"

Della nodded slowly. "Yes, I've seen the crates. So Art knew what the journal entries meant." Her world was spinning out of control.

"Yeah, he understood. That's why he hid it like I told him to."

Della's mind churned. Art had kept secrets and thought he could manipulate powerful men. He had mortgaged the farm without her knowledge. Financial pressures had turned him into someone she did not recognize. Her mouth tightened into a thin line. "You still haven't answered my question. Did having that list get Art killed?"

Lila dropped her cigarette on the stone floor and ground it with her heel. "Filthy habit. I really should stop." She must have felt Della bristling because she continued in a rush. "Look, I don't know for sure if the list got Art killed. I don't think Anders knew I copied it, but if Art was stupid enough to say something about having it, then, yeah, that's probably why he was killed." Lila cocked her head and gave Della a searching look. "You've got to understand this. Anders Aldridge doesn't take kindly to the word *no*. If you know what's good for you, you'll get away from him as fast as you can."

Della stuffed her fist into her mouth and bit down on her knuckles. Lila tried to put an arm around Della's shoulders, but she shook it off. Her life was completely upside down. The man she adored was murdered, and more than likely, she would lose the farm with no hope of the insurance paying. Even when she sold the farm to Mr. Adams, the money from the sale would have to go to pay off the mortgages before a clear title would transfer. She would be left with nothing—no home, no job, no money, and no answer as to why Art had died. She had to find Auggie. He would help her figure out what to do next.

Mustering as calm an attitude as she was able, Della stood and smiled. The ruse of two girls talking had to be resumed. "This has been delightful getting to know you, but I really can't ignore our other guests any longer." She extended a hand, which Lila took. "I look forward to having lunch one day soon."

Lila squeezed Della's hand. "Me, too. You know how to get in touch. Give me a call."

Della nodded. "Will do. I hope you enjoy the rest of the evening."

Della pushed her way through the crowd, but there was no sign of Auggie or Luke. She approached the butler. "Have you seen Mr. Breckenridge? I want to make sure he's having a good time."

The butler was a perfect picture of neutrality, but his eyes said he did not, for one minute, believe she wanted to ensure her cousin's enjoyment of the evening. Through lips that barely moved, he replied, "I believe I saw Mr. Breckenridge going into the walled garden."

Della wandered up the stone path leading away from the pavilion and turned left into the Chinese boxwood garden. Beyond it, walls of stuccoed brick stood guardian to roses and a lovely pergola with a bench positioned so that the winter sun shone on it during the middle of the day. Della had looked forward to enjoying it when the weather turned to what passed for winter in South Florida. Now, she sought something entirely different within its sheltering walls.

She glanced over her shoulder to make sure no one was watching. Instinct told her Auggie had chosen the seclusion of the walled garden for reasons he would not appreciate becoming public knowledge. Lila had said he was hiding something, and Della suspected she might be right.

As she walked, Della mulled over her relationship with Auggie. While she could list off the details of his life and family history, it was possible she might not know him in at least one important way. She had been so consumed by her own troubles, she had never once stopped to think about who he was as a person. Until now, he had only been Art's cousin come to rescue her—her knight arriving on an iron steed, her security in the face of tragedy and danger.

The pieces began clicking into place as recent memories flashed through her mind. The way he looked at certain people. His disappearance from the farm when he should have been there. The fact that he lived such a single life, unmarried and looking unlikely to ever make that commitment.

She reached the wrought iron gate entry and pushed it inward. At the far end of the garden, Auggie sat on the bench, but he was not alone. He appeared in animated conversation with another guest, the young man who had interrupted her initial conversation with Auggie. The two men were so focused on one another that they were unaware of her presence. Should she interrupt them? While she watched, the younger man cupped Auggie's face and drew it to his. Their kiss said everything Della needed to know. Her needs could wait. She backed away from the gate and closed it.

As she slipped away into the main garden, another realization dawned. Her upbringing and Florida law dictated she should be disgusted and appalled by what she had just witnessed, but surprisingly, she was neither. In reality, she had never thought about such situations, but the law could now affect someone she cared about. It made her consider the consequences if Auggie's secret was uncovered.

Auggie was her friend and cousin by marriage. He had shown her nothing but love and consideration. He treated her like family, even though their in-law relationship might be considered at an end. No, where Auggie was concerned, the only thing she felt was fear of what would happen if his romantic leanings were ever discovered. He stood to lose everything—his law practice, his friends, the respect of his community. Even his family would probably turn against him. He risked prison and disgrace, but the heart was not always so easily controlled by law or societal expectation.

Della had some experience with the expectations issue. Her mother and uncle had not approved of her marriage. Auggie had been their staunch supporter leading up to the wedding. She now had a greater understanding of why he had come to their defense with such fierceness. He knew what it was like to be separated from what his heart desired.

She needed time to process how to deal with what she had seen. Was it better to tell Auggie or leave things as they always had been? The coward in her said let well enough alone. Until there was good reason to divulge knowledge of his predilections, she would remain silent.

She exited the garden and headed back toward the pavilion. If ever she needed a drink, it was now. Halfway between the house and bay, she saw a welcome figure striding toward her.

Luke marched to her with as hard an expression as she had ever seen. He grabbed her arm and pulled her into the relative darkness of the other side of the garden. "Where have you been? I've looked for you for at least fifteen minutes."

"I *might* ask you the same question. I've looked for *you all* evening." Della was too tired, confused, and overwhelmed to keep a civil tone.

Pleading flooded his eyes. "Aldridge has fired me, as expected. Told me to clear out or he would file a trespassing charge. If he knew I was talking to you or anyone on staff, he would be furious. The only reason I haven't gone is because I had to see you. You've got to get away from him and the villa. Something is going down tomorrow, and you don't need to be involved."

"What is it, and how do you know?"

"All I can say is find Auggie and leave. Go to the farm and stay there."

# CHAPTER 33

Della met Luke's plea with squared shoulders. "As much as I appreciate your concern, I'm not going anywhere as long as there's a chance of finding out why my husband was killed. Art died here at Villa Lucca. It stands to reason the answer to his murder is also here."

Luke's fists balled at his sides. "Of all the stubborn, foolish things I've heard, this has got to be the worst. I'm going to see if I can get your cousin to talk some sense into you."

He started to walk by Della, but she stepped in front of him blocking the path. "No, please leave Auggie alone. He's taking an early train tomorrow, and I think he needs time to say goodbye to someone."

"Yeah, I know who he's been seeing." Luke's mouth thinned. "Another reason for both of you to get away from Aldridge and the villa. He's not above blackmail if it gets him what he wants. You really have no idea what he's capable of."

Della couldn't let things stand as they were. "Luke, I appreciate all you've done for us and for being my friend. I would do as you ask if the situation were different, but I can't let it go. I've got to know why Art was killed."

Luke scowled. "Is that what I am? A friend?"

He seemed to have heard nothing else she had said. Her throat tightened as she choked out, "I'm a recent widow. What more do you expect?"

Luke raked his fingers through his hair. "Nothing. Forget I said anything." His gaze drifted toward the house. "Look, I've got a job to do, but I also want to keep you safe. As long as you're at the villa, I'll be nearby."

"How?"

His eyes snapped back to her. "Leave that to me. Now, I think you'd better get back to the party before your boss gets suspicious."

As he turned away, Della grabbed his hand. "Thank you. I mean it. Please be safe."

"Good advice. Too bad you refuse to take it." With that, he marched away into the dark.

Della plastered on a smile and headed to the pavilion where Aldridge waited for her. "You've been gone a long time. What were you doing?"

Scrambling for a satisfactory reply, she chose partial truth—easier to remember than a complete lie. "I needed a breath of air, a few moments away from the crowd. So many guests make the pavilion rather close."

He glanced around the area with a satisfied smirk. "That may be, but no one refuses my invitations. Politicians, business leaders, the idle rich, the socially prominent . . . they all come." He gestured toward the crowd. "They come to see who has been invited and to mix with those they would otherwise shun. They find my more, shall we say, colorful guests highly entertaining." He cupped her elbow. "Come. Some of our guests want to leave. We should bid them good night." He guided her to the side of the pavilion closest to the house.

As the crowd began to thin, Auggie worked his way to them and shook Aldridge's hand. "Thank you for a lovely evening. It's been a great party."

With a broad smile, Aldridge cut his eyes at Della. "Mrs. Monroe did an outstanding job. Sorry you're leaving so soon."

"I've got an early train to catch. Don't want to sleep through my alarm." Auggie leaned in and kissed Della's cheek. "I'll call you from South Carolina when I have news. In the meantime, I'll work on bringing the estate to a close. Take care, and remember I'm only a train ride away if you need me."

Della nodded and hugged him. She didn't trust herself to speak.

By 3:00 a.m., only a few guests and the policemen in plain clothes lingered by the bar and buffet tables. After the band played "Show Me the Way to Go Home," they began packing up their instruments, the sign that the evening was truly at its end.

Aldridge kept Della by his side as they saw the dregs on their way. The last man to approach them had a strange effect on her boss. Although he had stated his desire to personally speak with each guest before they departed, Aldridge hesitated before extending his hand.

"Saunders, I wasn't aware you would be here tonight. I hope there are no hard feelings. It was business. Nothing more."

Della glanced at Aldridge from beneath her lashes. This man Saunders was in the address book, so she had sent the invitation like she had to everyone in it. Aldridge had said nothing about excluding anyone. As she pondered, it dawned on her that the name was vaguely familiar as well. She recalled the overheard telephone argument between Aldridge and someone he addressed as Saunders. What's more, she had seen this Saunders before, but she could not remember where or when.

The man addressed as Saunders scowled. "So, ruining a man and sending him into poverty is just another day's business for you, is it?"

Aldridge bristled. "See here, man. I lost a bundle on that deal myself. You can't hold me responsible for the downturn in the market."

"Really? Then explain why you didn't think it was important to tell me when you were going to pull out? We were supposed to be partners—fifty-fifty. That's what you promised." Saunders's volume grew with each comment.

"So, sue me." Aldridge's voice was soft, but his tone was hard and aggressive. "Of course, in order to do that, you will need to have something in writing . . . say, a contract."

Saunders stiffened while red flooded his face. "We had a gentleman's agreement. You shook my hand and said there was no need for anything formal between friends. You bastard, you lied." His last words would have been heard as far as the road running several hundred yards in front of the house.

Della edged several steps away from the men, who now leaned toward one another with balled fists. Saunders, younger and larger than Aldridge, was a victim of deceit and a ruthless disregard for others, just like Art had been. It would serve Aldridge right if Saunders beat him senseless.

Aldridge's eyes narrowed. "I did not so much lie as make a serious misjudgment. For that, I apologize." His tone lacked any semblance of regret.

"Not good enough. I want my investment back—in full. You've got the money. It will mean very little to you, but it was everything I had." Desperation and rage colored Saunders's screech.

Aldridge's expression hardened. "Then you should not have risked it. Look, we've been over this enough times. I'm not going to tell you again that you get nothing."

"But you promised it was safe."

"And it should have been, but even I cannot always see the future. We both lost money. Speculation always carries risk. You must accept your loss."

"Like hell I will." Saunders pulled a pistol from his coat pocket and slammed it against Aldridge's temple.

Della screamed and stumbled backward. Stunned but still conscious, Aldridge dropped to his knees. His lips moved, but no sound emerged. He seemed frozen by the shock and surprise of being so caught off guard. The expression in his eyes said the situation had taken on the quality of the unreal for him, as though he watched from afar as another man was in danger of losing his life. Saunders bumped Aldridge with the gun, but he still remained silent. Whatever Saunders hoped to hear, it would not be forthcoming. With an anguished howl, Saunders placed the gun against Aldridge's forehead and fired. Blood, brains, and hair splattered over Saunders and the pavilion's stones.

Della glanced down at her skirt. Although she had stepped back, it had not been far enough. Ugly, red splotches marred its delicate fabric. She glanced at Aldridge, lying in a pool of his own blood. Bile rose in her throat, and she quickly looked away. The whole episode had taken no more than seconds, but it had moved in slow motion for Della. The look in Aldridge's eyes as he fell would be something she would not soon forget.

Footsteps pounded from behind. Someone shoved her aside. Luke tackled Saunders, wrestling him to the ground. Gripping Saunders's wrist, Luke hammered it against the stone floor until there was a sickening crack. With a scream, Saunders released the pistol, which landed at Della's feet. A kick sent it skittering over the stones away from the struggling men. Other men joined Luke, and soon, Saunders was hauled to his feet and handcuffed.

Barnett pushed his way through the small group of policemen, members of the band, and villa staff gaping at the murder scene. He planted himself in front of Luke. "Got an interesting call from Washington, Singletary. Good work, but the next time your boss sends an undercover agent into my jurisdiction, a heads-up would be appreciated."

Breathing hard, Luke bent over and placed his hands on his knees. "Clean out the dirty cops in your department and there won't be a next time."

"Already done." Barnett jerked his head toward Saunders. "Or it will be by the time we get this joker booked and into interrogation." He motioned to a couple of his officers. "Get this guy to the station. I'll be there by daylight. The rest of you men start interviewing witnesses."

Della saw what might be her only chance. "Wait. I need to ask this man a question." All eyes turned to her in silence. "Please, I need to know. Please let me speak with him."

Barnett rammed his hand in his pants pocket and withdrew a balled up scrap of cloth that he ran over his face and the back of his neck. He studied Della for a moment, then nodded. "Okay. You've been mostly honest with me. Considering all you've been through, I guess you deserve to ask a question, but keep it short."

Della stepped over to Saunders, who stood between two officers gripping him by the arms. "I'm Della Monroe. My husband was killed here back in the summer. Do you know anything about that?"

To her surprise, Saunders looked at her with what seemed to be pity. After a moment, he gave her a false smile filled with bitterness. "I'm going to hang anyway, so you might as well know the truth. I'm sorry and ashamed. I never meant for anyone but Aldridge to die. Hitting your husband instead of Aldridge was a mistake."

"So, you didn't kill my husband on purpose?"

"No. I'd never heard of him until I read his name in the paper the next day. Like I said, I'm sorry. I didn't mean to kill anybody but Aldridge. He took everything I had. He destroyed me and didn't care."

Barnett stepped to her side. "That's enough. You've got your answer. We need to get on with tying up the details from tonight." Over her head he shouted, "Nobody leaves until they've given a statement."

Luke came to Della. "Are you okay?"

She wrapped her arms around her midsection to calm its churning. "Other than an intense feeling of déjà vu and about to be sick, I guess I am. How about you?"

He gave her a small smile tinted with irony. "Other than muscles that are going to yell at me tomorrow, I'm good. My job here is done."

An emotion she did not expect and did not want to acknowledge made her pulse skip. "So, uncover agent. Federal?"

"Yep. US Marshal Lawrence Shelton at your service."

"Lawrence? Luke isn't your real name?"

"Of course not. We never use our real names undercover. Disappointed?"

"No, I just liked you as Luke. Do people call you Larry?"

"Friends and family do."

When he didn't comment further, Della asked, "*Surely*, you can tell me more about yourself than that. Like, how did you wind up working at Villa Lucca?" She didn't try to keep her tone neutral.

He ignored the edge in her voice but did not meet her gaze, either. Instead, he stared at the bay and let out a long breath. "Not really. Too much depends on the department's strategies being kept under wraps." Looking at her again, he was quiet for a moment. "I guess you deserve at least a little explanation. I was sent to infiltrate Aldridge's operations in Miami. In the process, I discovered he and Shoemaker were paying off cops to protect their bootlegging operation. The bootlegging was only the latest of Aldridge's criminal ventures. He was a gangster, pure and simple, one we've been tracking for a long time."

Della rolled her lips inward as she thought about what to say. "So what's next for you?"

"I'll clean up things here in Miami, then head back to Washington."

"Will you go undercover again?" Della blinked several times to keep unexpected tears from escaping. She was still mourning Art, but it was clear she had become attached to Luke/Lawrence. Dammit. She did not need that kind of complication in her life. She could only deal with one loss at a time.

"I doubt it. My face is pretty well known by now. I'm afraid I'll be assigned to a desk job for a long while."

"That's good, I guess." Several seconds of awkward silence passed. Della searched Luke/Larry, but he refused to say anything more. "Well, I'm really tired. I'm going to the house, change out of this rag, and try to get a little sleep. Please tell Barnett where he can find me."

"Sure." He stared at his feet. "Will you let me know when you leave for the farm?"

"Yes, but how do I contact you?"

"With Aldridge dead, I'm going to stay here at the villa. You've got the number."

"Okay, but I need a favor."

"Anything."

"Give me a ride to the depot? Auggie is going to leave my car there when he goes to catch his train, which is in about"—she glanced at her watch—"two hours. That is, if you can. If you aren't too busy."

"No problem. I'll make time."

"Thank you. You've been a good friend. Okay, well, bye for now."

Della passed by him and headed toward the gardens. As she reached the path leading away from the pavilion, she could have sworn she heard Luke, for she could not think of him as Larry, mutter something. It sounded very much like, "For you, I'll never be too busy."

# CHAPTER 34

Della trudged through the back entrance and into the grand hall. Seated on a chair with an expression like the sword of Damocles would descend at any moment, the butler growled, "I've quit. So has the housekeeper. The maids are with the cops. If you want something, you can damn well get it yourself."

Della ignored him. She was too tired to deal with anybody's angst, anger, agony, anxiety, annoyance, or any other negative emotion one might name. She made for the grand staircase and the sanctuary of her bedroom and a big tub of steaming water. Barnett could come find her when he wanted her.

She ran the tub as full as she could without it overflowing, shucked off the ruined gown, and stepped in. She soaked until the water began to cool, then did a quick wash. Clean and dressed in her most comfortable nightgown, she slipped between the sheets and closed her eyes.

Damn. Her body might have been beyond exhausted, but her mind was suddenly and infuriatingly wide awake. She twisted, rolled, plumped pillows, adjusted bed linen—sleep remained as elusive as joy at a funeral. Leaning up on her elbow, she grabbed her alarm clock. 5:30 a.m. Auggie's train was at 6 a.m. With luck, she might catch him still at the farmhouse. She grabbed the telephone on her nightstand and gave a sleepy operator the number.

He answered on the second ring. "Monroe residence, Breckenridge speaking." His voice said he was irritated.

"Auggie, it's Della. Don't be a grump. I have good news—sort of."

"Dearest, make it quick. You caught me with my hand on the front doorknob."

Della filled him in on Saunders's declaration that Art's murder was an accident. Nothing Art had done had brought about his death.

"Well, that is good news." Della could hear the smile in his voice. "As soon as I get home, I'll file a motion by wire to have this Saunders deposed. The insurance company will be forced to pay. Now, I really must run."

She returned the telephone to its place and sank back into the pillows. Tension that had been her constant companion since Art's murder eased a little with the knowledge that at least some of her problems would be solved. She fell into a peaceful sleep.

•　　•　　•　　•　　•

The clock on her bedside table jangled loudly and insistently. Opening one eye, she squinted at its luminescent face. 7:00 a.m., her normal time to wake up. She must have pulled the alarm stem out of habit. Go back to sleep or go downstairs? The police would want to interview her at some point. Might as well get it over with.

She swung her feet onto the floor, pulled on her robe, and went downstairs to the drawing room to await interrogation. Although she could no longer be considered a suspect in any of the tragedies at the villa, experience with Barnett portended their interaction would be unpleasant. She plopped down in the corner of a sofa and laid her arm along its raised side. Resting her head on her bent elbow, she soon dozed off again.

Someone shook her shoulder. "Della, wake up. A policeman wants to take your statement." Luke, no . . . Larry stood over her.

She stretched her arms high above her head and rolled her shoulders. "Yuck. I sincerely hope this is the last time I ever have to see or talk to Detective Barnett."

Larry's lips narrowed, but the corners turned up. Something she had said amused him. He held out his hand and helped her to her feet. "Barnett left a couple of hours ago. He seems to have completely lost interest in you."

"Thank goodness. By the way, what time is it? I feel like my days and nights are all mixed up."

Larry glanced at his wrist. "It's nearly eleven. Quarter til. Come on. They're set up in the dining room."

When they reached the grand hall, they met Rollie Shoemaker in handcuffs being led away by two burly policemen. He glared at Larry and might have said something but was pulled away with a jerk.

Larry glanced at Della. "I guess he's not too pleased that one of his dirty cop buddies turned state's evidence. His bootlegging days are over."

They continued on to the dining room. At the door, she stopped with her hand on the knob. "Larry, will you be here when I'm finished with the cops?"

"Yeah. I'm not going anywhere. I promised you a ride home, and I keep my promises."

Della gave him a small smile and passed through into the room where she found a young officer seated at the table with pen and pad before him. He stood and pulled out a chair for her.

After all the accusations and suspicion on Barnett's part, Della's interview was decidedly anticlimactic. An officer took notes as she explained how Saunders was invited to the party because his name was in Aldridge's address book. He had told her to invite everyone, and she had.

She recounted what she observed between Saunders and Aldridge and what Saunders said to her when she questioned him about Art's murder. Della asked if Saunders had been responsible for the bomb in the boathouse. The officer confirmed he had confessed to that as well. The officer asked a couple of questions to clarify his notes, then said someone would contact her when her statement had been typed up and ready to sign.

That was it. She was free to go and do whatever she wanted. The police would bother her no more. When it was time for Saunders's trial, someone would be in touch if she was needed to testify. Since he had acted and confessed before multiple witnesses, she might not be needed at all.

Larry met her in the hall when she exited the dining room. "What are your plans now that you have no one giving orders?"

She tilted her head. "I've given it absolutely no thought. I think I'll take your advice and start packing."

"Will you be leaving for the farm today?"

"I don't think so. I'm exhausted. I'm not going to push myself. I'll work until my mind has calmed down enough for sleep. As tired as I am, I may sleep for days. What about you?"

Larry shrugged. "I've got a mountain of paperwork to complete. I'll stick around here until you're ready to leave." He should have walked away, but he appeared frozen in place with his eyes fixed on Della as though she was the only thing he saw or wanted to see.

Under such scrutiny, her gaze flitted about the space, finally settling on the view seen through the back entrance. "Look at that. The pavilion is a mess. The caterer and rental service will be chomping at the bit to get their things back." She placed her fists on her hips. "With the housekeeper, butler, and maids all having quit and left for God only knows where, I guess that job falls on me. I'll have to ask the police when they can start clearing."

Larry focused on the area beyond the doors. "Yeah, I forgot to tell you. Barnett said you can call the rental people and caterer when you're ready. Might be a good idea to do it now. The Weather Service in Washington has issued a storm warning for South Florida."

"A storm warning. Great. Perfect way to end my first and only foray into society hostessing." Silence fell between them. Larry did not respond to her attempt at a joke. Della cast about for something to say. "I guess I'd better go make those calls. Any idea when the storm will start?"

"Not really. All they can tell us is it's headed this way."

"Okay. Well, I'd better see to the rental people now." Like a dunce, she was caught in a cycle with the same thoughts coming out every time she opened her mouth. She shot Larry an apologetic smile and fled to her office to make the calls.

Instead of packing, she spent the afternoon making sure that the caterer and rental service people left with everything that had arrived the day before. She could have left it. Supervising the cleanup was no longer her job, but it kept her from having to interact with Larry. Just thinking about him left her confused and anxious. After a quick sandwich taken alone in her room, she packed a few things and fell into bed. Sleep came instantly.

•   •   •   •   •

Della awoke with a start. Wind howled, and rain lashed the windows. Things were crashing on the stone patio below her second-floor balcony. Thumping and dragging sounds came through the ceiling. She listened for a moment, then the source of the commotion dawned on her. Heavy, clay tiles on the roof were being ripped from their anchors and blown over the edge. She reached for the bedside lamp and clicked the switch. Nothing. The electricity was out.

A tremendous shattering of glass sent her flying over the edge of the bed and onto the floor. Even in the dark, she could make out the shape that had just broken through a window. A huge tree limb now protruded into her bedroom. It seemed impossible, but the house actually shook with the force of the gale. The storm had arrived, but it was worse than just an ordinary South Florida storm. Much worse.

# CHAPTER 35

Her door flew open, and a beam of light flashed around the room. "Della! Where are you?"

"Over here. On the floor." The light landed on her.

"Are you okay?"

"I'm not hurt, but I'm pretty shaken up."

"Come here. We're going to the wine cellar. It's walls are solid, and it has no windows."

She felt in the dark for her slippers, catching her finger on a shard of glass. Sucking on the injury, she continued to grope for something to put on her feet. "What time is it?"

"About one o'clock. Come on. The roof could go at any minute."

Stuffing her feet into her damp slippers, she followed the beam of light and crept toward Larry. He grasped her hand and pulled her to her feet. The sound of breaking glass accompanied their flight down the grand staircase and into the first floor service hall. Larry rushed to the wine cellar door and opened it.

He swept the flashlight beam over the racks. "Thank goodness there was no time to restock. We'll just pull what's left to the floor. Don't want them falling on our heads."

With the task completed, Della and Larry sank down beside one another with their backs to an empty rack. Larry held up a bottle of Pol Roger Vinothèque and two glasses. Popping the cork, he said, "We might as well enjoy what we can. I'm afraid tonight is going to be one hell of a ride." He handed her a glass, then extinguished the flashlight. "Better save the batteries."

After finishing the bottle between them, Della's head dropped onto Larry's shoulder. As much as she wanted to stay awake, her interrupted sleep schedule and the champagne made her eyes too heavy to hold open.

•   •   •   •   •

Della dreamed of throngs jostling for standing room on the pavilion until someone fell over the balustrade and rolled into the bay. She pushed through the onlookers to see if she could offer aid, but suddenly, she was the one in the water. Oddly, it was only ankle deep, but it was rising. Her eyes flew open.

Larry was already on his feet, lifting her to stand beside him. "The house is flooding. We need to get to the second floor."

"But what about the roof?"

"We'll have to take our chances. The water is coming in fast."

By the time they got to the grand staircase, the water had reached their knees. They raced to the second-story landing.

Timber cracked, and a section of roof flew away. Water and debris rained down through the hole. A crash at the end of the hall where the balcony overlooked the bay drew Larry's flickering flashlight beam. The French doors had blown in, bringing a new deluge.

Larry slipped his arm around Della's shoulders and pulled her close. "We'd better get out of this hallway. The linen cupboard in the back upper service hall may be our only refuge." The flashlight took that moment to die. Larry gave it a fierce shake, but the thing was as dead as last night's stuffed flounder.

Feeling their way along the walls, they made it inside the linen cupboard. A fierce gust slammed the door shut. Miraculously, the linens and space were dry. Larry felt along the shelves and pulled down towels and blankets.

Della dried herself as best she could without disrobing and wrapped herself in a blanket. They sat huddled together for heaven only knew how long. After what felt like hours, there was a sudden change. One minute, the wind howled and the house shrieked. The next, a deadly silence descended.

Della sat up and poked Larry. "Do you see that? There's light coming in under the door."

Together, they crawled to the door and cracked it open. The sodden hall floor was littered with leaves and sticks blown in through a shattered window at its end. Otherwise, that part of the house had somehow managed to stay together.

Larry glanced at his watch. "6:10. This is only the eye. I don't know how long it will last, but this may be our only chance to get food and water for several more hours. Want to risk it?"

"Do you?"

"I think we'd better."

They slipped into the hall and headed for the service stairs. As Della and Larry approached them, the sound of water lapping against walls greeted them. The bay now sat halfway up the staircase.

Della gasped. "Will the water get any higher?"

Larry took her hand. "I don't know. When the eye passes, the storm could very well push more water inland from the bay. We'd better get back to the closet."

They huddled in that damp, dark space for hours. Crashing glass, howling wind, sheets of rain, and the shrieks of a dying building accompanied their vigil. When a change in pressure sent the closet door flying off its hinges, Della screamed and buried her face in Larry's shoulder. He wrapped his arms around her and held her fiercely.

She had no idea how long they sat clinging to one another. She felt Larry's lips against her hair with a start. She tried to pull away, but he held her firmly and whispered, "No. Don't. We may not make it out of here alive. I won't die without telling you how I feel. I've loved you almost from the start. At first, I chalked up my feelings to wanting to protect a vulnerable girl, but as time passed, I saw you quite differently. You are not only beautiful, but brave and smart as well. You are everything I've ever dreamed of in a woman. I guess you don't feel the same, but it is important to me to have said it."

Della did not trust herself to reply. It was too soon, much too soon. If they lived beyond today, then she would tell him. For now, she would take the only comfort she had—the strength of his arms around her.

At what she estimated was midmorning, it sounded like the wind shifted direction. By noon, the wind and rain began to diminish. By 6:00 p.m., they had stopped altogether, and a watery sun peeked from behind scuttling clouds.

Larry stood and helped Della to her feet. "The hurricane's passed. I think we'd better see if we can get out of the house. I don't know how stable it is after the pounding it took. We'll use the grand staircase since it's constructed of stone."

Della swallowed hard. She didn't trust herself to look at him, so she simply nodded and kept her eyes trained on the floor. They picked their way through debris over flooring that squeaked and moaned. Where the roof had been torn away, sunlight turned broken glass into a sparkling carpet. They reached the grand staircase, which was still intact. Only a few inches of water now covered the foyer below. The bay had retreated as the storm diminished.

Larry tested the banister and first step. "I think it's safe." Holding her hand, he led her to the first floor.

Della stood in the foyer's center and gaped at the destruction. Not a single window or French door had survived intact. Valuable antiques lay broken on top of each other, jammed against walls in heaps. Artwork had been stripped from walls and lay strewn over water-soaked floors, their frames shattered and canvases ripped. Uprooted trees and what must be part of the roof blocked the path to the front door.

They turned to the back entrance where the light was partially blocked by a large keel. Larry pulled Della's hand. "Looks like the garden room may be the best exit."

When they finally got outside, Della turned toward the bay and pointed. "Oh my gosh! The boathouse and dock are gone. It's like they never existed."

Larry nodded. "Looks like the yacht and boats are what's blocking the back entrance to the house. The cars are probably destroyed, but let's see if we can get one started."

In the parking area, they found Larry's MG filled with silt and covered in debris. The same was true for Aldridge's Bentley. When Larry tried to crank the Bentley, sparks flew and smoke rose from the engine.

The danger had passed and the bay had receded, but Della found it difficult to be relieved. Destruction and chaos lay everywhere she looked. "I wonder if my farmhouse survived."

"Has it been through hurricanes before?"

"Yes. It was built in the 1880s."

"They used really sturdy materials back then. They built things to last. Being as far inland as it is, maybe the damage isn't too bad."

"How on earth can I get out there to check on it? The storm shutters won't have been put up."

"I suspect your Mr. Adams took care of that. If we're going to get away from here, it looks like we'll have to walk."

Della looked back at the house. "We can't stay here."

"I agree. Let's see what we can do about getting downtown. Maybe some of those buildings survived. There'll have to be shelters set up somewhere." Larry eyed her. "Do you want to try to get something else to wear? And you need shoes."

Della glanced down at herself. She was still wearing her nightgown, which clung to her body in damp folds. "If we got down the grand staircase, maybe we can get back up. I won't go into town dressed like this unless I must."

They retraced their steps and ascended the stairs with caution. Larry went first, testing floorboards and moving debris out of the path. When they arrived at Della's bedroom, the door hung by one hinge. The room was in shambles, but the floor appeared safe enough. He stepped back to allow her to pass.

Della found her suitcase still in the chifforobe. She took it to the bed and opened it. "I packed only the clothes I brought with me. By some miracle, everything is only a little damp." She withdrew a simple day dress, socks, and a sturdy pair of walking shoes. After dressing quickly, she joined Larry in the hall. "I'm ready."

"Do you want to take your case? I'll carry it for you."

"I don't think so. By the time I can wash what's left, everything will have a serious case of mildew."

"Can't they be hung to dry?"

"In this humidity? Not likely. Let's go. This place is getting on my nerves."

If the villa had made her anxious, the walk away from it was one hundred times worse. The storm had passed, and the heat of summer had returned in force. By the time they picked their way around uprooted trees, bits of torn-apart outbuildings, and waded through ankle-deep, waterlogged sand to the road, Della and Larry were wet through with sweat. Della's heart sank as she stopped at the end of the driveway and viewed the road, or what she thought might be the road. Where Ingram Boulevard once ran, there now lay nothing but sand and debris as far as she could see.

Larry grabbed a stick and pushed it down into the sand. "We'll never make it through this. The sand here is at least two feet deep and unstable. No telling what it's like between here and downtown."

Della sank down onto a nearby fallen palm trunk. "What on earth are we going to do? It'll be dark in another couple of hours. Should we return to the house and wait for help?"

Larry shook his head. "No. We need to get where other people are. That's where help will be." He sat down beside her. After several moments of silence, he tugged at his shirt collar. "Damn heat. Ever paddle a canoe?"

Della blinked and stared at him. "Yes, as a kid with my dad. Why?"

"If one of the canoes or small fishing boats survived without too much damage, we might be able to paddle our way into town." He stood and held out his hand.

Taking it, she replied, "We don't really have a choice, do we?"

"Nope. Let's see what we can find that might pass for seaworthy."

They slogged their way to the back of the house where they found the motorboats, yacht, and several smaller craft shoved against the porch pillars. Considering the battering they must have taken, it was hard to believe the two stories of porches had not caved in. Larry turned over several small craft, all with holes too large to stay afloat, even with constant bailing. The last one he rescued from the pile had survived with only small dents visible. A little digging unearthed the handles of the paddles strapped beneath its seats.

Larry, breathing hard, bent over with his hands on his knees. "Looks like this one will have to do. We'll get pots and big spoons from the kitchen. We'll take whatever food and drinks are still usable. There's no telling what we're going to find in town. Help me turn it on its side so we can dig the sand out."

Della pushed until her head swam. With one last shove, the canoe tilted onto its side. "We've got to have something to eat and drink before we set out."

Larry nodded. "You're right. The canned food in the pantry should be okay if it hasn't been washed out to sea."

The kitchen turned out to be in better shape than they feared. The pantry still held cases of canned goods and bottles of Coca-Cola. After a quick meal of sardines, Coke, and canned peaches, they set to work on digging out the canoe. The sun was setting by the time they finished their task and began shoving the canoe toward the bay.

Larry searched the waterfront. "There. Beyond the walled garden, the bulkhead is only about a foot above the water. That's probably our best place to launch. Are you doing okay?"

Between deep breaths, Della choked out, "Yeah. Never been better."

Larry chuckled. "I've always liked a girl with a sense of humor."

When they reached the low point in the bulkhead, they pushed the canoe into the water and placed their provisions in the middle. Larry climbed down and took Della's hand.

Before she stepped in, Della looked back at Villa Lucca. "It's hard to believe."

When she didn't continue, Larry asked, "Believe what?"

Della's head moved slowly side to side. "All this destruction. Less than forty-eight hours ago, three hundred people danced and drank here. Now the place is in ruins."

"Yeah, that's pretty much how hurricanes operate."

She crawled into the canoe but looked back over her shoulder. "Do you think anyone will want to restore it?"

"I doubt it. With Aldridge dead, there isn't anyone left who cares about the place." Larry tossed a paddle to Della. "We'd better get going."

She picked up the paddle but did not put it in the water. Her eyes drifted back to the villa. She could not bring herself to move just yet. The future she thought she would have—everything she and Art had dreamed and hoped, like Villa Lucca—lay in ruins, but unlike the gangster's palace, her existence must continue. She owed it to Art's memory and what they might have had.

Exhaustion clouded her mind, but one thing was clear. She'd had enough of deception and intrigue and other people's demands. She wanted her life back. Although it could never be what she had dreamed, she was determined to take back what was hers. "I want to go home. I don't want to stop until we reach the farm."

"And how do you propose we do that?" Larry's voice was sharp with irritation.

"Hear me out. The Miami River runs within a mile of the house. If we can make it up the bay to the river's mouth, we might get to the farm by morning."

"What if we can find shelter when we reach downtown? It would be better to stay there at least until daylight."

Della put the paddle in the water. "Okay. Let's see what we find."

# CHAPTER 36

Moonlight played over mounds that had once been the bay-front mansions of Coconut Grove as Della and Larry paddled up Biscayne Bay toward the Miami River's mouth. Only hours before, the bay had surged inland as though it was determined to swallow the entire peninsula. When the hurricane subsided, there was nothing to hold the bay waters on the plots of ten or more acres each, so the bay retreated like a naughty child worn out by a tantrum. Now, it was flat, calm, and at peace. The atmosphere's fury was spent. The earth and her inhabitants could come out of hiding.

From the front of the canoe, Della pointed and called over her shoulder, "There it is. See where the land disappears? That's the river's mouth."

A few minutes later, they turned inland and stopped. Della gasped at the scene. She looked over her shoulder at Larry. "My God. The river is filled with wreckage."

Larry grunted as he leaned forward for a better view. "Yeah, it's got a lot of stuff piled up, but we might find a channel if we're careful. We need to get out of the bay and find someplace to stay overnight. Can you think of anything along the river strong enough to have survived?"

"Maybe the Granada Apartments building. It's right near the mouth."

They guided the canoe into the river proper, inching along between boats of all kinds that lay broken and piled atop one another. From behind her, Larry called, "Do you see it? Is the building still standing?"

Della rose to her knees in order to see over the debris piles. "It should be about thirty yards up on our right."

"Do you see a gap where we can put in and walk?"

Della strained to see. "Nothing but wreckage jammed against the bulkhead. There's no way to get near the place."

The Granada's seven stories, normally filled with light and signs of life, now loomed over them in complete darkness. The Howell Towers behind them were the same. It was as though they had entered an unexplored jungle where a great civilization that had once existed now lay in ruins.

Della looked over her shoulder at Larry. "Maybe we should try to get farther inland."

They spent the rest of the night gliding past wreckage, bumping into unseen obstacles, and slapping at clouds of mosquitos that had survived the hurricane just fine. Della's palms stung from burst blisters on hands unaccustomed to using a paddle. Her arms, back, and shoulders screamed with each drag of the wood through the water. Dehydrated and hungry, her head swam. It was tempting to suck up water from the river, but goodness only knew what was in it. As the sun rose over the upper river, a scene of complete desolation greeted them. The wooden buildings that once lined the banks looked like a children's game of pick-up sticks.

Della pointed at an opening in the bank. "There. Pull in. I've got to have something to drink, or I'm going to pass out."

The canoe bumped against the bank. Della scrambled out and collapsed onto the sodden ground. Larry pulled the canoe onto the solid earth and grabbed the flour sack that held their provisions.

He dumped the sack's contents at their feet. "I hope you won't object to a repeat of last night's gourmet meal—sardines, canned peaches, and Coca-Cola. A meal fit for a queen."

Della opened one eye and wrinkled her nose. "This queen will eat just about anything you put before her but be careful with those Co-colas. I want to drink them, not wear 'em."

Larry pulled an opener from the sack and put it to work. Della took a bottle and downed its dark, sweet contents in a couple of gulps.

Larry watched her between his own gulps. "Careful now. All that fizz may not sit well on an empty stomach."

Della stuck out her hand. "Give me those peaches, and it won't be empty." After gobbling a few bites, she wiped her chin with the back of her hand and watched Larry from beneath her lashes. He really was an amazing man. If she wasn't still in love with Art, Larry would be perfect—brave, kind, smart, capable, and very good-looking. As it was, her heart was not ready to make such a drastic change. It needed time to mend, to let go of the dream that could now never be.

When he caught her watching him, heat rose in her cheeks. Her eyes darted to the open area behind them. A dike lay between the river and a road winding away through open fields that at present looked more like swampland. Flat, dark earth, wet. Nothing unusual for inland South Florida.

Her heart beat a little faster. Something about the area looked familiar. She stood up for a better view. With a tremble in her voice, she pointed and said, "That road over there—I think it's the way home."

"Are you sure? It wouldn't be a good idea to wander off and get lost."

She eyed the road and shouted, "I know it is. The farm is only a mile that way."

The walk home took twice as long as it would have under normal conditions, but Della trudged along at a pace that surprised even her. At the end of her driveway, she stopped and leaned against the gatepost, breathing hard. After catching her breath, she ran the rest of the way. She came into the yard and stopped to determine if she still had a home. The roof had held, and the windows were intact. Smoke curled up from the kitchen chimney. Thank goodness she had convinced Art to keep the old, woodburning range when the electric stove was installed.

Other than a couple of trees uprooted, broken limbs lying about, and water standing in low places, the house and yard looked no different.

Larry reached her side in a few strides. "Well, would you look at that. It's still standing."

The door opened, and Mrs. Adams stepped onto the porch. "Oh, thank goodness. How on earth did you get home? We've been so worried."

Della flew up the steps and into Mrs. Adams's arms. "I thought we might not make it, but Larry, Mr. Shelton, saved me."

Mrs. Adams peered over Della's shoulder. "Larry Shelton, huh? I always knew there was something fishy about you. Well, come on in away from the skeeters. No need in getting bit to death. I got a pot of soup on the stove. You must be about starved."

Once Della and Larry were seated at the kitchen table, Mrs. Adams dropped her head until her chin almost touched her chest. "I hope you don't mind, but we had to come here. Our house is too damaged to stay in."

"Is everyone all right? Is anyone injured?"

"Praise the Lord, we're all unhurt, other than a few bruises and scratches."

"Of course, you must stay here with me until we get things sorted out. There's plenty of room." Della stopped while a crease formed between her eyes. "Where are Mr. Adams and the children?"

"They're checking on the herd. Those cows were plenty upset, I can tell you. Won't give good milk for a week at least. We could hear them bawling even over the worst of the wind."

"The herd survived?"

"Mr. Adams and the boys put them up in the barns when the storm warning went up day before yesterday. My man believes in taking care of his animals, and we been through plenty of bad storms." She placed bowls on the table. "You eat up, now. And then use some of the hot water on the stove to wash in. The well's hand pump is still working good. Glad y'all didn't do away with it when you got running water to the kitchen."

Della grabbed Mrs. Adams's hand. "Thank you for everything. You're a godsend. After we eat, Mr. Shelton and I both need to rest. We've not really slept in about forty-eight hours."

•   •   •   •   •

Larry looked at Della over the rim of his coffee cup. "I've been here a week. I think I've imposed on you and the Adamses long enough. My bosses in Washington are probably wondering what's become of me."

"You're not imposing. I think Mr. Adams hopes you'll stay until the farm is back to normal, no matter how long it takes. He appreciates the help."

He was quiet for so long that Della thought he would say no more. There was no need for awkward silence between them after what they had been through together.

She started to speak, but he stopped her with a hard stare. "What about you? Do you want me to stay?"

The time that she dreaded had arrived. Her tongue refused to form words because she had no answers, or at least not ones he wanted to hear. Her life and her emotions were too confused to make promises.

"I guess your silence is my answer." Pain filled his eyes. "Look, I meant what I said when we were huddled in that closet. I'm in love with you and probably always will be. If you tell me there's no chance for me, then I'll accept it and try to get on with my life. But if there's even the smallest chance, I would like to know."

Della dropped her gaze as she thought about his request. She was attracted to him. She could not deny it. But was attraction enough? Her great fear was that her love for Art might never allow her to love another man. It was too soon to know what path her heart might take. She needed time to heal from her old love before she could think about forming a new one. If this were another time, another place . . . if she had not met and married Art first . . . if, if, if.

Larry got up and moved a step away from the table. She could not let him go like this.

She jumped up and grabbed his hand. "Don't leave. Sit down. Let me explain."

Her feelings, thoughts, fears, and hopes tumbled out in a flood as though a dam long in need of repair finally crumbled. She wasn't sure if she was making complete sense, but she just let her mind wander where it wanted until she had said everything.

Larry listened until the flood of words and emotions subsided. His eyes fell to his hands without meeting hers. "I see. I think I've known all along that I expected too much of a recent widow. I see I was right. What will you do once Auggie gets the estate settled?"

"I've told Mr. Adams that he may buy the farm as soon as we can get an appointment with the bank. Because of the generous life insurance policy, I will be able to cosign a loan for him. I think it's what Art would want since there is no way I could make a go of the farm alone."

Larry still did not meet her gaze. "And after that?"

"Auggie will give me a home until I can figure out my life. I have a degree, after all, and I want to use it. If anything good came out of my time at the villa, it is the realization that I am a good art historian. I want to put those skills to work."

He finally raised his eyes to meet hers. "I see. Any idea where that might be?"

Della shook her head. "My choices will be limited because I'm a woman, but I'll find something. I'm determined to see what I can achieve on my own. It's the only way I'll be able to move forward with my life."

The small smile lifting the corners of his mouth was in sharp contrast with the pain in his eyes. "I can see I have to accept your decision. I guess I understand it, but I don't have to like it. Will you be offended if I keep in touch with your cousin?"

"To what end?" Despite knowing she was making the right decision, Della could not extinguish the spark of hope his words ignited.

"If there is ever a chance for me, I don't want to miss it."

# EPILOGUE



*1929*

Della sat on the foyer floor, studying the original blueprints and interior designs of Charleston Museum's latest purchase, the Heywood–Washington House. The sun pouring through the open front door provided better light than one of the rooms with their dirty windows. Restoring the 1772 mansion to its original glory was a task Della anticipated with enthusiasm and a touch of anxiety. It was the first big project she would oversee since joining the staff two years ago.

The museum director, Laura Bragg, being great friends with Cousin Auggie, had been persuaded to give her mostly untested art history degree a chance. She owed Auggie her new life, one which she was enjoying immensely. Only one thing was missing, but she did not dwell on it. She had managed to start over in a new city in a job she loved.

The sound of shoes scuffing on the entrance steps brought a smile. Laura must be coming to check on her. They had agreed to meet in the house to discuss Della's initial thoughts on the restoration.

A shadow fell across the blueprints. She cupped her hand over her eyes. Through the glare, she could see that her visitor was male. She stood up, dusting her hands down her skirt. When her eyes adjusted, a flutter rose in her chest.

Larry held his hat in his hands. "Miss Bragg told me where to find you. I hope you don't mind."

Della stammered, "How are you here and not in Washington?"

Larry ruffled his hat brim through his fingers. "I've quit federal work. With the public agitating loudly for the repeal of the Volstead Act, my future there didn't look all that bright."

"So, what are you doing in Charleston?"

Larry gave her a half smile. "Our mutual friend in Abbeville suggested there might be a place for me with Charleston PD. He hinted that with his connections and my experience, the job is mine if I want it."

Della fought to keep her voice from trembling. "And do you? Want it?"

"That depends on whether you'll have lunch with me."

Della threw her arms around his neck and kissed his cheek. "Yes, of course I will. I can't think of anything I want more."

One day very soon, she would send Auggie a carefully worded thank-you note.

# ABOUT THE AUTHOR

Linda Bennett Pennell has been in love with the past for as long as she can remember. Anything with a history, whether shabby or majestic, recent or ancient, instantly draws her in. It probably comes from being part of a large extended family that spanned several generations. Long summer afternoons on her grandmother's wraparound porch or winter evenings gathered by the fireplace were filled with stories both entertaining and poignant. Of course, being set in the American South, those stories were also peopled by some very interesting characters, some of whom have found their way into Linda's work.

Linda resides in the Houston, Texas area with her sweet husband and an adorable Labradoodle, Lulu, who is quite certain she's a little girl, not a dog.

*"History is filled with the sound of silken slippers going downstairs and wooden shoes coming up."*
—Voltaire

Facebook: https://www.facebook.com/AuthorLindaBennettPennell

Website: http://www.lindapennell.com/

Twitter: @LindaPennell

Goodreads:
https://www.goodreads.com/author/show/7166661.Linda_Bennett_Pennell

Pinterest: https://www.pinterest.com/lindabennettpen/

# OTHER TITLES
# BY LINDA BENNETT PENNELL

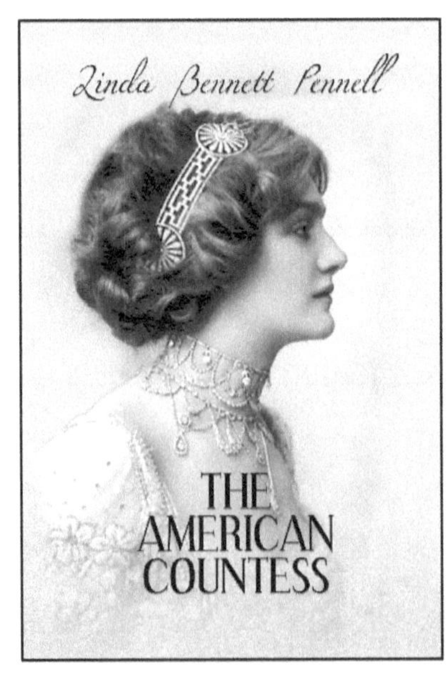

# NOTE FROM
# LINDA BENNETT PENNELL

Word-of-mouth is crucial for any author to succeed. If you enjoyed *Miami Interlude*, please leave a review online—anywhere you are able. Even if it's just a sentence or two. It would make all the difference and would be very much appreciated.

Thanks!
Linda Bennett Pennell

We hope you enjoyed reading this title from:

www.blackrosewriting.com

Subscribe to our mailing list – *The Rosevine* – and receive **FREE** books, daily deals, and stay current with news about upcoming releases and our hottest authors.
Scan the QR code below to sign up.

Already a subscriber? Please accept a sincere thank you for being a fan of Black Rose Writing authors.

View other Black Rose Writing titles at www.blackrosewriting.com/books and use promo code **PRINT** to receive a **20% discount** when purchasing.